THE EXISTENCE OF BEA PEARL

Candice Marley Conner

OWL HOLLOW PRESS

Owl Hollow Press, Springville, UT 84663

The Existence of Bea Pearl

Library of Congress Cataloging-in-Publication Data
The Existence of Bea Pearl / C.M. Conner. — First edition.

Summary:
Sixteen-year-old Bea Pearl doesn't believe her brother is dead, even when everyone else has given up on finding him. She decides it's up to her to figure out where he could be. With minimal clues and her own shaky convictions, Bea Pearl is determined to unravel the mystery of his disappearance.

ISBN 978-1-945654-74-9 (paperback)
ISBN 978-1-945654-75-6 (e-book)
LCCN 2021932611

OWL HOLLOW PRESS

To Momma and Daddy,
for giving me the best kind
of swamp-wild childhood.

I wouldn't have been able to dream up this story without it.

1

Fake Funerals & Catfish Barbs

We are a murder of grounded crows, shrouded as we are in our black. The raw, red clay rectangle in the ground fills my vision, shoving out every other color besides shades of shadow. My eyes refuse to take in the scene, though the casket on the plastic carpet is empty, its plush pillows undented by my older brother's body. I force myself to listen to the words hanging in the air, catching ragged bits like "Jim Montgomery is by God's side for Eternity" and "Isn't our God great to want us next to Him forever?" The utter and complete wrongness of it all almost knocks me back. How could they abandon Jim when he's still alive? He's waiting on us to stop playing around with this stupid, sad funeral and get searching.

Pressure builds inside me. The black crepe dress constricts and slides around my chest and neck. I whisper something, or maybe it comes out as a yell. Momma bursts into more heart-wrenching sobs and tries to crawl into Daddy. Something touches my hand, and my first instinct is to snatch it away. I dart to the side, pushing against the solid blackness just wanting—needing—to get away from this atrocity. It gives, throwing me off balance as I pitch forward and take off running, deeper into the graveyard. I chuck my heels at a live oak cloaked in Spanish moss, finally hiding behind a crumbling mausoleum. A mourning cherub has its head bowed, perhaps in shame of the event unfolding, its poor wings caught in concrete forever. Time spins like a falling, dead leaf. I can't hear the god-awful drone of the officiant, thank goodness. I desperately need peace.

Though I don't deserve it. I was there. The last one to see Jim alive.

"Bea Pearl?"

Someone calls my name, but I'm incapable of answering. My best friend's head pops around the side of the sepulcher, the weakening Alabama daylight still bright enough to make her blonde hair shine as if with angelic light. I scowl at her. She drops my heels covered in graveyard dirt at my bare feet.

"It's the stupidest thing my parents have ever done, getting Jim declared legally dead," I spit out once I find my voice. The safest emotion for me is anger. Otherwise, my life would be spinning like Alice's Caucus race when she first realizes she's stuck in Wonderland. All those giant tears were in vain, and this time the subsequent flood would be my fault, too. I'm stuck in Jim-less land, and the Jabberwocky that I must battle lives inside me.

Honey sits on the moss-covered cement bench beside me and takes my hand. I squeeze back. "You know why they did it," she says.

"But it's only been six months." Half a year of waiting for news. Of making a nuisance of myself in the horrible weeks that followed so that I'm banned from the police department. Endless search parties. Of coming home horse-fly bit and hollowed out on the inside. Of the fear of failing him. If I really tried and couldn't find him, then he would be actually gone. "By declaring him dead, no one will keep looking for him." My voice is as crumbly as the old gravestone next to me. A centipede buries itself in a crack.

Honey nods and swivels slightly to face me. "That's true. But *I* think *they* think it's the only way to get you to live again. They want you—and themselves—to have closure. To lay him to rest. It was an accident, a crazy, random, wrong-place-at-the-wrong-time situation."

We've had this conversation before. When the search parties soured and withered away. When I did too. "The only way I can live again is when Jim returns," I force through clenched teeth. "He's not dead."

Because if he really is, then it's my fault. And I don't think I can live with that.

"I miss him too," she says and lays her head on my shoulder, and we both cry. Because I can't hold the tears back any longer. Jim deserves for me to cry over him, and who knows, maybe another flood will bring him back.

After a while, Honey's tears turn to hiccups and then she surprises me by letting out a giggle.

"What's so funny?" I ask.

"Beth's face as she was trying to crawl out of the grave."

My jaw drops. Beth's a new girl, by Georgefield standards anyway. In a place where no one leaves—except if you mysteriously disappear in a flood surge—and no one moves in or if your grandparents weren't born here, you're considered new. She moved here with her parents a couple years ago, during our eighth-grade year. "What the hell was she doing in there?"

This time Honey laughs. "I'm sorry. I know, I have the worst, most inappropriate reactions, but I can't help it. Her face!" Her shoulders are shaking, she's laughing so hard.

I'm too confused and heart-shattered to find anything humorous. She must notice my expression because she wipes her eyes with the back of her hand and straightens her shoulders. And then I recall that blackness I pushed against when escaping that farce of a funeral. "Oh, Jesus Tap-dancing Christ. Did I knock her in?"

Honey explodes into fresh laughter, scaring a couple crows who take to the sky, cawing out their displeasure. "Brother Matthew slipped trying to help her out."

"He fell in, too?" I'm both amused and appalled. Not nearly as much as being forced to bury my not-dead brother in the first place. Jim would've enjoyed this, appreciated the Monty Python humor in the situation. Too bad he's not here to see it. My lips tighten.

Honey's trying to calm herself down again. "What is it, Bea?"

"Jim's somewhere, and I'm going to find him."

"But your parents want closure."

I nod. "That's what they say." I'd overheard a conversation before the funeral that it would be better for the town if he could be put to rest. No use making everyone suffer when he could lay in peace. I snort.

Honey raises her eyebrows like she knows a tempest is stirring inside me. A line of shelf clouds waiting on the horizon. "Why do you think they declared Jim gone?"

I stand, brushing the moss and clinging graveyard off my black dress. "That's something else I need to figure out, isn't it?" She reaches her arms out to me, so I hoist her up. "Why did Jim stupidly go down to the river as it was flooding? Where is he now?"

Honey chews on her lip at my questions she's heard a thousand times in a thousand different ways, but her eyes are encouraging. "What're you going to do?"

I knock the dirt off my heels. "A resurrection of my own. I'm going to bring Jim back from the dead."

My parents haven't even commented on Beth's fall into the grave. It's as if they buried their last bit of life into that empty casket, trying to fill it up with something. But if I'm going to find out what happened to Jim, I need to start somewhere. I decide the best place for that is his bedroom.

The door creaks slightly, as if already accustomed to disuse. I take it all in: his basketball hoop hamper hanging from the closet door empty of dirty clothes, swim trophies adorned with deflated balloon-like swim caps and goggles. It's just as he left it, as if he could come back at any moment and demand why I was snooping in his room. I close the door behind me.

Clues will be impossible to find in this mess, so I start by picking the clothes off the floor, checking pockets before tossing them into the basketball hamper. Mostly it's just spare change, gum wrappers, and gas receipts. Looking more closely, I find that a good number of the receipts are for marine fuel. Paid with cash. It's weird because we only have canoes on the property. Jim does eco-tours on the river since he knows them so well, but even those are in canoes. Why would he be buying boat fuel?

I toss the jeans behind me but it's a crappy throw and the whole hamper falls, the metal rim crashing into the hardwood floor. I wince. That's going to leave a dent.

A shriek comes from somewhere in the house and I instantly cower, the sound so wretched that goosebumps prickle my arms even in this warm, musty room. Momma's footsteps pound down the hallway and I wildly look around for a hiding spot. My reaction surprises me. It's just my own mom, right? But the pumping adrenaline tells me to run. I've done something very, very wrong and it's somehow worse than knocking a girl into a fresh-dug grave.

The door is thrown open so hard it bounces off the closet door behind it. I've only had time to move behind the bed and I crouch there, feeling and—more than likely—looking guilty as my mom scans the room with harsh eyes.

"Ji—" Her eyes settle on me and her bottom jaw drops slightly as if she can't quite catch her breath. "What are you doing in here?"

She's staring at the fallen hamper, but I'm pretty sure she's asking me. "Looking for clues," I whisper, unsure of the right thing to say, or even if a right thing exists. I clear my throat and try to sound more confident. "To find Jim."

That was apparently the wrong thing to say, because she lunges at me and I belatedly notice she's carrying a catfish. She and Daddy had been on the dock in an attempt to get her out of her bedroom and in the sunshine. I notice the fish because she raises it at me as if it's a weapon.

"Momma…" Incredulity floods my voice as I back up, throwing my arm up to keep from getting attacked by a fish.

"Don't touch his stuff!" she screams as she whacks me on the arm, a barb going deep enough that when she lets go, the fish stays, hanging like a remora from a shark. She collapses on the floor, crying into her palms.

I run.

Away from her, away from a musty room whose hinges shriek at us, away from the pain pulsing in my arm and the sharper ache in my heart at the sight of my mom breaking down like that.

Why does the possibility of Jim being alive seem to destroy my mother, while it gives me hope? A reason to go against everyone I know in search for him. I stop running when I reach the road to Honey's house, then rub the catfish's slime over the wound to stop the pain, mixing it with my blood. I'll have to be more careful at keeping my searching from Momma, maybe protect her broken heart a little better.

Even though secrets drive wedges.

Phone Calls & Snapchats

My brother's name hasn't been spoken out loud since the fake funeral and the fish attack. As I say his name into the phone receiver, it tastes like that sweet moment caramel goes from hard to chewy. "Jim." It's a short name. I try to savor the way my teeth click.

"Yeah, Jim Montgomery. Is he there? Is… is he okay?"

The voice on our landline isn't familiar. Maybe because I'm more focused on the echo of my missing brother's name in my head. "No." It comes out as a whisper. I clear my throat. "No, Jim's not here." I want another excuse to say his name out loud. As if saying it aloud will bring him home.

"Can I leave a message? When will he be back?"

I cradle the phone on my shoulder. "I don't know."

The wooden creak of a floorboard behind me makes me jump and I scramble to hang up.

Daddy enters the kitchen, empty coffee cup in hand. "Morning, Bea. Who was on the phone? Anyone calling in sick?"

"I don't know." I touch the empty spot on my chest. The catfish incident made it clear we don't talk about Jim. Daddy might be willing to listen at some point, but now his focus is on putting Momma back together again.

Why would the caller ask if he was okay? What does he know? My throat aches. Maybe he simply doesn't know our town pretends he's dead.

Daddy refills his cup. "Telemarketers." He shakes his head. "The girls from your cheerleading squad are taking pictures in front of Lake George right now."

My eyes slide back to the phone. I run my tongue over my teeth, unsticking them from my lips. I should've asked who was calling. The caller must know something if he's asking after Jim. The missed chance crushes me.

"Shouldn't you be out there?" His spoon scrapes the sides of his coffee cup as he swirls it around.

Then the kitchen is quiet. If the phone rings again, it will echo against the silence. His spoon clanks against the spoon rest. I turn to look at him. His thick eyebrows raise expectantly. "I didn't know about it."

Daddy frowns. "Oh. Are they being rude? Should I go get your mother?"

I sigh. "I'm not cheering this year, remember?" Ever since Jim disappeared, lying low is the easiest way for me to deal with uncomfortable stares and loud whispers. I honestly don't know how school—or anything—will be now that there's a stone with his name carved on it.

"Right. How could I forget? You don't cheer anymore. You haven't picked up your camera in months when last year your dream was to be a photographer and it never left your neck." He winces, then his face darkens. "You'd better open the concession stand since Honey's busy taking pictures with y'all's friends. I don't want to dock your pay."

I glance at the phone one last time before sliding my feet into my flops. Daddy was never an angry person 'til this past year. His good nature, Momma's happiness, and their combined hope for Jim are all bouncing around in that padded, airless death box. That's where the Old Bea resides, too. The one who used to cheer and take pictures. I wanted to change the way folks saw the everyday world around them with my photographs. It was a lofty dream, and now it's buried six feet under too.

I wonder what happens to dreams when they become worm food. Do they get mixed in the soil and help flowers bloom brighter? Or do they poison the dirt until nothing can grow?

The morning August sun is bright as I open the wooden door of our house, but there's a slight breeze peeking from beneath humidity's antebellum skirts. It's a short walk, crossing the front yard and parking lot to Lake George and the concession stand where I work with my best friend since preschool. But it's enough time for two thoughts to jumble inside my head and hitch my breathing:

I don't want to stop existing like my brother.

I don't want to be allowed to disappear.

What's left of my family lives and works at Lake George, at the junction of the Talakhatchee and Chatothatchee Rivers, close to the Alabama/Florida line. A very happening place for a very un-happening sixteen-year-old girl. During the summer, Honey and I run the concession stand, scooping ice cream, popping corn, and grilling hotdogs for the hungry anglers, swimmers, and sunbathers. Her older brother, Lucas, is a lifeguard like my brother Jim is, or was, or... Lucas helped out on so many of the search parties. When even he stopped showing up, stopped responding to my texts, that's when I knew everyone had given up.

High-pitched laughter drags at my attention. My former cheerleading squad is posing in front of a camera with the lake in the background. The lighting will make their faces look overexposed.

It doesn't bother me that no one told me about the pictures.

Well, maybe a little that Honey didn't mention it. Perhaps she thought it would hurt my feelings. But I'm the one who took a break after Jim disappeared. To hang out with shadows instead of real people.

When Honey catches sight of me and waves me over, Sara puts her hand on Honey's arm. Sara's hair has gotten lighter over the summer, an almost white that looks brittle and fake next to Honey's thick, sunshiny waves. She and Beth are best friends, so I expect some sort of fallout from knocking Beth into the grave.

The breeze over the lake blows in my direction, pushing Sara's voice closer. I've gotten good at listening to the quiet. "She can't come over here."

I slow down to empty the gravel out of my flops. Toby, our Lab mix, lopes over, as excited to see me as if I'm the one who is missing. The sadness in my throat loosens as I scratch behind his ears.

"It was an accident. Of course, she can," Honey says. "Not to mention she *lives* here, silly."

Does she mean the accident of Beth falling in the grave or Jim being snatched away from me during the flood?

Sara smiles so wide the morning sun reflects off her teeth, forcing me to avert my eyes even at this distance. "I mean she can't be in the picture."

"I don't see what the big deal is," Honey shrugs and then fluffs her hair. "She was part of the squad last year and you were friends."

"Yeah, and now she's all weird. Listen, it's nice that y'all are still friends for old time's sake—"

Sara stops talking when Honey snaps around to face her. I can't make out what she says with her back to me, so I veer towards the concessions. I don't want my pay docked on top of all this unpleasantness. When I was little, I used to cover my arms and legs in mud from the river and watch it fracture as it dried before peeling it off to see the skin print left in the clay. I try to imagine my skin thick like that, but Sara's words still seep through the cracks. Occasionally the mud had ants in it, and her words are ant bites that won't wash off fast enough.

My phone dings. It's a snapchat picture of Beth in Jim's grave but with my picture over it and the freaky mermaid filter so my face looks eerily like the whatever-she-is that has been popping into my sleep since this past spring.. *Everything's better down where it's wetter! You should join your brother!* the caption says, followed by the devil emoticon. I screenshot it before it disappears even though I should ignore it. How dare she twist a song from The Little Mermaid against me, especially if she's too lazy to even make it rhyme. Adding *before you kill your mother* would make it work.

A few minutes later, Honey joins me in the little painted wooden snack bar, flinging her bag in a corner. It hits the floor planking with a thud. I smile, then look over my shoulder through the wide counter window. "They're still taking pictures." I point out. Obviously, as they're hard to miss.

"Yeah, screw them. I need to get to work."

"You don't have to defend me. I don't care."

"Oh hush. How did you hear?"

"I was downwind."

She nods as she stacks yesterday's cups from the drying rack into neat piles, ready for the day. It was a sophomore class project of Jim's to make Lake George as green as possible. So, a few years ago, we started using washable food containers—not a Styrofoam cup or plastic spoon or straw in sight. It meant extra work for us, but we get paid by the hour, so we don't care.

I hand her my phone, screen showing the snapchat.

"Wow, is this from Sara?" When I nod, she continues, "So, instead of helping her bestie out when she *accidentally* gets knocked into an open grave, she takes pictures. Beth's really got it good in the Best Friend department."

"Yup. You can delete it. I shouldn't hold on to it. It'll just make me crazy—or crazier."

"Aww, can't I have a little fun with it?"

My shoulders slump as I look at her in disbelief.

She laughs. "I want to figure out how to get your picture off and restore it to the unedited version. We can caption it: *Beth looking for her next boyfriend.*"

"Gross."

"Got worms? Then snapchat me up!"

My face starts feeling crumbly, so I turn away. I don't know why I'm reacting this way because Jim isn't down in a lonely grave.

"Shoot, that's insensitive." She sighs and hands my phone back to me. "I'm sorry, it's deleted. Maybe you don't have it so good in the bestie department either."

I scoop myself some pistachio ice cream and hand Honey vanilla in a waffle cone.

"Good call. Stuff my face so I can't talk anymore." She winks as she takes the cone then pulls out a stool for each of us. She gives me a sideways glance after a few moments of silence. "Please don't let Sara get you down. Are you worried how Beth's going to retaliate? 'Cause I ain't afraid to pull that girl's whale tail up over her head."

Her cage fighting moves look like a cheerleader being attacked by wasps. I can't help but smile. I can always count on her to bring me to the surface of whatever funk I'm in, and since my brother's disappearance, she's definitely earned her best friend status.

"Something else besides Sara's crappy photoshopping skills is bothering you. Did you have another dream?"

I shake my head. When I told Honey about my dreams earlier, I thought she might think something was wrong with me.

They are probably nothing more than my overactive imagination reacting to my closed off parents and fear over whatever happened to Jim. But what if they're not? What if they're bits of repressed memories, reorganized and seemingly directed by Tim Burton?

With the school year fast approaching, my summer has disappeared, and I lose a little bit more of myself with every passing day. I'm not crazy, but maybe I'm going there and at least one person should know where I'm headed. Of course, with Honey eager to hear my dreams as if we're discussing a new Netflix series, she might be headed to Crazy with me. Which is fine because I like her company. Maybe we can get discounts on travel arrangements if we bring a buddy. More likely, she just sees it as something different to talk about on hot, quiet days in a small town in lower Alabama.

I take a few licks of my ice cream for courage. It's just going to eat at me if I don't say anything. "Someone called for Jim."

Honey swallows her last bit of waffle cone as the lightness leaves her face. "Who answered?"

"I did."

"Who was it?"

"Didn't ask. Heard someone behind me, and thought it was Momma. I hung up." I don't want to be the reason Momma gets that scary, white-lipped, spaced out look again.

"What did they want?"

"To leave a message, I guess. I wish I had asked who called."

Honey grabs a broom and sets to sweeping out a corner like there's a fire ant bed in it.

Sometimes crazy is a good thing. People tend to gravitate toward a certain passionate personality of wild abandonment, because those types do fun and exciting things without warning. In the South, people display that over-the-top personality on their front porch. Now people think of me as a deranged individual that needs to hide in the attic with the winter coats.

"Someone besides us must think Jim still exists." I brandish my waffle cone at this hint of justification. "He asked if Jim was okay."

Her mouth twitches as she struggles to maintain her blank expression, her facial features exaggerated by the extra make-up from the photo shoot. It makes her look older and more somber than the lighthearted person she is.

"Okay, *I* know he still exists, and you humor me. I need to find him." The urgency in my voice startles me, causing my fingers and toes to tingle. All that stupid funeral did was bury hope. How did my parent's think it would bring me closure? Why does everyone who experiences tragedy think closure is the only path to recovery? Why should I scrape my brother out of my life like he never existed? With the mysterious voice on the phone, I realize someone *is* looking for him. "So, I'm going to, too," I whisper, while that shelf cloud from the funeral snaps with lightning and summer thunderstorms, urging me on.

After vanquishing the invisible ant bed, Honey looks at me with a sad little smile that I can't quite read. "It was on your house phone?"

I nod.

"Star sixty-nine tells you the last number that called. Daddy had to do that when one of Lucas's girlfriends fell in love a little too hard and would call the house in the middle of the night when Lucas wouldn't answer his cell."

"That's a great idea." I stand.

"But it only tells you the last number," she cautions as I take off running to the house.

I dash in front of a pick-up that I first thought was parked but realize too late is moving slowly. My shoulder brushes it so I give an apologetic wave but don't stop. The sun reflects off the windshield. I should pause to explain about parking, but I don't have time for sightseers. A flip flop flies off as I transition from gravel to the yard. My ankle gives but I right myself and keep going. I need to make it before the phone rings again. I have to know who called.

I reach the first step to the porch. To make it to the kitchen, I still need to go through the screened-in door and past the living room. I wrench the door open. The hinges shriek at me as a splinter stabs into the fleshy part of my thumb.

The shrill ring of the phone is so abrupt it makes me flinch.

The screen door crashes behind me. Momma sticks her head around the corner, phone to her ear, cord twisting around a finger, the expression on her face telling me to quiet down. "Yes, we'll be open 'til ten tonight. No reservations, though call aheads are fine if your party is over eight." A pause. "Great. We'll see y'all then." She hangs up and looks at me with an expectant expression. "Need something, Bea?"

I sputter. "Why didn't they call Daddy's line if they were calling for the restaurant?" I'm furious at myself for hanging up earlier. Angry at the fact that the first shard of hope I've had in months was snatched from me.

Momma blinks. "Well, both numbers are in the phone book. Are you expecting a call?"

I look down, not sure how to answer.

"Where's your phone?" Momma puts a fist on her hip and sighs. "Did you lose it?"

My brain's moving too sluggish to think of any better excuse for why I tore into the house, so I nod. But when she turns in profile and I hear her press numbers, I realize she might be calling me. Snatching the phone out of my back pocket, I throw it behind me.

Adele's "Hello" fills the air. Momma turns to me. "Sounds like it's in the living room. Check between the couch cushions."

"Yes, ma'am. Thank you."

3

Sand Dollars & Slippery Banks

A shiver runs through me despite the August heat as I sit up in bed and open my window. In the predawn hush, the only illumination comes from the streetlight in front of the restaurant. The east is a forgotten dream of a sunrise. So still. So secretive, like I might be the only person on this earth. But Jim's out there somewhere, and maybe he's feeling like the world forgot him too. Melancholy catches in my throat and I sigh so deeply Toby startles, then shimmies his tailless rear end.

Rubbing the goosebumps on my arms. I lean against the sill, thinking about the dream. It started the same as all the others that I've had since Jim first disappeared. I'm working the concession stand and a pale girl walks up to the window. She has light hair, not blonde like Honey's, but more the color of moonlight reflecting off Lake George. Her eyes are the blue-green iridescence of bluegill scales and their intensity makes me uneasy. I stand there: waffle-cone in one hand and scoop in the other.

Waiting.

We look at each other and I wonder if I stare too long into her eyes, my own green eyes will become more like hers. Too mesmerizing. A dangerous sort of glittery. I glance away and that's where the dream ends. Usually. Tonight though, it continues.

In this new part of the dream, it looks like Venice's watery roads, except people are paddling by this reverie version of the concession stand in canoes rather than gondolas. I hand the girl an ice cream cone while avoiding her too-bright eyes and she lays her coins on the counter. I pick them up. The texture is rough.

Sand dollars.

Not the bleached white kind you'd find at the beach. These were fossilized thousands of years ago when this whole area was underwater and filled with sea life. When our present-day rivers are low enough to expose the limestone banks, people can find all sorts of saltwater shells and sharks' teeth. Once, Daddy found a dark brown monstrosity that was a whale's tooth.

But what does dreaming of sand dollars mean?

I've been thinking about the dream all morning and haven't forgotten a single detail. My preoccupation has me burning hot dogs and dropping ice cream.

"You okay, Bea?" Honey wipes rainbow sherbet off her sandal.

"Sorry." I catch the sticky rag she tosses my way since the sink is closer to me. "Do sand dollars mean anything to you?"

"Like from the beach?"

I shake my head. "No, the limestone ones from riverbanks. Oh, haha. Sand *dollars*, river *banks*. Funny."

Honey drops her shoe. "Orange Mini Gophers. Is this the latest installment of Bea's Crazy Technicolor Dream-Memories?"

Referencing brightly hued, miniature rodents began way back in elementary school. We swore we'd never be one of those

O.M.G Girls— the hair-flipping, gum-smacking, giggling-uncontrollably-at-stupid-boy-jokes types. The world needs all types of people, but we decided we were not interested in behaving that way. Anytime we felt the urge to O.M.G something, we used the acronym for the first words that popped in our head instead. It's silly, but we thought we were very progressive in elementary school. Now it still crops up occasionally.

I purse my lips and nod. "The sand dollars were a new part to the same old dream."

"Do you think Jim was in financial trouble? Maybe your, ahem, joke was on target."

I consider. "He'll start college this year. That's a heavy burden. But he's been telling Momma and Daddy he has a basketball scholarship."

"Maybe he never had a scholarship, and he was getting his tuition money by doing something illegal instead. Like selling fossils? It's against the law in Florida, so maybe he brought some over the state line?"

"Jim wouldn't do anything illegal," I ground out through clenched teeth. When I remember that Honey isn't saying it to be mean, I relax. "Would Lucas know if Jim was in money trouble?"

"I'll ask. But if you're dreaming about fossils, maybe it's time to take yourself to where the fossils are. You should go down to the Shelf." Her eyes widen. "I mean, if it's not too painful."

The Shelf is a large limestone shelf in a bend of the Chatothatchee to the northwest of our property. When the river's low, about ten feet of limestone is visible and covered in fossils. Hence, the reason why Honey suggests I check it out. Parts of it have been hollowed out by acidic rainwater, so there are sections where the river can be seen flowing just a foot or two beneath the shelf.

The last place I saw Jim alive was near the Shelf.

Limestone shelves are a favorite place for alligators, sturgeon, and all sorts of secretive animals. They are also dangerous because swimmers can drown under them since the current is usually much swifter in the bends. It makes me nervous to take Toby when we go down since Labs can't resist the call of the water. As much as I love him, I will not go under one of those shelves.

"You wanna come with?" I don't have to work at the restaurant tonight. Since it is summer, it doesn't get dark until almost eight, so there will be a few hours of daylight left once we close for the day.

"Babysitting the Lopez twins," Honey says wistfully. "But you'll be okay?"

I nod. I think so anyway.

Lake George flows into the Chatothatchee through creeks and swamps until it meets the river, which empties into the Gulf of Mexico near Panama City Beach. Jim, Lucas, and a couple of their friends once rafted from Georgefield to the beach, and he said it was treacherous in the narrow parts with an uncomfortably fast current. He told Honey and me you'd get accustomed to the sweet breeze from the tupelos, the mullet jumping and one-upping your buddies, then, wham! The current could knock the boat right from under your feet if you were standing. Back in the steam-boating days, the Chatothatchee was an important water thoroughfare, but runoff from all the farms has made it shallower.

I tie Toby to the dog run by his kennel since I don't want to have to rescue him from under the Shelf. He whines, letting me know how he feels about me going on an adventure without him. I'm unhappy in equal measure because I'm afraid I'll bump into the water sprite that visited me in a dream and left a clue about my brother near the last place I saw him alive.

Whew. I can do this.

I drag my feet as I cut across our back field. The little hike feels rejuvenating with a tiny bit of coolness in the breeze that hints of fall.

Once I hit the tree line, the temperature drops a few degrees and I take time to appreciate the sunlight spilling from leaf to leaf. Deer tracks are pressed in the sandy spots and passionflowers nod off on their vines. The whole path is flocked by glinting ruby and emerald hummingbirds. It's so peaceful with only the sounds of birds chirping, wind meandering around the flat river birch leaves, and the rhythmic trickling of water.

It was different last time I was here.

It was March, cold and raining. A premature dusk and hair sticking to my eyelashes made it hard to see. I told Jim not to go down to the river, but he just brushed off my concern like I was a gnat and continued on anyway, west of the house and through the field, just inside the tree line.

"It hasn't crested yet!" I yelled at Jim's back.

"Go back to the house, Beep."

"But you need to help sandbag!"

"Go home. I have to get something."

Get what? What on earth was down there that he was going to risk a flooding river? We still had a ways to go before we reached the river proper but I could already see water. It was monstrous and rabid with the thick foam we call cow spit clinging to brush and tree trunks. I wanted to stop running after him and go back home where it was dry and warm and safe. But I knew that if I did, if I let Jim do this alone, something bad would happen. I was scared for him.

My brother hesitated at the water's edge, then plunged in anyway, the muddy water lapping at his waders. I gave a cry of frustration and ran faster, my rubber boots slapping my calves.

He made a sharp turn to the north and I gasped. Didn't he know there was a drop off there in the sand, now covered up with rising waters?

"Jim! No!" I yelled.

Jim finally looked back at me, but he must have slipped on the sandy bottom anyway because he fell to one knee, his waders filling with water, dragging him down.

I was close enough to touch him. He reached for me but missed my hand. I lunged and felt something tug at my neck. He looked at me with wild eyes. "Bea, behind you! Run!"

But if I broke eye contact, he'd slip underwater and stay there.

There was a rushing sound as a wall of water smacked into me, lifting me up at the same time my boots were held down by something sinister and dark. I lost sight of him, holding my breath, kicking until the boots came off, and then I was able to claw my way to the surface. The swirling currents slammed me into a tree. My shoulder throbbed, but I still paddled to Jim's last known spot. I treaded water in a circle. The water was so disorienting. Fire ants floated by on their own pontoons. A water moccasin swam past in oddly elegant strokes.

I yelled for Jim. I thought I heard a faint response so I paddle-walked towards it. The water was chest-high now, deeper because of the surge that snuck up behind me. I needed to stay within the tree line. At least here I could touch the bottom, but the closer I got to the river birches, the deeper and angrier the water became.

Then, a boat motor buzzed over the sounds of water.

Someone's here to help us! I swam toward it, pretending it was just me and Jim practicing our freestyle in the pool. Looking up to orient myself to the sound through the dripping rain and tree branches, I saw someone in an aluminum boat hoist a limp body wearing a blue Lake George T-shirt and waders into the boat. I laughed giddily, they found Jim! *Waving an arm in the air to get their attention, I got caught in another swirl of current. It slammed me headfirst into a thick oak.*

Everything went dark.

With a throbbing head and shaking hands, I pick my way down the embankment and follow the creek to the now tame river contently within its banks. If I had kept my mouth shut, hadn't called to him, he wouldn't have slipped. That thought has eaten at me like hungry mosquitoes since March, but now I push it away.

The sandy cliffs tower over my head like a swamp cathedral, then open up as the creek empties into the river. I take off my flops to feel the cool creek water.

The river flows over the limestone shelf until it spills down the eroded holes. I peer into a hole but only see a rush of silvery water pouring down. My memory of that March event seeps coldness into my soul. Fear lingers as I imagine a pale arm reaching up and pulling me down into the dark void. I back away quickly and slip on the stone, landing painfully on my butt.

"You okay?"

Nearly jumping out of my skin, I slide down even further, brain working overtime. The masculine voice reveals that it's not the sprite from my dream since most water spirits are females. Or maybe it's a pooka. Those are male, right? But pookas are water spirits who turn into horses so if there's a horse talking to me, I now have one more worry to add to my list. A merman? Those only live in saltwater.

I guess it's easy for my mind to wander when I see a stranger in the middle of the woods.

Finally, I stop sliding around and turn to see who spoke. An unfamiliar boy about my age stands on the bank proper, now about ten feet away since I slid so far. By sight, I know all the guys who live in Georgefield because we've gone to the same school since kindergarten or I've seen them at Lake George. His familiar blue eyes remind me of the sparkle-eyed girl from my dream.

I don't think dreams can hurt me. Or is that ghosts? As I catch my balance, I notice his eyes are more of an icy blue like a clear winter sky. He's gorgeous. I freeze and stare a moment too long.

He steps over a knobby cypress knee, getting closer. "You okay? Need some help?"

"You startled me!" I sputter, aware that I look like a wobbly foal with my legs splayed out for balance. My cheeks turn red as I spy a lovely greenish-brown smear of algae and mud on my shorts.

"You fell before you knew I was here," he points out. "You're awfully close to the edge. Limestone thins the closer you get to the drop off."

"I didn't intend on getting this close. And I know this already. I live here!"

"It's all right," he says soothingly, as if he's a horse whisperer. Pooka whisperer? "You're making it worse with all that squirming. Will you get away from the edge?"

I really am trying to get to safety. This close to the edge there is more algae, making it impossible for my bare feet to get a grip. Not only that, I hear the distinct sound of a chunk of limestone hit the water's surface. A sound that surely is a dinner bell to the nearest hungry gator.

I imagine the gator chomping down on my leg, pulling me deeper underwater, twisting as we go. I'll be so disoriented by the pain I won't know which way is up. Or, what if it's not a gator but Grendel who takes me to his underwater cavern and Grendel's mother is sitting there holding Jim captive?

Think of something else!

That guy has some really muscular arms; he should take his shirt off.

That's it! Stop thinking, Bea Pearl!

I banish my jumbled thoughts and instead crouch frog-like to find handholds. Unfortunately, this shifts my center of balance and cracks appear on the shelf.

The guy dashes up the creek, away from me. I curse him until he reappears with wild scuppernong vines he twists together to make a rope.

"Now grab on. If the shelf falls, don't let go. I'll pull you out."

He tosses the rope vine toward me and a bigger limestone chunk near my right foot falls with a heavy *kerplunk*. I swear eyes look at me from the water. Grendel? An alligator?

"Stop looking down. Look at me. Grab the vine and belly crawl towards me," he commands.

"There's something down there!" I say, clutching the vine with both hands.

"Yeah, probably a moccasin or something."

Totally forgot about snakes. I slither towards the bank faster, hand over hand on the rope vine until I reach sandy soil. He grabs my wrists, pulling me up to safety. We stand, boots to bare toes, and my pulse beats faster now than it did when I was about to go over the edge.

"Thanks," I say softly. "I'm Bea Pearl."

He studies my face for a moment, as if looking for something. "Colin." Then he drops my hand and walks into the woods. Not towards Lake George but following the river downstream. Blood pounds in the hand he held.

His voice, I belatedly realize. That's what is somehow familiar. I stare at Colin's back until he disappears. We're far enough away from Georgefield that people aren't usually walking along the river. They may be in boats— fishing or canoeing— but not out for an evening stroll. The junction, with its boat ramp, is within walking distance, but it lies around a couple of bends and on the other side of the river.

Where on earth did this Colin guy come from? Maybe he has a canoe stashed downstream. Maybe he's a guardian angel sent by Jim or the water sprite. Had the dream led me here so I can meet Colin because he knows something about my brother? Did I hear him speak in my dream, a little tidbit resting on the sleepy edge of my consciousness?

I tear off a papery piece of River Birch bark and scrape some of the algae and river muck off my feet. If I wasn't so dirty, I might just chalk this whole surreal event to my imagination. A twig breaks but I don't pay much attention to it until a prickly sensation scurries up my spine. It feels as if intelligent eyes are watching me.

Deer, opossums, armadillos, beavers, and otters can snap a twig before running off, but this watching prickle is an entirely different sensation. I distance myself from the limestone, not wanting to startle and fall again. I really wish Honey was here instead of babysitting. The woods are too quiet now. Not a single bird is singing and that worries me more than the twig snap.

"Colin?" I call out, cringing at the sound of my high-pitched voice. This stranger is going to think I'm incapable of doing anything on my own.

"Toby?" Maybe he chewed through his rope.

"Jim?" Hopeful but doubtful.

Brush rustles and I pinpoint the sound. On top of the sandy knoll a couple feet over my head, a scuppernong vine grows over a bush creating a thick bramble of leaves. And peering out, not blinking, are two forward-facing eyes, watching me intently. Eerily human-like.

Not Jim.

Backing away, I retrieve my flops and then, without bothering to put them on, I run home so fast the mosquitoes can't catch me.

Gentleman Callers & the Sheriff's Office

An artesian-fed swimming pool sits alongside the concession stand by Lake George. People swim in the pool but avoid the lake because of alligators. Occasionally, a boy on a dare will jump off the fishing and canoeing dock. The lifeguard stands are tall enough that Lucas—and Jim, at one time—blows his whistle and threatens to call the kids' parents. When the reluctant boys emerge, they huddle with their acne-covered friends and regale them with tales of how they *almost* jumped on a gator. Their friends hand out high-fives and thumps on the back, telling them how brave and crazy they are.

Toby once jumped on an alligator, and now doesn't have a tail.

If Jim got attacked by an alligator during the flood, wouldn't we have found some evidence?

Lake George Restaurant is built over the water with a dance floor made of beautiful golden pine planks. Its walls are lined with windows so customers can watch fish jump as they eat fried breams or grilled catfish with hush puppies and coleslaw. I work there in the evenings along with my mom and dad, the cook known as Mr. Catfish (whom I doubt remembers his birth name), and various girls and boys that come in from nearby Georgefield and Briar to wait tables and dance with folks on their nights off. Briar seems to have grown dangerous for its young people in the past couple of years. Though maybe it has always been like that and I'm more aware of what's around me know that I'm in high school.

"Junior was up there talking to your dad when I clocked in." Honey catches my eye as I tie on my apron.

"Talking about what?"

"Fish. You."

Snorting, I realize that she's trying to get my mind off Grendel-monsters. "What do fish and I have in common?"

Honey gives me a wicked look. "According to Junior, y'all are both delicious. Especially covered in tartar sauce."

"He did *not* say that to my dad!"

She laughs, almost rocking herself off the stool.

Junior can have the fish. I don't need anything new in my life—even if I were interested—until I figure out what happened to my brother. Coming to work every day keeps me busy and the busy keeps me sane.

"Remember those boat fuel receipts you told me about? I asked Junior but he had no idea why Jim would be buying it. Lucas had no clue either and didn't recall him being at the boat ramp any more than usual."

"Thanks for asking. I didn't even think to ask Junior."

Honey shrugs. "He's been around a lot this summer."

"Did Daddy hear y'all?" I ask quickly before she can tease me again.

"No, he'd already walked off toward the back."

We fall silent, doing our respective tasks like clockwork as we get prepped and ready for the day.

"I don't think an alligator would attack during a flood," I muse, catching sight of the dock again as I refill the napkin dispenser on the long front counter.

"Um, what?"

"If Jim got eaten during the storm. The gator would try to get to safety too, right? But, they're opportunistic feeders…"

Honey looks slightly squeamish. "Uhh…"

"So, it might bite him if Jim got too close, but I don't think the gator would want a full stomach. It wouldn't be able to move fast enough *and* digest him, you know?"

"Lord, Bea Pearl. You're going to make me lose my breakfast. Anyways, didn't you say you saw a boat pick him up?"

Yes, the reason I still hold out hope. The reason why I'll never have closure. The sheriff's office told me they never found out a lead on the rescuer, so everyone thought I made it up, a delusion to soothe myself until a blood-stained shirt of Jim's was found once the waters receded. In the face of all that disbelief, it was hard to give my hope a voice. It made me fear that I was failing my brother. It looks like Honey believes my side of events. I smile.

"Speak of the devil—is that Junior coming out of your house right now?"

I look to my left, out the window that faces our home. The big concession window allows a view of the restaurant, lake, and partial pool, while this smaller one faces west. "*We* weren't speaking of him, *you* were," I mutter as we watch him fly down the three steps off my front porch and hightail it across the front yard.

"He sure is moving fast for a gentleman caller."

I narrow my eyes at her while still watching him. "You're reading too many romances again."

"What else is he doing inside your house?"

"I have no idea." I nibble on my bottom lip, then stand. "Guess I'll go ask."

Honey tugs my arm. "What if he was looking for a token?"

"Like a knight?" I blow a raspberry and shake my arm free. "Again, lay off the romances. No one's in the house, so he shouldn't be either."

"You want to ride with me to the library after work?" she asks as I push the door open.

The library is across Commerce Street from the police department. *Opportunity*. "Yeah."

Junior almost trips himself up when he sees me bee-lining for him. Do I make him nervous because he likes me as Honey thinks, or did he just realize he got caught?

His hands are shoved all guilty-like in his camo cargo shorts, and when he stops in front of me his eyes dart everywhere except my face. "Hey, Bea Pearl. I…"

"…Was in my house," I supply, helpfully, when he stutters to a stop.

His head and Adam's apple bob. "Yeah," he gestures behind me to the restaurant then points over his shoulder at the house. "Your dad had me run an invoice over."

"You work here now?"

His free hand goes right back to the pocket like a startled rabbit to its burrow. I grimace as I realize that my tone sounded a little raptor-y.

"Just trying to be helpful," he murmurs.

My face colors. Honey—with all her bodice-ripper-reading—may be right. I shove my own hands in my cut-offs pockets and roll a gravel rock around with my flip flop. When I look back at his face, he's studying mine. My cheeks itch.

"Well, I left my pole baited…" This time he gestures with his elbow, now looking like a gimped up rabbit, so I nod and move to the side. He takes a step so we're side-by-side and stops again. "It was good talkin' to you." Then walks toward Lake George.

Crap. Honey's going to be insufferable.

As she pulls into the library's parking lot a few hours later, I'm wondering how to get across the street without her noticing. She may believe me about a rescuer, or at least a boat, but I'll bet she won't approve of the wild hare I thought of, especially since it seems like she agrees with Momma and Daddy on this closure bull.

Honey lays her books on the return desk and chats with the librarian. Next to the front door, stairs lead to the basement where we used to have our summer reading programs. Now, shelves of outdated books for library sales fill the space.

Honey taps my arm. "You going downstairs? I'll be in the romance section."

"Duh." I hoped she would. She can't see the front door from there. I head towards the stairs, but as soon as she turns the corner, I retrace my steps. A quick glance at the front desk shows the librarian with her back to me. She'll hear the door chime as I exit, but maybe the excuse that I left my library card in Honey's car will not make her suspicious.

Once outside, the muggy air seems to slow me down. Or maybe it's because I'm sneaking around behind Honey's back. Or maybe it's the memory of what happened last time I went to the police department.

I cross the street, walking past the plate glass windows for Galstrup's. My parents used to take Jim and me for Coke floats to celebrate good grades, or to soothe hurt feelings and skinned knees. My already unsure feet falter when movement inside catches my eye. A man is throwing his arms out, getting in the face of a girl about my age. I walk closer and pause. Yikes. It's Beth, the girl I accidentally pushed into Jim's grave. With the way she's crouched low on the stool, it looks like he's giving her a hard time.

I look ahead at the police department, then back at the window, wondering if I should help. Just as I'm about to head to the door, a lady walks up to them, exaggerated eyebrows visible even from here, and the man seems to calm down. Of all people, I should know better than to get in someone's family drama. Especially when Beth turns my way and glares once recognition hits. I'm the last person she wants to see.

Taking a quick step back, I resume my mission, wondering if Honey realizes I'm gone yet. The fountain splashing in front of the police department makes a queasy feeling well up in my stomach. It didn't end well last time I was here. I run my tongue along my teeth and go inside.

"Bea Pearl!" The receptionist, Mrs. Lou Ann from church, looks at me in surprise. "Why, I haven't seen you in a blue moon. What brings you down here and why haven't I seen you at Sunday school?"

I've never been good at small talk. Especially since I've gotten out of the habit. Even to a nice old lady who brought—and probably still brings—chocolate chip cookies to Bible Study for as long as I could remember. My fingers twist with nervousness so I hide them behind my back. "I want to tell Chief Hoyle that someone called for Jim. Asked to speak to him."

Her pleasant smile disappears as she pushes her glasses up her nose. The colorful beads looping around her glasses click as she looks around furtively. "Well, who was it?"

"I don't know. I tried to star sixty-nine, but I was too late." Oddly, my eyes start to water.

"It could've been anyone, darlin'. A magazine salesperson. A Pakistani askin' for his credit card number. What did your parents say?"

"I didn't tell them. I…I thought y'all could trace the call? What if it's the person in the boat that rescued him?"

"Bea Pearl, I thought you stopped all that nonsense."

I step back in surprise. "Ma'am?" Without warning, the sounds around me grow loud: the fax machine chirping, the bubbling of the water cooler, the insistent phones ringing, the faraway clank of metal from the holding cells.

Past Mrs. Lou Ann's desk, Sheriff Oakwood exits his office at the end of the lobby. He catches my eye and frowns. I remember that look. Like he'd put me away forever if he could. He hands a file to someone and walks in my direction. Starting to panic, I suck in air.

Mrs. Lou Ann pulls me into the ladies' bathroom.

My hands are shaking as I push hair out of my face. "So, that's it then? Y'all won't help me anymore since that mockery of a funeral." I try not to spit out the last word. It's not Mrs. Lou Ann's fault, after all.

Mrs. Lou Ann looks at me with sympathy as she rubs my hand in her wrinkled, veiny one. She has massive gold rings on each finger. I focus on those to get my breathing steady. "Not a soul came forward sayin' they rescued him. Not a sane soul would be out in a johnboat in a flood anyhow. And nothin' done in the Lord's name is a mockery, young lady. Your parents already lost one child. They can't lose you, too."

I have to bite my lip hard at that reminder. "Please don't tell my mom I came down here," I whisper, afraid if I speak any louder my voice will crack like a levee.

"Oh, child. As long as you let the dead lie in peace."

I focus on the beads from her eyeglass chain as they catch the light. "Did the police ever figure out why he went down to the river in the first place?"

She shakes her head, chain swinging like hound dog jowls. "You're hurtin' yourself with all this nonsense you keep dredgin' up. Sheriff Oakwood's got everything under control."

Hurting myself? I tug my hand away. Her expression makes me recall the last time I was here and the way everyone in the office stared at me as if I was insane. Daddy pulled me out, past the fountain while I screamed for Jim.

My face flushes.

She sneaks a peek out the bathroom door. When she faces me again, her pleasant smile returns. "Now, I don't want to see your pretty li'l self unless it's at church or I'm at Lake George eatin' soma that fried catfish with my Bunco ladies." She pulls me out of my hiding place and gently pushes me past the main doors. "Off with you."

A framed newspaper clipping catches my eye on the way out. THERE'S A NEW SHERIFF IN TOWN, the headline reads. The date seems to jump out at me before I'm pushed into the humidity. It's the same time frame as those marine fuel receipts I found in Jim's room. Is it a coincidence or a clue?

The doors swing shut, locking in the cool AC. Squeezing my eyes shut, I try to stop the tears of frustration. Does Mrs. Lou Ann think I'm hurting myself because I won't stop looking for answers or because I was the only other person there that day besides Jim? Something's going on. What aren't they telling me? The way Oakwood looks at me through the door makes me wonder what I'm missing. Was Jim involved in something bigger than what I thought? Am I in danger?

And what about the way she said Oakwood has everything under control? I shiver.

An Open Window & a Swarm of Fireflies

At dusk, I cross the parking lot, stomping from the restaurant to the house, scraping cocktail sauce off my Lake George T-shirt that *accidentally* landed on me when the server carrying it tripped. Sure. It'd be more believable if the girl hadn't had a dish rag apparently coated in tartar sauce when she pretended to clean it off. I smell like horseradish and relish and feel like a giant walking, talking, and annoyed hotdog.

The screened door hinges screech at me as usual but it's the dull thud coming down the hallway that cements me in my tracks. I stop so suddenly the door smacks into my side. Toby growls behind me then shoots inside, morphing from lazy teddy bear to hellhound in 1.1 seconds. Someone who doesn't belong is in this house. I need to get Daddy.

But when Toby snarls, attacking Jim's door, I grow cold. My tingles get overwhelmed by what-ifs. Could my brother be back from whatever hell he's been stuck in for the past six months? I dash down the hallway and wrench open the door.

The room is empty. Empty of specters. Just a dog sniffing wildly at an open window. Jim's room smells like dust and the rubber of basketballs that cast lumpy shadows around the room. I can almost imagine Jim's presence from all the times I crept in as a kid because I had a bad dream.

Enough moonlight streams in the windows to make the shadows bigger. If I stare at the dark lump of a pillow on his bed, I can almost see the slight rise and fall of his sleeping form.

I blink to let my eyes adjust to the dark. I reach out, expecting a warm body. Jim. Then my hand sinks into nothing.

Toby whines. I sense that something is wrong other than Jim being gone. Flipping on the nightstand lamp, I let out a gasp. Without the mask of twilight, I realize that this isn't Jim's normal disarray. I walk to the other side of his bed. Crap is strewn everywhere. Drawers have been dumped out, like someone was looking for something. But what? I wonder who has been here. Sticking my head out of the open window, I gaze towards a dark field lined by woods. The view is lit by moonlight not yet freed from trees. His bedroom faces away from the parking lot and restaurant.

Something is going on no matter what everyone around me thinks. Between the phone call this morning and Jim's trashed room, I know *someone* is looking for Jim or something that belonged to him. I plop on Jim's bed. How do I tell my parents someone broke into Jim's room without my mom losing her mind again?

It takes me a long moment to rouse myself, to collect my wits enough to pull my phone from my back pocket and dial Daddy.

"What's up, Bea?" Daddy says over the phone. His tone is clipped with impatience. I'm bothering him but he's trying to hide it. Perhaps I'm interrupting a clogged soft drink dispenser, a spilled tray of broken glasses, or over-fried pickles. My eyes flit back over Jim's stuff on the floor.

My breath feels fluttery, like my lungs can't suck in enough air for speech. "It's Jim—Jim's room," I clarify before he thinks I'm just being hysterical again like at the funeral. "Someone tossed it."

A pause. "Lock yourself in your room. I'll be right over."

I look around wildly. It hadn't crossed my mind that I might be in danger. Instead of going to my room, I lock Jim's door since it appears to be empty of intruders. Who knows if mine is safe since I've haven't searched it yet?

The front door shrieks and crashes. Daddy's footsteps echo down the hallway. He calls out my name, probably when he realizes I'm not in my room. I sit cross-legged on the side of Jim's bed facing the door, not getting up until Daddy pounds on it.

"Bea! Bea? Open up. It's me." The irritation is replaced with something else. A thread of fear, and maybe even a skein of anger.

I unlock the door and then resume my sentry post, guarding Jim's room. Daddy looks me over, running his hands from my head to my shoulders, checking me before taking in the mess.

"What happened?"

"I heard a thud and Toby went berserk at the doorway." I gesture helplessly. "But the room was empty, and no one was here. Nobody, not even Jim." My voice is getting soft and sing-songy which isn't good, but I can't seem to help it.

"I'm going to check the rest of the house. You stay put."

Daddy presses three numbers as he walks out the door—911, I assume—and time slips by a little more, winding around voices and the tinny static of walkie-talkies. Toby whines as he's dragged from my side and down the hallway. Momma's voice is sharp and hollow at the same time. How is that possible? How can it reverberate so shrilly? It echoes off the basketballs, bouncing on the rubber.

Dry hands grasp my arms and I'm escorted to my room. I sit on my bed primly, the horseradish and relish filling my nose. I take off my shirt and lob it to the floor. As I follow the slow arc it makes, times slows so much that I can see the folding and un-folding of the stained shirt. It hits the floor without a sound and time speeds up, doubling up to make up for the lost seconds. And then I'm at the door, cheek pressed tight to the wood in a tank top I don't remember getting into. The voices are muffled but I can still make out the conversation.

"No sign of forced entry anywhere," says the sheriff's voice, a baritone thick with snuff and full of menace. "Not on y'all's front door, kitchen door, Jim's room, or on the windowsill. If someone did come in, this window was left open for them." A pause, a soft hiss of static, and a clanking that could be a read-justing of a belt. "I hate to be the one who says it, James, but this might be another cry for attention from your daughter."

Another? I gasp, my cheek rasping against the painted wood. How dare he!

Momma sighs. And the sound hurts because it's threaded with annoyance, a current of how-could-she-do-this-to-*us* winds through the soft expulsion of air. The sound makes me throw open the door.

"Someone breaks into our house and your answer is to blame *me*? Well, that's just the stupidest thing I've ever heard. About as stupid as declaring Jim dead in the first place" I glare at Momma whose face is too pale, the apples of her cheeks look feverish in contrast. The starkness in her gaze makes me avert my eyes in instantaneous regret, though when I look at the sher-iff's I-told-you-so expression, I spit words at him. "Great piece of detective work." The sarcasm is so heavy my words sink un-der the weight of it, rather than strike him in the heart as if slung on an arrow. Why is Sheriff Oakwood always the one that comes when we have trouble? Shouldn't it be Georgefield's chief of po-lice, Chief Hoyle? Come to think of it, I haven't seen much of him since Jim disappeared. I always hoped he was busy chasing leads.

Daddy looks as if my words struck him instead. I step back and slam my door. Breath heaving, I press my lips together so I can make out their response. Footsteps fade away as Oakwood says, "You may need to get her professional help before she hurts herself, or you guys."

Momma's murmur of agreement makes me want to howl in frustration.

But that would be a crazy-person response.

The next day after I serve the last customer during lunch rush, while most of the teenagers and families picnic on tables and blankets under the pine trees, Lucas walks up to the concession stand. I get his usual—hot dog smothered in barbeque sauce— ready for him.

"What's he holding?" Honey leans against the counter. Once the cops left last night, I called her immediately to fill her in on everything. I needed her reassurances to calm me down from my near hysteria after my own mother refused to believe that some- one broke in. I needed someone to be on my side.

I join her at the window to see something in his hand about the size of a naval orange but white, bone white. "No idea."

Lucas sets it on the counter, his grin wide and mischievous. Then, he turns it around. Two large, empty eye sockets stare blankly at us.

"Get that thing off the counter!" Honey yelps, backpedaling so I stand between her and the skull. Relief floods through me as I realize it's too small to be Jim's. Horror takes over when I real- ize it's the size of a baby's skull.

Lucas laughs. "It's not a baby if that's what y'all are think- ing. It's a swamp monkey."

"Those do not exist," I say firmly.

"There's no proof either way," Honey looks dubiously at the skull.

"Good grief, are you serious?"

"Serious as a fadeaway jumper at the buzzer for the win," Lucas says. "You never heard those stories about the circus rail-car that overturned back in the '50s and all the monkeys escaped?"

"What? No."

"True story," he says. "I've never seen one, but I've heard stories about them."

Honey nods. "Mama's friend Terri swears she saw one on their Senior Skip Day, but Mama says it was the wine coolers. Where'd you find it?"

Lucas gestures behind him to a group of boys at one of the picnic tables. "They found it while bream fishing in a swamp off the Talakhatchee. Figured y'all would want to see it. Ah, you got my dog ready. Nice."

He scoops up his food and the skull before heading back to his lifeguard perch.

Honey grabs my arm so abruptly I jump. "What?" I screech.

"Bea, what if it was a swamp monkey you saw yesterday at the Shelf?"

"The idea of monkeys loose in the swamps freaks me out as much as the idea of a Grendal-monster because I was planning on forgetting any of that even happened."

Honey shakes her head sadly, but with a hint of something else. "You pick the weirdest things to believe to be real. But things that could happen, you pretend don't exist."

My throat tightens. I hate disappointing people, especially my best friend. That's all I seem to do lately. But it's a small price to pay if I can ever find Jim.

She throws both hands out, fingers splayed and eyes narrowed, and I step back, thinking she's going to push me. "This whole thing with your brother. I wish I could just knock some sense into you."

"I thought we were talking about swamp monkeys. What's this have to do with Jim?"

"There you go, pretending something that doesn't exist is real. You're making yourself miserable and I'm tired of seeing you do it to yourself. Why can't you move on? He. Is. Gone. There's no savior. Your brain's playing tricks on you."

My eyes prickle with tears that I hide behind the ice cream freezer door. The kernels in the popper burn, the acrid smell filling the small building. Does this mean she doesn't believe me about the break-in either?

She tugs me toward her, bobbing her head until I look at her face. "Stop focusing on the what-ifs and think about your what-nexts."

I wrench my hands away and the ice cream scoops clatter to the floor. "That's what I'm trying to do!"

Her mouth tightens. "No, it's not. You're so worried about your past, you might miss your future."

I know she means well but I can't stand this. I cross my arms to shield myself from her words. "The past is the only place with Jim. How can I move forward? He's not there." I turn away from her.

"Lunch rush is over. You can handle things from here." She unties her apron and rushes to her bike. I watch her ride away feeling bewildered, hurt, lost, and angry.

Miserable, I can't even successfully pull off a fake smile when I work that night at the restaurant. When I accidentally screw up the second order in a row, Momma sends me home. She can barely stomach to look at me, so I'm sure she's glad for the excuse to get me out of there. I haunt the house, blazing a trail between my bedroom and Jim's. His room is still in shambles, so I put it back to normal-Jim-chaos.

What Honey said about me not knowing pretend from reality messes with me. It feels like a riddle. I get out a notepad and sit on my bed with Toby for company and make a list to organize my head.

Things I think aren't real: swamp monkeys.

Things I'm on the line about: ghosts, water spirits, and mysterious boys named Colin.

Things I think are real: alligators, Toby, I had a brother though now he's gone, and a best friend named Honey.

Should I move that last one to the maybe list? What if she doesn't want to be my best friend anymore? I'd be even more alone than I am now. As my throat tightens, I know I'm pathetic for being so upset that she's mad at me. It's a vicious swirl of sadness I can't figure how to crawl out of. What's worse is that a part of me—the self-preserving selfish part—knows she's right. I need to focus on the what-nexts. She's not right about the moving on part. I know in my heart he's not gone forever.

Toby whines when I push him off the bed to make more room for the scrapbooks, searching for pictures of the four of us—me and Honey, Jim and Lucas. I stare at each markered, stickered page as if it's a Da Vinci code waiting to be cracked. The last page is of the previous Christmas. We wore reindeer headbands into the woods. Honey gripped a pine tree as she did a toe touch, while Jim and Lucas attacked its trunk with a saw. I took the picture. Honey was beaming, Lucas laughing at something, but Jim…

What was Jim looking at?

At first glance, I thought he was looking at Honey but now I see the angle is wrong. Looking past her, he wears an expression that could've been alarm or surprise. Could he see something the rest of us missed? Was there something in the woods? Something more alarming than maybe-swamp monkeys and scary enough to make an almost-man vanish into thin air? Something that would force my parents to declare their own son dead?

I stick a finger underneath the picture, trying to pry it out but it rips. I bite my lip in frustration, then howl, startling Toby.

What clues could an old picture tell me anyway? I need some air.

The setting sun casts shadows on the porch, tempting bats and moths for a game of hide-and-seek. Toby leaves me to join the fun. Green tree frogs appear on the windows, stretching their voices for the night's performance. I'm not in the mood to appreciate it. Momma and Daddy walk over after the restaurant closes, Momma handing me a take-out box gone cold. I pick at it. When I feel them watching me through the sheer curtains of the living room window, I tell them I'll be at the dock.

Everything is wrong. The lightning bugs still dance their tipsy dance to the songs of bullfrogs and cicadas. The moonflowers still make me think of what Heaven must smell like. Even the Big Dipper is in the same spot it always is.

But it's all wrong.

The coyotes in the woods know something's off. Their mournful, lonely howls stir the sadness within me and tears well up in my eyes. I sniffle and wipe them away with the hem of my shirt.

What would I be doing if Jim were here? We'd be on the dock searching for a cool breeze as the winds blow across Lake George. Our backs would lean against the wooden steps to watch for falling stars. Last year, every shooting star carried a wish for my crazy, frizzy hair to smooth out. This summer, I'd wish for my brother back.

Jim would've brought a mason jar with holes poked through the lid. Catching lightning bugs on the walk from the house to the dock, we'd both be amazed at how such an ugly bug could be so beautiful when it let its light shine.

I listened to his stories about the constellations over and over. In late winter, before they sank too low, he'd tell me about the seven stars all huddled together in a bunch used to be sisters. How Zeus turned them into stars because they were so sad when their daddy, Atlas, had to carry the whole world on his back. Or he'd tell me how Orion eternally chased them through the heavens while quoting Tennyson. I whisper Jim's favorite lines.

Many a night I saw the Pleiads, rising through the mellow shade,

Glitter like a swarm of fire-flies tangled in a silver braid.

I remember thinking how marvelous it would be to have seven sisters since it was only the two of us.

Now it's only me.

Most important, if he were here, I wouldn't be so alone.

I'm feeling extra lonely on this quiet evening beside the bait lean-to where Daddy sits in the shade selling shiners and crickets to his customers. Canoes bob sleepily in their berths. The figure stretched out in one is just... oh crap, someone's out here.

"Mr. Catfish?" I scramble to a crouch, my toes prickling with adrenaline in case I need to run.

"If I say anything, am I going to have to rescue you from the lake?" Colin asks wryly.

"Since I think you might be real, you're probably imaginary," I relax a little. I mean, if he was going to hurt me, he'd have let me fall under the limestone shelf.

"Not sure what that means, but okay." He steps out of the canoe and sits next to me on the dock.

"I'd ask what you're doing out on our dock, but since you don't exist, you really aren't." His closeness surprises me, makes my tongue flippant. It's so...companionable. Doesn't he know that most people stay away?

"Aren't what?" he asks.

"Here." His eyelashes are long for a guy. "Do you have a message for me?"

"Did you hit your head on the limestone? A message from whom?"

I ignore the insult. "My brother—Jim Montgomery."

A cloud must have scurried across the moon because his eyes seem to gleam for an instant. "No…"

"Then why are you here?"

"According to you, I'm not."

I push my hair back in frustration, but he seems amused, so I drop it for now.

"Were you crying?" he asks.

What guy asks that? "That's none of your business."

He shrugs and gives me a sideways glance.

And for some reason, that undams my mouth. "Let's see, my best friend's mad at me. My brother's been missing since March. No word if he's okay or where he went."

"What do your parents say?"

I laugh bitterly. "That I need closure. Now, I hate that word. And that I'm just a cry of attention away from a nuthouse." Might as well get that aired out. "My dad acts like I'm torturing my mom, like I'm overreacting. Overreacting? Because I'm worried about my brother who disappeared into thin air?"

"Then they must know something."

"Yeah, but they won't talk to me about it. No one will." And the weight of it all crushes me.

"We'll figure it out," he says, a casualness to his tone like it's something simple. A task easy enough to be finished in a moment. He makes it sound like we're already friends, and I can't stamp down the hope that wells inside me, sending a warm prickling from my fingertips to my toes. Lifting the weight.

Suddenly, Momma calls my name, an edge in her voice that hints at pinched lips and too wide eyes, and the burden settles back onto my shoulders. I walk across the parking lot to the house, sneaking glances back to where Colin has disappeared into the darkness. It isn't until I'm brushing my teeth that the obvious hits me. Something that I should've thought of immediate-ly, but the feel-good tingles must have masked.

Why on earth would a stranger, especially this beautiful stranger, want to help me?

6

A Found Object & a Hidden Truth

Right after my Cheerios, I head over to the concession stand to set up. I'd rather keep busy than make myself a nervous wreck. If Honey doesn't come in, at least I won't be behind in the prep work when I open for the day.

The concession stand opens for lunch and snacks, while the restaurant serves dinner. Daddy's already checking on things at the fishing and canoe dock, so I walk over to ask for the restaurant stockroom key.

"Morning, Daddy."

"Morning, Beep." He washes out an empty bait bucket. "You need to get into the stockroom?"

"Yes, sir."

"Know whose this is?" He holds up a leather bracelet.

"Not mine. But it does look familiar. Maybe I saw it on a customer yesterday?"

"You mind giving it to your mom to put in the lost and found box next time you see her?"

"Sure." Is this Daddy's subtle way to get Momma to interact civilly with me? 'Cause she'll probably say I stole it. I grimace and slide it on my wrist, trailing behind him. The raw-edged, suede leather cuff doesn't look like anything special. Daddy unlocks the restaurant's main doors, while I enter by myself, not turning on any lights since the morning sun beams though the windows.

There's something creepy about being alone in a place that is usually full of people and energy. My footsteps echo hollowly on the wooden floors, so I walk a little faster. I pull the chain to the light in the claustrophobic stockroom that's floor-to-ceiling with dry goods for the stand and the restaurant. Loading myself down with bags of popcorn kernels, sugar, and tea, I realize why that bracelet seems familiar.

It hits me that I saw it when I franticly grabbed a hand as I was pulled by a scuppernong vine rope from a slippery riverbank. The bracelet belongs to Colin.

I shift my arm to study it closer but realize too late what a bad idea that is as the tea container slips, displacing the bag of kernels. I drop everything. The sugar bag busts on impact. A rare snowy day in lower Alabama.

Damn, damn, damn!

Sugar crystals crunch under my flip flops as I search out a broom to clean up my mess. The broom handle whacks a clipboard hanging from a nail on the wall and causes it to fall, scattering sheets of paper among the popcorn kernels, sugar, and tea bags.

My fingernails dig into my palm as I swallow my frustration, sinking to my knees and sorting through the mess. The crystals dig into my knees, surprisingly painful for something so small. I clip the papers back together and rehang it on the wall when something flutters to the ground.

I catch the moss green paper in my hand carefully, as if I'm trying not to spook a butterfly. It's creased but legible enough to make out the word 'swamp' printed on one side. The stylized font makes it seem like part of a company name or logo. I flip it over to the other side:

5 am 4/27

The handwriting is sloppy and long, like Jim's. A tiny turtle with a basketball shell doodled in the corner confirms it. Jim always drew those. I chew on my lip. A time and a date. Does it have anything to do with his disappearance?

I slide the slip of paper into my pocket, a small smile stealing over my lips. A torn logo, a time and date, a phone call, and hope. It's not much to go on but it's so much more than I had just a minute ago. I finish cleaning up the mess, then scoop up the supplies before heading back to the stand.

The clock on the wall shows the time Honey usually arrives. I take out the scrap of paper and look at the turtle again, tracing the ridges of ink. My breath comes out shaky, so I busy myself with warming up the rotisserie and pouring kernels in the popcorn maker.

"Hi." Honey pauses in the doorway.

"Hey." I'm relieved but hesitant that she's here. I try to gauge if she's still angry.

"Sorry for going off like that. Being all weird."

Relief floods through me. "It's okay. Tough love is hard to give and take. I agree with one third of what you said."

She stashes her bag underneath the stool. "We just see things differently sometimes. It was asinine of me to react that way. You forgive me?"

"As long as you're calling yourself an asshole, then yes, of course."

Honey laughs. "Good, because I don't want to get another date to the dance last minute."

"Crap, that's tonight?"

Honey playfully rolls her eyes. "Anticipating that response, I already picked out a dress for you at Rosie's. After work, you're going to try it on. Just think. This officially starts our sophomore school year." She helps herself to a cup of fresh popcorn, munching thoughtfully. "The *last* popcorn of the *last* Friday of our summer. But the first time we get dresses together for a school dance this year."

Little—otherwise insignificant—things suddenly take on a bigger meaning. Milestones that are passing by too quickly until you look back and realize what they signified. And then it's too late. It's just a memory stored somewhere in a brain so full of hidey-holes that they never resurface. Like the last time Jim and I ate popcorn together, or the last time we raced in the pool, or the last time we fought over something stupid. But I didn't know at the time they would be our last.

"Bea? Are you okay?"

I wipe away tears I hadn't realized were there. "Yeah." They weren't our lasts, I remind myself, because I will find him.

"You know we'll eat popcorn tomorrow and it'll be our last popcorn of the last Saturday of our summer."

I grin and throw popcorn at her. She catches it in her mouth and laughs triumphantly.

Ah, it's great to have my thoughtful, bossy best friend back. I pull out the scrap of moss green paper and run my fingertips along the torn edges. Would showing this to Honey make yesterday's fight resurface? Now I almost wish she had been late to work so I could look up the logo without her presence.

I hunch over my stool and pull out my phone, trying my best to project indifference. A Google search pulls up logos for a brewery, a pizza place, a BBQ team, and a catering company—a surprisingly large amount of food-related businesses. Surprising because swamps don't make me immediately think of food. They're pretty to look at and I love to spend time in them, but they never make me hungry. I mean, stuff rots there.

"Whatcha doing? Texting Junior?"

I pause in my scrolling to give her a slitted look. "Pretty sure that will never happen. No... something... for the restaurant, for Daddy."

Her phone buzzes. Normally a vague answer wouldn't suffice, but she nods absently at me, fingers and thumb already flicking away at the screen, an odd, self-conscious but happy smile on her lips. I'd ask her about it but it's the distraction I need. I scroll down further.

So far none of the fonts match up, but swamp logo was a pretty unspecific thing to search. The only logos that are the same moss green color are for some kind of hospital system and... potpourri. Seriously? Since when do folks want their house smelling like decomposing vegetation? Though the lettering of the potpourri business looks the most similar and the address on the masthead is the closest, a post office box in Louisiana.

I sigh at this dead end, this non-clue, this scrap of paper Jim could've taken off Daddy's desk or somewhere random. I slide it back into my pocket anyway. There could still be some potential here with the date and time. Mostly, it's just something of Jim's that I can hold on to.

After we sell the mess out of some ice cream because of the heat, Daddy lets us close up earlier than normal and ride into town. Honey parks in front of the Piggly-Wiggly and we walk next door to Rosie's Boutique.

The door chimes and the scent of roses surrounds us as we enter the shop. We approach the counter where Miss Rosie has two dresses waiting for us to try on. Honey's gown is a beautiful sky-blue strapless dress with ruching on the sides, and she picked out a green-after-a-storm Grecian-styled dress for me.

"That color's gonna look so pretty with that Auburn hair of yours," Miss Rosie says. "And Honey, yours matches your eyes perfectly. Those poor boys won't know what hit 'em!"

We go into our dressing rooms to try them on. I stare at my reflection once I change. The dress does look nice, I have to admit. It makes me look like I have curves even though I'm on the small side but proportional, so I'm not unhappy with my appearance. The green compliments my tan from lying out those couple of hours each day between working the concession and the restaurant. In the winter, my skin becomes pale and even my freckles grow faint.

My hair is out of control as usual. It escapes from headbands, ponytail bands, and everything else I use to tame it. When it's lightning during thunderstorms, my hair actually stands on end. I am a sight to behold, and not in a good way.

"Bea Pearl, I hear that sigh. Come out so we can see what you look like," Honey commands.

I pull back the heavy curtain and stand next to Honey in front of the tri-fold mirror.

"I did good!" Honey exclaims, clapping.

Miss Rosie laughs.

Honey taps a finger to her chin as she assesses my dress in the mirrors. "Gold jewelry for you." She postures and pouts at her reflection. "And pearls for me. What do y'all think?"

I adjust the tiny silver bee charm hanging from its chain around my neck and rub at the empty spot. Jim gave it to me on my thirteenth birthday. He described it as my name necklace, as he pointed to the bee next to the lumpy freshwater pearl. When he disappeared, the pearl had gone missing, too.

"Oh." Honey's watching me fiddle with my necklace, so I drop my hands to my sides, bunching the delicate fabric. "I shouldn't have mentioned pearls. And duh, you don't have to wear gold. I know you don't want to take off Jim's necklace…"

I shake my head and glance at Miss Rosie, who looks uncomfortable, as if she just ate an entire family platter of greasy fried catfish by herself.

"When'd you get that bracelet?" Honey asks. "I haven't seen it before."

The roughness of Colin's cuff contrasts oddly with the dainty, feminine dress. "Oh, Daddy gave it to me." Well, he handed it to me, to be exact. I'm not going to tell Honey about Colin because of her getting angry out of the blue earlier. It's weird keeping something from her, and it doesn't sit well with me, but I don't want to inadvertently tick her off again. The easiest thing is to keep quiet about it.

"Was it Jim's?" Honey asks, cringing when Miss Rosie cuts her eyes at her. The shop keeper's bottom jaw juts out like she's appalled.

"Y'all just change out of those dresses and I'll bag 'em up for you," Miss Rosie mutters, turning away from us and walking towards the front counter.

"Oops. I made it ten times worse, didn't I? Why can't my mouth just stop before I try to eat my own foot?"

I sigh. "I better get out of this dress before I mess it up."

We change, pay for the dresses, and run to the Pig for hair-spray.

"You're coming over to my house to do your hair before the dance, right?" I ask as we get back in her car. I really mean help me with my hair, but she doesn't correct me.

She glances at my messy bun and grins. "Yup."

Honey and I sit on the piano bench in front of Momma's vanity. Honey takes her rollers out and her corn-silk hair swirls into perfect waves. Mine are tight corkscrews that surround my head like the burning bush from Bible Study. Momma tries to loosen the curls by brushing them. I jerk my head away.

"Let's try braids," Honey suggests and she and Momma braid it up until they declare me a Grecian goddess. I'm thinking Medusa is more accurate. I'll avoid my reflection in the mirror and in Jim's truck windows just in case I turn myself to stone .

Every time I grab Jim's keys off the hook next to the back door, Momma gives me a pained look like I'm dragging my nails down a chalkboard just to aggravate her. But she never says anything, because otherwise I'd have to borrow her car. She takes a picture of us before we head out for the evening.

My smile sticks to my teeth as I look at the camera. I watch it so closely I see the shutter blink.

Momma looks at the screen. "Goodness, Bea. What an odd look. Smile, huh?"

She takes another. This time I'm sure my look is faraway because there's something about that camera that I can't place. I shake my head. Maybe it's a picture I need to find. I have a feeling that what I need is hidden in a memory. Or a dream.

"Relax, Bea," Honey says, my arm in hers as we walk out to the truck. "It's just a dance."

7

Spectral Jerseys & King of the Lost and Forgotten

I would rather be anywhere else than at this dance while Honey is having the time of her life. Maybe if I was as good as her at dancing and making boys laugh, I wouldn't feel so out of place.

At some point, she'll tuck my hand under her arm, and we'll flit from person to person. She'll say things to me like: "Oh. Such-n-such was staring at your shoes! She's jealous." Or "Did you see So-n-so looking at you! Mmmm-hmmm, he's interested, all right." And I'll snort and look toward the exit.

For now, Boy-Who-Plays-Football slides up beside Honey and asks her to dance. I head over to the refreshment table to hold a glass of punch, so my hands have something more to do than flutter nervously like a blue jay with broken wings. At the punch table, Sara tells me, with a smile that makes me uneasy, that Junior actually does want to dance with me. Odd that Beth isn't with her.

My face flushes but I nod. I blame it on feeling the teensiest bit of envy at how much fun Honey is having. I once liked to dance, and I miss that free feeling. But I don't know how to reclaim it because it feels like it no longer exists for me.

Sara leads me over to Junior as if I'm a virginal sacrifice. We dance for one whole song but don't say a single word to each other. It shouldn't be so awkward—it's not like he's disrespectful or smelly or arrogant. Regardless, misery curls around my shoulders like a fancy fur stole. I would rather be elsewhere, even curled up in a ball on the rug in Jim's room. Not exactly at the moment though, since half his room has been destroyed. I peer up at Junior's face through my lashes.

Is it a coincidence he was running errands for my dad in my house the same day it got broken into? I bite my tongue as I mull it over. The sheriff did mention the window could've been left open to allow someone inside while he was trying to throw me under the bus. But all Jim and Junior have in common is basketball, and balls are a stupid motive for breaking into someone's house.

The song ends. I breathe a sigh of relief when he lets go of my waist. My hands drop from his shoulders. He opens his mouth like he's going to say something but decides against it and walks away.

Probably because I made the whole situation incredibly uncomfortable and couldn't come up with a Single. Thing. To. Say. But really, why didn't *he* try to say anything himself?

Honey still flits among the dancers on the gym floor. As another song begins, I cross my arms as the space around me between the corrugated cardboard columns fills up. Then I uncross them so I don't look defensive. I rest my hands on my hips and feel awkward as if I'm trying to figure out how to use someone else's appendages.

There's a murmur mixing with the beat that sounds like my name. Pivoting, I peer into a darkened hallway behind me that leads to the classrooms. I hear it again. Now I know I'm not imagining it.

"Hello?" The hairs on my arms raise, chilled, as if this part of the gym has the only working air conditioner.

Someone whisper-yells my name. A locker door slams farther down the hallway. Looking back to the dancers, I scan the crowd but can't find Honey. What if she's messing with me? "Not funny, Honey."

What if it's the same person who called looking for Jim? I'll go as far as the water fountain. The dull grey gleams from the darkness. Not caring if I look defensive, I wrap my arms around myself and half run to the fountain.

It hums and gurgles as it circulates water. What if it's the water spirit from my dream? "Hello?" Addressing the water fountain feels incredibly silly. Pausing for a polite amount of time in case it responds is ludicrous. Music and light spill out the open doors of the gym so it's not as dark in the hallway as it seemed from where I stood in the gym.

There's another wing of classrooms just beyond the fountain. A rustle catches my attention as someone—something—shifts. I hear small clicks, so I turn around in time to see something big and pale hurtle towards me. The number eleven fills my vision, overwhelming me.

I scream. Jim's basketball number.

Everything is white. Something silky fills my mouth. The sound of giggling and the click of heels against linoleum fades. The quiet calms me enough to stop screaming and feel around.

It *is* Jim's basketball jersey, formerly hanging in a display case across the hall from the school office. I rub the mesh between my fingers, beyond ready to be home. I ball the jersey, shoving it in my purse.

Running back to the gym, a steady clicking noise makes me jumpy until I look down and notice the gold chain on the toe of my shoe is broken, flopping around like a tap-dancing tilapia. Crap. I borrowed these shoes from Momma.

Please let me find Honey, I chant to myself. The first person I see is Sheriff Oakwood, acting as a chaperone. He's in uniform except for his hat, and his scalp gleams through his comb-over, reflecting colors from the DJ's disco ball. He is his own mirrored ball. He's smacking a flask against his palm as he talks to a small huddle of senior boys. I try to casually walk past but I'm still too jumpy to look nonchalant. My heart is still pounding, my breathing too fast, and I'm sure my eyes are more bug-eyed than wide-eyed. Since when does a sheriff chaperone a school dance? Usually Chief Hoyle or a deputy attends school events but it's mainly a goodwill, community-type appearance, not this.

"Bea!"

I shriek, then bite my lip as Oakwood frowns in my direction. Crap. That's far from casual.

Honey touches my elbow. "Bea. You look like you've seen a ghost. What's wrong?"

Sheriff Oakwood stares at me, as if deciding he has enough cause to have me committed.

"I need to go home."

"Sure." She links her arm in mine. "Let's go."

I reluctantly show Momma her broken shoe once I get home after dropping Honey off at her house. Momma takes it much better than I anticipated.

"Does this mean you danced my shoes to pieces?" she asks with a wink. She sits with Daddy on the couch in the living room watching some reality show. "Did you have a good time?"

I shrug. Is she asking me because she really cares, or because it's a requirement in some Mom Manual? "It was all right.

I danced a slow dance with a boy and then one of those huddle dances that girls do when they get into big groups and sway and sing really loudly and off key."

"Dancing sure was different in our day," Daddy begins and I groan inside knowing this might be a long story, one of those we-had-to-dance-uphill-there-and-back-in-the-snow-with-a-bobcat-taped-to-our-toes type tales.

"Who was the boy?" Momma asks.

Normally I'd think this was none of her business but since she just saved me from Daddy's story, I owe her. "No one important, Junior Batchelor."

"I thought I'd seen more of him and his buddies around here lately," Daddy says.

I shake my head. "Oh, no you don't, you two. There's nothing going on."

Momma shimmies her shoulders and winks at Daddy which irritates me into saying something I know I shouldn't.

"Y'all better give Jim this hard of a time when he comes back with—" I stop when Momma blanches. Daddy, on the other hand, looks as if he dove face-first into the cooler of cherry hunch-punch Ronnie Haster snuck into last year's town festival down by the river.

"To. Your. Room." Daddy forces the words through clenched teeth.

Ashamed, I run down the hall to my bedroom but not before I see the look of tender concern on Daddy's face as he scoots closer to Momma.

That concern sitting starkly on my dad's features has me easing the door closed, rather than slamming it like I'd prefer. I flop down on my bed. I don't understand why mentioning Jim does this. They'd rather pretend he never existed. My insides are as tangled as a midair mockingbird fight, the way they make me feel ashamed for bringing up my own brother. Why should I feel despicable?

Not just them though. Miss Rosie's reaction earlier today to Honey's comment about Jim is normal. It took me a few months after Jim's disappearance to figure it out, unfortunately. I'd see a former teammate of Jim's at the Pig and as soon as I'd mention something about my brother being back in time to help coach the underclassmen, the basketball player would look everywhere but at me and then mumble something about a sale on pork rinds before running off. It got to where I stopped talking about Jim and then quit talking to people in general.

Maybe I'm trying to see if I can disappear like Jim did. Just stop existing, too. Can I find him, if I'm here one day, then *poof*? Is there a place where all things go once they disappear? Maybe I'll find Jim robed in a mantle of misplaced socks, gilded with shiny keys, reading glasses piled precariously high on top of his head like a crown, perched on a throne of loose change. King of the Lost and Forgotten.

Once I stop existing, will folks from town even notice I disappeared? Perhaps they might pass each other in the grocery store aisles and ask each other whatever happened to that Bea Pearl. One day, she was a cheerleader and then she disappeared.

Then the other person would say, "Oh yeah, the girl at the top of the pyramid. No, she faded away; it took all summer for her to disappear. She stopped talking because no one would talk to her. She faded 'til she didn't exist anymore."

And the first person would say, "Huh. Well, they'd better find someone else, 'cause you can't have a cheerleading pyramid without the girl on top."

They'll forget they were talking about me in the first place as they ramble on about my replacement, and I'll fade away some more as the talk turns to Friday night football.

I know such conjecture is silly. Without many clues to puzzle out, my brain has to swirl something around. My hands jerk as I remember Ronnie Haster, a classmate of Jim's, getting in trouble almost a year before Jim disappeared. Ronnie told us about mysterious boats run aground up and down the Chatothatchee and Talakhatchee, abandoned in tree roots with rents in the metal bottoms. He was going to refurbish them and sell them on Craigslist to buy more Everclear for his soon-to-be-famous cherry hunch-punch.

I knock my fist against my forehead. Why would my brain have pulled that memory to the surface? I have more important things to focus on.

Taking off my dress, I lay it on a chair in my room. Pulling on my sleep shorts and an old Lake George T-shirt, I slip Colin's bracelet back on. It might not be the best idea, but I'm feeling pretty miserable. I find that slip of paper with the doodled turtle and look at the numbers again before turning off my nightstand lamp.

A lightbulb goes off in my head, illuminating a possible connection. Hatchee Fest is always the last weekend in April. It happened on April 27th this year. Five a.m. was before the fun run, or the worm fiddling, or the greasy pole. Why was Jim planning to be there so early? The flood swept him away a month and a half before that date, so what happened in his absence? I tuck my hands under my chin, but my brain is done for the night, proud of itself for the two exhumed memories. There are no more links to make.

I sniff the leather of the bracelet on my wrist. It traps the smell of boy and sunshine and woods and the tiniest bit of earthiness like baked mud. Inhaling it is the only way I can relax, the only way I can let go of the pain clenching my throat, enough to drift off to sleep.

8

Boiling & Bunning

The next day, the family rises earlier than usual in preparation for our Sixth Annual End-of-Summer Picnic. It's a big deal with hot dog eating contests, swimming and canoe races, and a fishing tournament. I'm glad there's something to keep my parents too busy to be ashamed of me.

We pull a couple of picnic tables together for our pre-festivities meeting. All the Lake George employees are there: my parents, me, Honey, Lucas, and an extra lifeguard since there will be more people in the pool than usual. Mr. Catfish will run the hotdog contest, then the fish fry later this evening. Posturing next to him, a few of the girls from town are in bikinis and shorts so short and tight I worry their butt cheeks might catch on fire if they walk too fast. The four of them have bleached blonde hair with brown under layers that reminds me of the soft-serve ice cream when we mix chocolate and vanilla. The contestants seem to eat, swim, and paddle faster when the shorts-challenged girls cheer from the sidelines. Daddy has the girls serving snacks and judging the races.

Momma hands out tank tops for us to wear while Daddy delegates our duties. Barely awake, I keep catching myself staring off into space.

"Beep, Honey, and Catfish will have kitchen duties." Daddy's voice is a honeybee drone to my sleepy ears. "We don't want to run out of hot dogs this year. I want to have enough for the paying customers, too. Sammie, Kiki, Mae, and Tonya, y'all will help Marg with the decorating. Lucas and Tim, I need y'all to power wash the sidewalks near the well box. I noticed there was still mud we must've missed this spring."

Daddy's directions startle me. I sit straight up and look around, sure I must have misheard. "What did he say?" I whisper to Honey.

She looks at me knowingly. "About the mud?"

I shake my head, impatient that she didn't hear what I did. "No, no, no, no. He wants Lucas and Jim to help him?" I'm breathing way too fast. Daddy frowns at me though continues with his instructions.

"Bea, calm down. He said 'Tim'. That's Lucas's friend from Briar who's helping out today as the extra lifeguard," Honey whispers.

"Bea Pearl, why don't you and Honey go ahead and start on the prep work?" Daddy glares at me.

Honey smiles brightly as she links her arm in mine, pulling me to the restaurant.

"What just happened?" she exclaims as we walk inside.

I'm still a little shaky. "No idea. I was watching that swallowtail and only half-listening to Daddy. I could've sworn he said Lucas and *Jim*. I got so confused, wondering if I imagined this whole summer without Jim. That it was just a horribly bad dream."

Honey purses her lower lip then hugs me. "Think of how much worse it could be."

"What on earth could be worse?"

"Your dad could have assigned one of those booty-licious girls to work with us."

I snort. "You noticed that, too?"

"I felt bad for those shorts!"

We laugh and that confused, shaky feeling sloughs off as I'm sure Honey intended. It's such a relief to laugh with her— even if I feel a tinge of guilt that it's at someone else's expense.

Honey adjusts the flames under one pot as I fill another with water.

Last year the hot dog eating contest was such a success, we didn't have enough hotdogs left over to sell. That ticked Daddy off, so he ordered way more this time which means we have a lot of boiling and bunning to do.

"Saw that you danced with Junior Batchelor last night," Honey begins casually.

I roll my eyes. "Not you too."

"He's bought something at the concession stand almost every day."

"Huh. You sound just like my parents."

Honey sticks out her tongue. "I'm just making an observation."

"You danced with Nick Ledger." Another synapse sparks. At this rate I may actually connect legit clues. "Oh, that's who texted you yesterday when you had the weird look on your face, isn't it?"

"I did not!" She brushes a hand across her face, a grin peeking out. "But, yeah. He didn't text me at all the day before, which was one reason why I snapped at you. Deepest apologies, again—I suffer from boy angst." She shakes her head and shudders with mock chills. "Anyway, he's second string quarterback and I'm going to be co-captain of the squad this year. It makes sense. Especially if we still like each other our senior year. Then he'll be quarterback and I'll be captain. I have it all planned out. You're our best flyer and you'll be my co-captain. Junior's on the basketball team…"

"Your idea of romance boggles me," I shake my head as I lug the pot to the stove.

Honey giggles. "It's a match made in Football Heaven. He's cute, I'm cute. He's a good kisser." She bats her eyes, looking at me expectantly, and I can't resist the bait.

"What! Y'all kissed? When?"

"He danced me behind one of those cardboard columns. It was very romantic."

"Sounds like it," I say skeptically. "As long as y'all don't end up being romantic behind some azalea bush because, knowing him, it'll be covered in poison sumac."

Honey smacks me in the arm with a raw dog in mock indignation. "Really, Bea!" Then she gestures toward Colin's bracelet. "With Miss Rosie being all weird yesterday you never told me if that was Jim's or not. You usually only wear your necklace." She nods in the direction of my pearl-less bee necklace.

I forgot to take the cuff off this morning. And now I'm in that same predicament: lie to my best friend or tell her and have her mad at me again. "Your pot's about to boil over."

"Oops." She turns down the flame. "So, I was right?"

I nod without looking at her. I didn't say anything so technically I didn't lie; just let her think what she wanted to. But I still feel pretty shady.

"Do you want to talk about the way Miss Rosie acted? Or what happened at the dance to make you look so scared?"

"What's there to talk about? Besides you and Co… I mean, you, that's how everybody reacts. It's not weird if everyone does it. You and I are the different ones." Flustered, I really want to change the subject. I don't know if it was the way Jim's jersey was 'given' to me, or the look on Oakwood's face that has me more anxious.

Honey arches an eyebrow, most likely over my near slip-up, but I walk out the kitchen mumbling about going to get more buns. Instead, I march past the stockroom and out the main door. I need air.

The restaurant sits on stilts over the lake and connects to land by a wide gangway with benches on each side for customers as they wait for tables. There's a candy machine on one side filled with bird feed so folks can feed the ducks below. Kneeling on the wooden bench, I look down to the water. The ducks congregate in my shadow and quack expectantly, but I don't have any quarters.

"Hey."

I smile, thinking it's Colin and feel a little embarrassed because he'll see that I'm wearing his bracelet. Plus, he didn't actually give it to me so he might think I stole it.

I shouldn't have worried because it's not Colin, but Junior, standing behind me.

My smile turns bland. "Hi. The Picnic starts at ten." We've already exchanged more words in this minute than that entire awkward dance last night.

"Okay." He adjusts his baseball cap.

"Are you going to compete in the hot dog eating contest?" I'm trying to figure out why he's here.

"If you want me to."

"Uh, it really doesn't matter. Concessions will be open pretty much all day. Up until the fish fry tonight. You seem to like hot dogs."

He shrugs, picking at his finger.

Suddenly, I remember him passing me a note at school. His hand, with a purplish thumbnail, held a white square of looseleaf. My hand, connected to a rainbowed wrist of knotted string bracelets, hovered over beige school-issue linoleum.

It was right before the flood, the day school got out early. He told me to give the paper to Jim, so I passed it on, too preoccupied with the weather to read it beforehand. I tilt my head to look more closely at Junior. Is there any chance the note is related to Jim's running to the river?

Junior seems to notice me staring and takes a step toward me, closing the buffer.

I abruptly look down at the gangway, then over my shoulder as if I hear Honey calling for me. "Okay… well, good luck if you are competing. If not, umm… I need to get back to the kitchen." I walk inside without waiting for him to respond, aggravated because he hogged my calming fresh air break. More importantly, I'm upset with myself because I wish I'd just read the stupid note. Now, I'll never know if it contained a clue. I snort at my paranoia.

"Where're the buns?" Honey asks.

"Argh, sorry. Junior was being annoying. It distracted me."

Honey flutters her eyelashes. "Oh really! And how did he distract you?"

I narrow my eyes, but without malice. "Not like that. He walked up but didn't really say anything."

"Aww, you have him tongue-tied. That's sweet."

"It's weird. Now stop it before I tell one of the booty girls to trade places with me." My irritation with Junior evaporates now that I can tell Honey's thinking about this rather than our earlier uncomfortable conversation.

Honey pretends to gag, and we boil, bun, and continue preparing for the contest.

Eavesdropping & Itchy Pearls

The fishing tournament is the first event of the picnic. It kicks off the festivities and runs all day. This afternoon, Daddy will have the fish tallies completed and then we'll have the big fish fry with the winning catches. The swim and canoeing races begin a little before lunch and the hot dog-eating contest is after that.

Momma and the Booty Girls did a great job with the decorations, I have to admit. All the picnic tables are covered in red-and-white checkerboard tablecloths with burlap-wrapped mason jars filled with daisies, coneflowers, and sunflowers. Festive bunting decorates the concession stand, restaurant, and bait stand on Daddy's dock.

Honey and I are stacking platters full of hot dogs for the five contestants when Momma and one of the Booty Girls walk up to the stand. "Bea Pearl, the Ladies' race starts in just a bit." Momma says. "Go change into your suit. I'll have Sammie help you, Honey, 'til Bea finishes."

I smirk at Honey, who gives Momma and Sammie a bright smile.

"Sure thing, Mrs. Margaret. Good luck, Bea. Swim like a nymph."

I grin and grab my bag, then head over to the ladies' bath-house. The first race is ladies' freestyle, then the men's, and then the kid's will be after that. I nod to the other girls once I reach the bathhouse. We don't have a swim team at Georgefield High, but I've been racing these same girls ever since we were old enough to compete at the picnic. Three of the girls I go to high school with, the other two have graduated, had kids, but they still have some skill. Their arms are ripped from toting grocery bags and babies all the time. I walk over to an empty spot in the bench and unpack my bag.

The bathhouse has a partition making a foyer right at the front door so anyone opening the door won't flash everyone. I hear the door squeak open and make a mental note to tell Daddy it needs some WD-40. The girl next to me, Lenise, stiffens and looks at me with eyebrows raised. She's never been mean to me before. We've always bonded because she can pull her thick, dark hair into a pouf atop her head and totally rock it when I just wish mine could look that cute. Now hers is braided tight to her scalp. Taken aback by her expression, I push my stuff away from her. Maybe I'm crowding her. Maybe she's afraid my crazy will rub off on her, that the rumors of me responsible for Jim's "death" are true. *I'm not a murderess, I'm just clumsy!* I'd like to scream at this entire town. God, I'd like to have *that* printed up on a sign, zip-tied to the chain link fence around the football sta-dium.

Lenise nods toward the door.

Whoever opened the door hasn't made it past the partition so only four ankles and two pairs of wedge flip flops are visible. Turning back around, I stop at the sound of my name. I try to ignore the conversations going on around me, because people who eavesdrop never hear anything good, but there's no helping it.

"—Bea Pearl and Junior." Thing One asks.

"No, I don't think they said a word. Sad. I feel so bad for Honey always having to baby-sit her. Thought maybe she would attach herself to Junior so Honey could actually have some fun. Ever since Jim's gone, Bea Pearl's just gotten weirder and weirder, sucking the life right out of poor Honey," says Thing Two, also known as Sara. Thing One is Beth.

"Oh-my-god, I know. I want Honey to hang out with us again! She's so fun… and Beatrice is such a whiney bitch," says Beth.

I've heard enough. With my face forty shades of crimson, I run to the toilets and lock myself in a stall.

Their high-pitched voices carry over the stall door as they come closer. I'm guessing they're in front of the mirrors, sharpening their claws and adjusting the padding in their bikini tops. Then it's quiet except for the low buzz of conversation from the changing room. I'm still shaking so I figure I'll stay in here until I hear Daddy on the megaphone. Or I might just stay in here forever.

"Bea Pearl, it's Lenise. You okay?" she asks through the stall door.

Surprised, I hastily dry my eyes, toilet paper sticking to my wet lashes. "Sure thing!"

"Don't listen to them. Sara's been after your spot on the squad and Beth wants to have Junior's babies." She pauses. "And um, the grave thing didn't help." I swear it sounds like she snorts. "They're just jealous. You and Honey have been best friends since preschool."

Opening the door, I try to smile at Lenise, but I think it comes out a little maniacal. I'm saved from saying anything when Daddy's voice calls the swimmers to the pool.

We head out of the bath house together. I try to forget what I overheard but it's sand in my oyster and won't come out. I didn't realize Beth dislikes me so much. True, I haven't apologized for knocking her into the grave yet, but I don't see any good way to start that conversation: *I'm not a grave-pusher, I'm just clumsy!* Anyway, it's not my fault she was standing so close to me or the hole. I don't even know how she knows me well enough to not like me. The few times I've seen her this summer, she's acted superior to me, like she knows something I don't. I chalked it up to everyone acting weird around me.

Luckily, swimming clears my mind so instead of wallowing in guilt over suffocating my best friend, I concentrate on the cool, sweet water and the rhythmic reach and pull of my arms. I may be clumsy at dancing, walking, and life in general, but I *am* as agile as a nymph in water. Or a hippo.

When Jim and I were little, we'd swim or practice our strokes every day. Every year, he'd win the kid's division with me not too far behind. Once in high school, he won the men's all four years. With my win last year in the women's division, I'm hopeful I can follow in my big brother's footsteps—or swim strokes.

By the time I reach an arm out of the water and pull myself up on the side, I've left that itchy pearl of guilt at the bottom of the deep end. Momma and Honey cheer on the sidelines and Lucas flashes me a thumbs-up from the lifeguard stand. Daddy gives me a big smile and holds my arm up in the air. I wish I could put that genuine smile in trophy-form. Then anytime I needed some reassurance—or hell, love from my parents—I could take it off the shelf and polish it.

"And we have our winner," he says into the megaphone. "Bea Pearl Montgomery for the Ladies' Freestyle!"

Sara's and Beth's lemon-sucking duckfaces makes me laugh.

I redress into my tank top and shorts and tie my apron back on. Sammie's impatiently waiting for me to replace her so she can join the rest of the Booty Girls as they flock around the pool to watch the men's race. That one really pulls the ladies out of the woodwork.

"That was the longest twenty minutes of my life!" Honey exclaims dramatically. "If we had to talk about her toenail polish for one more second, I was going to stuff a whole platter of hot dogs down her throat."

"Do I suffocate you?" Immediately, I wish I can take the question back. You don't ask questions you don't want to hear the answers to.

Honey looks at me funny. "I guess that depends on if you want to talk about your toenail color."

I smile in relief. "Cajun Coral. Same as it always is."

After the swim and canoe races, I'm manning the concession stand by myself as the hot dog eating contest is about to begin. Mr. Catfish places the hot dog platters in front of the contestants and Honey, Kiki, Mae, Sammie, and Tonya stand behind each contestant to keep count. Honey looks over at me and widens her eyes dramatically, giving a mock-scared look before leaning in to give her eater—a bird-boned, elementary-school girl—encouragement.

I laugh but then jump when the door to the stand swings open.

"Employees only," I say, turning around. "Oh."

Colin leans against the doorframe. "That's fine since I don't exist."

I smooth my hair back. "I thought about it and decided there's a possibility you might be real." I'm saved from looking suave when my finger tangles in a curl.

"Were you thinking about me? That's interesting."

My cheeks prickle like they always do when they're about to turn red. "That's not what I meant."

He walks the couple of steps toward me and lightly touches my wrist. I'm glad I'm not holding anything because it would be on the floor.

"And you're wearing my stuff."

My fingers falter as I untie the laces. Luckily, my voice isn't as shaky as the rest of me. "You dropped it on the dock and since I never know when I'll see you again…"

"Keep it. Looks better on you."

I tuck my arms behind my back, oddly pleased.

"What made you decide I was real?"

He's teasing me, but I answer him honestly anyway. "Your bracelet. Daddy and Honey saw it. I figured that meant if it was real, then you are too."

"If other people see and believe in something, that makes it true? Based on that conjecture, the world was flat before it became round?"

"That's ridiculous."

"You think you'll fall off the earth one day because it's flat?"

I can't help but laugh. "All right, I see your point. Because three people can see a bracelet does not make the bracelet real. Just like people once thought the earth was flat does not make it flat."

"Or the bracelet is real, but real in different ways so each person perceives the bracelet based on their own experiences."

"Like Daddy thought it might be a girl's bracelet, Honey thought it was Jim's, and you and I know it to be yours. I can't believe we're having such a philosophical discussion about jewelry."

He shrugs his shoulders and grins. "I'm just that deep."

"See, that's what makes me think you don't exist. You're a manifestation of what I want ..." Oh crap, did I just say that out loud? My hand flies up to my itching cheeks as I turn an even deeper shade of red than before. "... Of what's lacking in other guys." I don't know if that fixes what I said or makes it worse.

His grin broadens even more at my obvious discomfort. "You find your boyfriend lacking?"

"My what? Oh, Junior. Not my boyfriend." I shake my head. There's a roar behind me, I turn to look out the counter window, grateful to have an excuse to hide my tomatoey cheeks.

"Looks like they have a winner," Colin observes.

Honey holds the little girl's arm up in triumph. The other four contestants look overstuffed and grumpy. Except for the guy on the end staring at Tonya's knotted tank tucked under her bikini top.

"Where did that little girl put all those hot dogs?" I wonder. I turn back to Colin and the concession stand is empty.

As if he had never been there. I grin and twirl his bracelet around my wrist.

10

Pained Looks & Parasitic Wasps

Everyone working is getting worn out. The picnic is always exhausting but this year it seems more so, maybe because of Jim's absence. It's the first year without him. He was always here, there, and everywhere. Helping. Making people laugh. I watch the faces of people enjoying themselves and no one seems to miss him. An odd, lost sort of anger rises to my face, making pinpricks that feel like deer fly stings. I run my hand over my cheeks, but nothing buzzes away. The pain is in my head. That makes me mad too.

Daddy's getting a quick bite to eat before heading back to the dock to tally up the results from the fishing tournament. I refill his sweet tea.

"Sure am glad we hired those extra kids today," he says. "Couldn't have done it without all the additional help. Guess I'm getting old."

"It'll be easier with Jim here next year," I say quietly.

He glares at me then glances around, as if looking for Momma. Honey takes a step back and sweeps the farthest corner of the building.

"Don't let your momma hear you talk like that. You don't want to set her off again. Think I'll go ahead and start those tallies."

I stare at his back in helplessness as he strides toward the dock, calling on his megaphone.

Honey gives me a sad smile but before she can say anything, a customer walks up. "Going to take Lucas some tea," she announces brightly.

"Hey."

"Oh, hi. Junior." Grrr.

"You upset I didn't compete in the hot dog contest?"

"What? No."

"Oh, you seem a little ticked."

Just because you keep popping up when I'm doing something important, like breathing or unraveling a mystery. "Oh, sorry. No, I'm fine." I give him a toothy smile.

He takes a step back. "'Kay. Just wanted to say you looked good in that race." His eyes widen. "I mean your form," he mutters. "All right. Your daddy is about to call the winners and I caught me a good-looking catfish. You wanna walk down to the dock and see?"

"Sure, if I didn't have to work but I can't leave the stand unattended," I say apologetically if not sincerely.

He looks at Honey, who's talking to her brother at the lifeguard tower. "Okay. See you at the fish fry?"

I nod and he walks down to the dock, following Daddy's path.

Beth can have him, no competition from me. I prop my elbows on the counter and rest my chin in my hands as I watch the crowd. One of the Booty Girls— Mae, I think— is painting kid's faces. Families are clustered everywhere around blankets and picnic baskets. Older kids jump in the pool, but most everyone has congregated down to the fishing dock to see who's won the prizes for catching the overall biggest fish, biggest catfish and biggest bream.

I finish washing the returned ice cream cups and spoons as Honey returns, arms full of dirty sweet tea tumblers. She sets them in the wide sink and wipes her hands on her apron. "Your mom said we could close up for the weigh-in since she figures no one wants to spoil their appetite for the fish fry. Let's head down to the dock."

We take off our aprons, separating ourselves from the crowd as we meander down to the edge of Lake George and sit on the grassy bank.

"What did Junior want?" Honey unsuccessfully hides her smirk.

I roll my eyes. "You know I can't take teasing. He just complimented me on my swimming and invited me down to see how much his catfish weighed."

"Did I call it or what? I knew before y'all even talked that he liked you!"

Before she strains herself patting her own back, I say, "Sara put him up to it."

"Says who? How do you know?"

"I overheard Sara and Beth."

"Oh," she pauses, thinking. "Is that why you asked if you were suffocating me? Did they say something?"

I nod, embarrassed.

"Good grief. Don't listen to them, especially Beth. She's like one of those stink bugs that injects poison into squash plants and kills them. Ooh, or a parasitic wasp that lays its eggs in a caterpillar and when the wasps hatch, they eat the host caterpillar."

I laugh. "Oh dear, I'd better let Junior know. I heard Beth wanted to have his babies!"

Honey giggles and we can't control ourselves. We both start crying, we're laughing so hard.

"Shh! Your daddy's announcing the winners." Honey hiccups.

"Let's get closer," I say as we help each other up. I don't care who won, I just want to see if Colin's there. He had to disappear to somewhere, right? As the laughing fit evaporates, I wonder out loud, "Why would Sara want me to dance with Junior if she knows her best friend likes him?"

Honey shakes her head. "That girl thrives on drama. Don't you remember when she started that rumor in seventh grade about seeing our science teacher making out with the *married* math teacher? I *know* their propensity for rabble-rousing is the only reason she and Beth are friends."

Daddy makes the announcements and there's cheering, but I'm not listening. I scan the crowd for the mysterious, brown-haired, blue-eyed boy. Dejection sits heavy on my shoulders when all around me are the same faces I've seen pretty much my whole life. It's not until Honey nudges me that I realize Junior walked up.

"Did you hear?" he asks, maybe for the second time.

Based on his pleased smile, I guess his catfish placed so tell him congrats.

"I saved a seat for you," he says shyly.

Since there aren't enough tables for everyone at the picnic, a designated "Winner's Table" is decorated to the hilt. Most people eat on blankets or sit in folding chairs with their plate on their laps, only the old folks eat inside the restaurant on picnic night. I already have a seat waiting for me since I won the ladies' freestyle and now that Junior won, he has a seat as well.

"Awesome," I say unenthusiastically.

"Oh, Sara and Beth are waving me over," Honey says. "I have sooo much to discuss with those two!"

I laugh. "Be careful!"

It's awkward sitting next to Junior. Luckily, the person sitting on my other side is the little elementary-schooler who won the hot dog eating contest, and she seems very excited to be sitting at the Winner's Table.

"I'm Emma Kate and I'm going into fifth grade and I do gymnastics which is how I burn off so much energy and can eat so many hot dogs, and I love hot dogs but I don't love fish, but I like hush puppies, so I'll eat those unless Mama makes me eat fish, so I won't seem rude."

I smile. "Hi Emma Kate, I'm Bea Pearl and this guy," I point to Junior, "caught some of the fish we're eating."

Junior waves and Emma Kate frowns. "I will have to eat some fish, then." She gives me her full attention. "My daddy is a peanut farmer, and my mama works in the hospital lab. Did you know peanuts aren't really nuts, they're legumes? Isn't that a funny word? It's French. I know who you are. Mama told me. You don't seem crazy."

I stiffen and feel Junior tense up too. "Thank you?"

"Yeah, when we went to the high school football games last year—I looove going to the high school games!—you were my favorite cheerleader. I figure since I'm in gymnastics then I can be a flyer too when I'm old enough. As long as my boobs don't get too big, Mama says. But Mama said you're not cheering this year because you're crazy and that makes me sad."

I shred a festive bit of crepe paper lying on the table, aware that my face is reddening as she speaks. How can I defend myself? I'm questioning my sanity, too.

"Oh, but Mama told me not to say that to you. I'm sorry. I don't know any crazy people except my Great-Aunt Tootie and she breaks into peoples' houses and drinks their beer. Do you break into people's houses?"

I can't help but snort. "No, and I don't drink beer either."

Emma Kate looks relieved. "Good! Are you really crazy? Mama told me your brother died and that's what made you sick. I can't imagine my little sister dead. Gives me the willies."

I look to Junior for help. He avoids my eyes and my opinion of him sinks lower so that anger mixes in with the sadness, confusion and hopelessness already moseying around in my head.

"Jim is not dead," I say through clenched teeth, still looking at Junior who's looking at his plate. His Adam's apple bobs but that's it.

"Oh, okay. That's just what Mama said." Emma Kate looks around at the picnickers. "Where is he?"

"I don't know. He disappeared." I push back my plate. "I'm done."

"Oh, please don't be mad! Mama told me not to say anything and I did anyways. My mouth needs a zipper on it, Daddy says. Please don't tell Mama I said anything!"

I stretch my lips into a smile and then a thought pops up, the bare bulb a bright light in the darkness that is my head. "I won't be mad only if you introduce me to your mom."

She chews a hushpuppy as she eyes me suspiciously. "Are you tricking me to get myself in trouble? 'Cause I don't need any help."

I smile for real this time. "If she works in the hospital lab, I want to ask her a question about my brother."

"My mama can help you not be crazy? And then you'll be a cheerleader again?"

"Maybe. I hope so." I climb off the bench seat as Emma Kate wraps hushpuppies in a napkin. Junior hunches over his plate. "Um... thanks for saving me the seat." I hope he doesn't offer to come with us.

He turns toward me, nodding, his eyes darting around as if he's unsure about what he should do.

"I'd feel bad if you didn't get to finish your dinner," I say.

"She's over there, talking to her Junior League ladies." Emma Kate points and marches toward them.

If it wasn't for that little girl's confidence, I would probably keep going and disappear to the other side of the restaurant. When I'm not walking fast enough for her, she grabs my hand, pulling me along.

"Mama." She tugs on her mom's arm. "Mama! I wanna introduce you to someone."

Her mother pulls her arm free. "Emma Kate! Really, you see me talkin'—"

She cuts herself off mid-sentence. The other ladies turn to look at me. Thank goodness Emma Kate doesn't let go of my hand. Junior League ladies are a social force to be reckoned with and I don't know what to expect.

"This is my mama, and Mama, this is Bea Pearl. The high school girl you said was cra—"

"Emma Kate!" She says sharply, and then laughs. "Excuse me, ladies." She walks past other huddles of conversation and we follow. Emma Kate skips along as I trudge after them with a heavy heart, although I'm hoping for answers.

"I'll just go ahead and apologize for whatever Emma Kate has said, she's a li'l pitcher with too big ears." She glares at her daughter but spoils it by ruffling her hair and kissing the top of her head.

I should have planned something to say. "She said you work at the hospital lab?"

"That's right."

"Is there any evidence that proves my brother's dead?" This comes out so soft I'm worried she can't hear me but her hand stills. She stops twisting Emma Kate's hair. "I was just wondering… I don't know why my parents…" I catch my breath.

"I'm sorry. I can't help you." Her eyes don't meet mine. She is pulling her daughter away from me when Emma Kate reaches up, tugs on my ponytail, and mouths *I'm sorry*. Then they disappear into the milling crowd.

What did I expect?

As far as I know, the only post-flood evidence is a Lake George T-shirt, covered in blood. I assume it's Jim's blood, and that's how they figured out who it belonged to, but really, all I know is what I overheard in those early days of search parties. If Emma Kate's mom worked in the hospital lab, she'd know about autopsies and stuff like that. Or un-autopsies for people who didn't die, contrary to what an entire town believes. But the words stick in my throat as if I swallowed a catfish bone. I'm not as brave as I thought I could be.

Fresh air. I need to breathe. Walking in the opposite direction, down to Lake George, I pass the dock and the restaurant building.

It's twilight now. Momma and the Booty Girls strung up light bulbs everywhere so looking back, the grounds appear magical. Lucas has his guitar out, while couples' shadows dance in the grass. On the other side of the restaurant, the only light spills out of the windows. I barely make out the tune as the restaurant blocks most of the sounds.

Plopping on the grass, I sigh heavily. Since the visit to the police department turned out to be such a bad idea, I don't know if I should continue this hospital lab angle. Though it feels like there's a lead here somewhere. I don't know if it's because I'm unsure of where to look next or because Emma Kate's mom acted like she was hiding something from me. But why? And what? Is it something so horrible she thought it would finish breaking me? Or—since she doesn't know me—could my parents have put a gag order on the entire town to keep me in a somewhat safer cocoon from the truth?

Will the truth of what happened hurt me more than Jim's supposed death? That's impossible to imagine. So, it must be because my parents think I'm guilty. That it's my fault. I shiver despite the heat and wrap my arms around my knees, thinking back to what Colin said earlier, that just because everyone thought the earth was flat didn't mean it really was.

My heart thumps faster. Is that what he's trying to tell me then? I probe the question. Maybe if I bother it enough, I'll get some answers. Why do I feel so strongly that Jim's still alive? A mystical brother-sister connection like what twins have? I don't think so. It feels more like a known truth. The sun always rises in the east until one day it decides to rise in the west. That just seems wrong—unnatural—and that's how I feel about Jim's disappearance. I wish Colin were here to help me sort out my head.

"I am."

I suck in so much air I inhale an entire swarm of mosquitoes. Colin sits next to me and pats my back as I choke on the bugs.

"Seems like I'm always saving your life."

"Saving me from mosquitoes?" I glare at him as soon as I catch my breath.

"From asphyxiation, West Nile, Zika," Colin shrugs with a mischievous twinkle in his eyes. "So, you wished I was here and now I am."

"What, are you my fairy godmother now?"

"Don't you have to have wings and a wand for that? No, you said it out loud. I was close by."

I'm glad it's too dark for Colin to see my face. As embarrassed as I am—as I always am around him, it's amazing how good his hand feels on my back. As if suddenly remembering it's still there, softly drawing circles, he snatches it back. "Close by? Are you stalking me?"

He laughs. "Didn't you say a water sprite sent me? It would make sense that I'd be near water."

"Makes as much sense as anything else does. Guess that means I'm stalking you."

"It is odd to see a girl like you wander off by herself on a night like tonight with the music and the dancing. I figured your boyfriend would sneak off with you."

"One, he's not my boyfriend. Two, I'm not that kind of girl." Though I can't deny how right it is to be here in the dark with Colin. Wouldn't mind sneaking off with him. I scratch at my too hot cheeks as my imagination takes off.

He leans back on his elbows. The light is too dim to read his features, but I feel his eyes on me. "Why'd you wish I was here?"

I sigh, hugging my knees to my chest. "Thinking about what you said earlier. About the world being flat and what my parents know."

"Your parents more than likely know the world isn't flat."

"Harhar. That girl who won the hot dog eating contest? Her mom works in the hospital lab and I'm almost certain she's hiding something from me."

"Yeah, that's what I've come up with also. Discovered there're two blood types on the shirt. The general consensus is the second one's yours, but surprise—no one actually knows for sure."

"Two? Mine? How'd you hear?"

"I told you I'd help you figure this out."

"About that offer... Why?"

"Why what?"

"Why help out the crazy girl you just met that you have to save all the time?"

"We didn't just meet, Bea Pearl." Colin's low voice causes goose bumps on my arms.

"Well, not 'just' as in today, but ..."

"No, as in this past spring. I was here when the Chatothatchee flooded."

I shake my head emphatically. "I would have remembered you."

"Maybe I just wasn't as real to you then as I am now."

"Please stop with these brain teasers." With the physical exhaustion of working all day and swimming in the race coupled with the emotionally wrenching eavesdropping of Sara and Beth and the conversation with Emma Kate, I'm unraveling. Tears gather, then hang heavy like rotting pears on a tree.

He sits upright and tilts my chin. He smells of sunshine. My breath catches as his face is close enough that I can make out his expression. It holds tenderness, concern, and something else I can't place but has my heart pounding, trying to lodge itself in my throat.

"Bea Pearl, I ..." He lets out a whooshing breath and takes his hand away to run through his hair.

I study his face but can't read his expression. Whatever he's about to tell me won't be good.

"I'm here as part of a school co-op with Fish and Wildlife with my uncle."

"Ah, the real reason why you're always near water." And why I've never seen him before. I nod in understanding and wait for him to get to whatever is causing that odd look on his face.

"I left an expensive piece of equipment at one of our stations and knew Uncle Rob could get fired if it was lost. It was my fault, so I went to get it."

Realization knocks me back like the flood surge. "You were the guy in the johnboat, the one who pulled Jim out of the river?" And then anger rolls in, hot waves licking at my face.

"Yeah."

I rise up to my knees in front of him. "You realize that no one believes that I saw a boat pick up Jim, don't you?" My voice is so soft and low, it scrapes along my throat. It would rather scream. "Not a damn soul came forward, so I was patted on the head, pretty much ignored, because there wasn't any proof. It's the whole effing reason my parents and the sheriff could declare him dead. And you knew what you did this whole time."

He hangs his head.

"So, where is he? Where's Jim?" He told me no one actually knows if that second blood type is mine. Could his be the unknown blood on Jim's discarded shirt? The thought horrifies me. My anger pushes it away.

"Bea, I wasn't supposed to be out in the boat. I hadn't told anyone what I was doing. The engine couldn't handle going against the current. I had to go a good ways before I found a place cleared out enough that I could pull up without getting knocked into trees. Jim was unconscious. I left him in the boat and walked back to the ramp. There was no way I could have carried him, because he was so badly hurt. I didn't want to make it worse."

"Badly hurt? Where is he?" I sink back to the grassy bank, my fury unsure, my hands fluttering nervously like those damn broken-winged jays.

"He was gone when I returned with the truck and trailer. No idea how or where." His fists clench. "We helped sandbag but then the field office moved us downriver to help out. When I first came back to Georgefield and heard he was dead, I felt guilty. What if I was the last person to see him alive? I called Lake George to ask about him but got hung up on. I told the sheriff's office—"

"They know? What did they say? Who specifically did you talk to?"

Colin shakes his head. "I don't know. A guy? He thanked me and said they'd look into it, but I never heard anything back."

My shoulders slump. "And they still don't believe me? What kind of proof do I have to have?" I blink tears away. Or try to.

Colin's watching my face. I turn my head away to hide my eyes. He gently touches my jawline but then drops his hand. "Then I saw you, found out he was your brother, and that you still believed he was alive. I thought since I didn't know where he was, I'd help you."

That phone call. The first time I felt hope. "So that's why that night on the dock you offered to help me find him?"

He nods, the concerned look on his face making me feel better.

He leans in, earnest. Our knees touch.

Then someone calls my name.

He cups my cheek with his warm hand for the smallest slice of a second. I let out a whooshing sigh and stand on my wobbly legs. "Over here," I holler. When I look back, he's melted into the darkness. I walk towards the lit restaurant gangway.

Honey meets me. "Your mom is looking for you." She looks behind me into the dark. "Oh, were you with someone? You look flustered." Her eyebrows raise. "Junior?"

"No way, just needed some breathing room. Is Momma mad?"

"Not any more than usual." Honey grimaces apologetically. "She acted surprised you weren't with me." She grabs my hand. "Lucas's rocking that guitar. Let's go dance after you check in with your mom."

And we dance in the grass until Lucas's strings break, the *something else* in Colin's expression guiding my feet and arms. I pretend I'm the Old Bea for a song. The thought that the second blood type might be mine—or Colin's, if he's not telling me the whole truth—is pushed back for a song. Just one. Don't I deserve just one dance?

Probably not.

Sandbars & Wasp Stings

Another dream with the sparkle-eyed whatever-she-is keeps me from sleeping restfully. I wake, sweating, and throw off the quilt. Daddy's remark about the mud on the well box runs circles in my head, chasing the dream. I can't sleep so I may as well make use of the time to search for clues. Even if it's three in the morning.

It's near water so maybe I'll see Colin. I smile and pull a T-shirt over my camisole.

Flashlight in hand, I ease out of the front door, careful to not let the screen door slam behind me. A cold nose on the back of my knee makes me gasp. Toby was at the mercy of a gaggle of toddlers during the picnic, so I'm surprised he's awake. He follows me off the porch, across the street, past the concession stand and to the pool.

It is dark and still. The humidity presses against my face until I can taste it. Bats swoop around the streetlight in front of the restaurant. I jump when there's a crash from the garbage bins but

I'm sure it's from the feral cats. Or raccoons. I turn the flashlight on to keep them from getting too close. Or to keep from stumbling into a tick-eating, toothy 'possum.

Being farther from the streetlight, it's even darker around the well box. My bare feet sink into the ground that grows more mucky the closer I get. Momma and I planted swamp irises in the wet dirt years ago, their dagger-like leaves catch the illumination from my light, throwing sharp shadows on the high walls of the well box. I walk around to the back. The mud line Daddy mentioned is gone.

I splay my free hand on the cool, white-painted cinder blocks. Then snort to myself. What, now I think I'm a telepath?

I aim the flashlight outwards. From the direction of the lake, eyes glow in the light but they're low to the ground. Gator, but far enough away that I don't feel threatened.

Something skitters across my foot. Pointing the light downward, I grimace as a roach the size of a matchbox waves its disgusting little antennae at me. I kick-hop. Maybe squeal a little. When I land, something jabs into my heel. Probably an iris root but I bend to pick it up. It's a lighter, nice enough to be engraved but now worn smooth to chicken scratch. I wipe the mud off onto my T-shirt, flick the lighter and watch a tiny flame ignite.

With the spark, another flame of memory, or perhaps a remembered dream, alights. I see Jim, head close to another guy whose face is hidden. The mystery person has a ball cap pulled low, a cigarette between his fingers as he gestures with his hands to get his point across. I can't make out what he's saying, since there's a loud ruckus of yelling and splashing behind me.

In the present, Toby growls, followed by a rustle of bushes too close for comfort. I grip the lighter as I make my way back to drier ground. One last look into the darkness before shutting off my flashlight and walking toward the front porch light.

No clue as to why Jim went down to the river.

But now I have a scrap of memory to hold onto to, a piece of a dream. Hopefully, I'm one step closer to finding Jim.

The next morning comes too early. I'm not prepared to appreciate my last day of freedom before my sophomore year begins tomorrow.

On Sundays, Lake George doesn't open 'til after church, but Daddy is nice enough to let Honey and me have the afternoon off. I'm a bit concerned about the possibility of being permanently replaced by one of the Booty Girls. I do love my job, but I also don't want to look a gift horse in the mouth. Honey planned a trip to the Sandbar, our own private, white-sand beach on the southern bend of the Chatothatchee, to celebrate our last day of summer.

I lie in bed as long as I can, but with the sunlight streaming through the curtains and my back starting to ache, I can't stay down much longer. Especially once I glance at the clock. It's almost ten, and Honey will be here soon.

I throw off my bed sheet. My feet and shirt are muddy. A tinny taste fills my mouth, and my heart tries to leap out of my chest until I remember my early morning search for clues. Taking deep breaths, I wonder how I can go from relaxed to full blown panic in two seconds flat. The lighter is still in my nightstand drawer, tangible, looking just as beat up in the light of day as it did last night. I grin.

Dressing in a swimsuit, blue jean cut-offs, and an oversized Lake George tee I cut into a cover-up, I braid my hair without brushing it, and then head to the restaurant with Toby at my heels. Neither Momma or Daddy are around, but the property is big enough so I'm not concerned over their whereabouts. Especially when the restaurant is already unlocked.

Finding an empty cooler, I drag it to the kitchen and load cokes and maybe a few beers—oops, what would Emma Kate think of me now—then cover them with ice. I throw in a couple packs of hot-dogs and sit out on the gang-way to wait for Honey. Toby barks at the indignant ducks below, his whole body wiggling with glee.

The *boom-boom* reverberates against the restaurant walls and echoes off the lake before Lucas's packed truck pulls up. Honey jumps out of the back, bright-eyed as if we hadn't just worked a twelve-hour shift.

"The sun is calling me! Wanna just take one truck so you don't have to drive down? Everyone'll fit."

"Sure."

Nick Ledger hops down to help load my cooler. *Interesting.* I cut my eyes at Honey, who smiles brightly in return. No wonder she's giddy this morning.

He even holds my elbow as I climb into the bed of the truck. Making nice with the best friend must mean he really likes Honey. I'll need to watch him more closely.

Honey sits next to me on the cooler as we drive past the house, down the grassy road through the pines and oaks to the river.

"Who all's in the cab besides Lucas?" I ask.

"Kiki, Tim-not-Jim, and that's Mae in Tim's lap."

"Oh, yay," I say unenthusiastically. "We get to hang out with the Booty Girls."

"Don't kill me, but Kiki isn't so bad. She and I hung out a little yesterday during the fish fry. And Mae's artistic—at least when it comes to face painting and flower arranging."

"Oh no, next thing I know, your butt will be hanging out your drawers."

Honey laughs. Nick looks pleased at the idea.

It hits me right then like a bug to the teeth that I'm doing the same to these girls that the town of Georgefield is doing to me—

reducing all the parts that make us whole to one thing. Their clothing choice doesn't define them. Holding out hope at my brother's existence shouldn't define me as someone who can't be trusted. I grimace, mad at myself.

"Wait. Am I the only non-couple?" Great. I narrow my eyes at Honey.

"We aren't a couple," she says, glancing at Nick. "Yet," she whispers to me.

Giving her a sour look, I duck to avoid a branch. The last bend in the road is the most overgrown, but that's how I know we're almost there. Suddenly, the trees end, and the hard-packed, grassy dirt gives way to sand.

Lucas parks the truck, and everyone hops out.

"Wow. This is fierce," Kiki says, looking around. We're on a high bluff of sand, as white and soft as any at Panama City Beach. Below the bluff, the sand levels out and the brown river flows by. A live oak leans over the water, a rope swing swaying gently from its branches, slam full of good memories. It's the perfect place to swim, not much limestone to hide gators, and no bends to speed and twist the current.

I notice Lucas looking wistfully at the swing he hung with Jim a few summers ago. The girls jump-walk down the sand bluff then and spread out towels on the sand as the guys carry the coolers down.

"The four of us— me, Jim, Honey, and Bea Pearl— have been coming down here as long as I can remember," Lucas says. Everyone turns to look at me.

I don't enjoy being the center of attention, especially when everyone's looking at me oddly. Do they think I'm a second away from freaking out? What if I have another bird stuck in my hair? I mean, it has happened before.

"It's okay," I say, running a hand over my head. "I miss Jim." I'm not going to mention the fact that he's coming back, I'll just play along to their flat earth theory.

"We were supposed to leave for college this fall," Lucas says. Kiki puts her arms around his bare chest.

I forget sometimes my family isn't the only one who suffers from Jim's disappearance. Instead of going off to school, Lucas decided to stay, work a semester, then begin school in the spring. I like to think it's because he's waiting for Jim to return, but it could be because he's still mourning his best friend.

"Why didn't you? What happened?" Kiki asks.

I hold my breath. Maybe someone will talk about Jim for a change. *Finally.*

"They gave away his scholarship," Lucas begins.

I'm surprised at the anger in his voice and the fact Jim lost his scholarship. I didn't know that.

"Some dude from Briar got it instead. They were both gunning for the same scholarship, and Jim's last stats would've made him a better shoe-in. The committee heard rumors of Jim dealing. Then his grades went down."

"What?" I look wide-eyed at Honey.

"He wasn't, of course, but you know how reputation is down here. The school didn't want anything to do with that. I personally think the guy from Briar started the rumor, but how can I prove it?" Lucas shrugs his shoulders.

Kiki cocks her head to the side. "Not saying anything about Jim, but I've noticed it's a lot easier to score lately." Everyone looks at her and she wrinkles her nose. "Not for me, or anything. I've just noticed it at out-of-town bridge parties. Something's different. My grandma always says thank goodness for Sheriff Oakwood keeping it out of Georgefield."

Mae nods, the feathers braided into her hair swaying with the movement. "It's that synthetic shit, too. It'll mess you up. I only do homegrown. Organic, non-GMO stuff, you know? Fresh from Mother Earth."

Honey's trying her best to keep a straight face. "Gluten free?"

Mae's eyes widen. "I don't know!"

"Sweet! There's beer in here," Tim calls out from my cooler.

"Compliments of Lake George, just don't tell Daddy," I say.

Everyone returns the smile. Nick high fives me and I feel normal—accepted—for the first time since spring. Folks are talking about Jim again; just that tiny bit of acknowledgement relieves some of the weight constantly holding me down.

That feeling of normal lasts all of ten minutes. Really, that label is misleading. 'Normal' isn't a word to describe my life now, so it should be called abnormal. I'm abnormally feeling like my old normal pre-Jim-gone self for ten whole minutes. It feels nice. Incredibly nice. I smile with my eyes. I laugh with my head thrown back at Tim's jokes. I'm bubbly happy for the budding romance of Honey and Nick and the-whatever-you-call-it of Lucas and Kiki and Tim and Mae. Ten minutes isn't enough time to get buzzed from the quarter of a beer so I know it's not the beer bubbles.

The echo of a boat motor breaks into our revelry.

"Waves!" Honey yells as she pulls me to the water's edge. That's a term used loosely on the river. No one grabs a surfboard and says things like hang ten. It's more like the gentle lapping of a giant brown-tongued cow. Exciting none the less.

The boat makes the turn and slows down. I shield my eyes from the sun to see the passengers, then groan. "Sara and Beth."

Honey grimaces. "Oops. They were sitting next to us when we were talking about coming here at the fish fry last night. I guess they felt invited."

I sigh. My abnormally normal feelings dissipate like dandelion fluff in a tropical storm. "This is public property. I'll just sit in the truck 'til they leave."

Honey grabs my hand, tucking it firmly under her arm. I pull back but it's stuck. "Oh no you're not. Lay on your towel. Drink your beer and let them know you don't care what they have to say."

"I can do that. But no one better give them my beers," I drag the cooler closer to my towel and sit on it.

The guy piloting the boat is a senior, but I don't know him well. He helps Sara and Beth disembark and hands their bags to them. The bags are huge and stuffed full. Great, they're planning on being here for a while.

Sara smiles too brightly as they wade to shore. "Hi y'all!" Her white hair is piled artfully messily on top of her head, just like Honey's. "Let's put our towels next to Honey! Bea Pearl, where's Junior hiding today?"

"Um, no idea."

Sara wags her finger. "Always need to keep an eye on your boyfriend! No telling what he might be up to."

Behind her, Beth arches a dramatically drawn eyebrow, and for the life of me I can't help but giggle. Really! Who draws on eyebrows to come down to the river? It looks like she has on false eyelashes and enough glittery jewelry to fill a pirate chest. And she's carrying heels. Good luck with those in sand and mud.

"Oh, we aren't together."

Sara gives me another alligator smile, nice on the outside but I can almost see the malice inside. "Well, that's too bad. I'm sure it wasn't you."

Honey tenses up beside me and Nick's turning his head back and forth as if he's watching a tennis match. My face prickles but I can't think of anything to say.

"That was sweet you to try to set them up," Honey says.

The way Beth's eyes narrow at Sara make me think Beth didn't appreciate the nudge.

"Tanning lotion?" Mae asks innocently, passing down her bottle. "Bea Pearl, your face is already pink, you wanna borrow my hat? I have an extra."

"Er, thanks." Catching the cap she tosses, I'm thankful to shade my blushes with the bill.

"Who wants to chicken fight?" Kiki grabs Lucas's hand, tugging him into the water, closely followed by Tim with a squealing Mae thrown over his shoulder. Sara reaches for Beth until she's stopped short by the frost in Beth's glare. Rolling her eyes, she snatches up the hand of the boy from the boat instead.

Then it's just Beth and me. I'm a clumsy buzzard perched on top of my cooler, while she's lying on her towel glinting like a diamond in a worm fiddling contest.

I should say something. "Junior and I seriously aren't an item."

"Good to know," she says without looking at me, pulling a phone from her bag, her thumb flicking madly.

"Honestly, I'm not interested in him. He's all yours."

She lifts her head to glare at me. "Just what I want, the crazy freak's hand-me-downs. Thanks."

Okaaaay, ouch. I watch the couples splash in the water and sigh wistfully. "So… I saw you and your parents at Galstrup's the other day. Everything okay?"

Her nostrils flare and lips curl as she looks at me in contemptuous disbelief.

I take a deep breath. "Sorry about knocking you into that grave." Why the hell am I even trying? Though the queasiness in my stomach lightens a bit.

She opens her mouth but then presses her lips together in a tight line, as her eyebrows vee together. "Have you gotten any beyond-the-grave messages from your brother?"

"Excuse me?"

Beth cackles, then her eyebrows take flight as she feigns innocence, "Oh, that's right! You think he's still here. Is he sitting beside me? Or maybe he's chicken fighting too?"

Again, I have no idea how to respond. No one has ever been this hostile to my face before. Avoidance from everyone happens all the time. But this? Tears sting my eyes and I'm again grateful for Mae's hat.

"Hey, Jim. What's going on?" Beth addresses a clam shell lying in the sand next to her towel. "Everyone knows you're dead except your crazy, messed up little sister. What do you think about that? Back in you go." She picks up the shell and throws it into the river. "You know the part that pisses me off the most? Junior can't even see what a delusional weirdo you are. Folks see you as a victim because you were stupid enough to get hurt, but I know it's your fault."

I stare at her with my bottom jaw hanging.

"Aren't you going to do something crazy? You're just sitting there like an idiot, catching flies."

Even though I know this is about her hurt feelings, mine are in tatters too. I have to get away from this parasitic wasp as Honey calls her, so I toss Mae's cap on her towel, walk downriver from the couples, and dive into the water.

I hold my breath.

The water is murky, a mixture of brown and green with iridescence from air and methane bubbles swirling with suspended flecks of mica. Sounds from the world above are muted as I swim deeper until the water changes from warm to cool. Suspended between the thermoclines, I pause. I can't tell if I'm crying because my salty tears are being welcomed and replaced by the fresh river water. Why didn't I demand she tell me what she meant by it being my fault? Obviously, she was trying to hurt me but maybe there some truth mixed in with the rest of her comments.

The Chatothatchee shifts, bends around rockier ground, finds a path of least resistance in softer sand and limestone. I let the current take me for a bit, feeling cathartic and finding comfort in the womb-like hold until my throat begins to burn. I unconsciously inhale water through my nose.

Swimming towards the surface, I break free, coughing. The current took me far enough past the Sandbar that I can't see anyone, but I can still hear the echoes of the victorious chicken fighters. I'm farther into the river than I want, so I head back to shore, careful not to swim too close to any limestone shelves. Swimming in the river by myself with only Beth knowing my location might be risky, but I'm still close enough to yell for help if needed so it's not too irresponsible.

The September breeze is chilly, shaded as I am by vine-covered oaks. There's no sand here, just bank created by trapped debris in tree roots. Full of spiders, I bet. I draw a shaky breath and sit on a fallen tree trunk with my knees pulled to my chest, losing myself in the glimmer of sunlight off the river.

"Thought I'd have to save you again," the water sprite says from behind me.

Sprites & Sprained Ankles

I am finally starting to realize that if I'm by myself near water, Colin will appear. My ghost, my water spirit, my merman, my fairy godfather, my whatever he is.

"Still need saving," I say with a little laugh, scooting over on the log to make room for him. "I don't know how I'm getting back."

"Current's too strong to swim against."

"Yup, and no shoes to walk back through the woods."

"Then I guess you'll have to hang out with me."

I look at his profile until he turns his head to observe me. He has a tiny bit of freckling on his nose and cheeks, almost hidden by his tanned skin. My fingertips itch to trace them so I tuck my hands in my lap before I embarrass myself. "My former company is a bit waspish so you're a welcome change."

"Sounds interesting."

"It's not."

Sitting in silence, the peacefulness helps the tenseness leaves my shoulders. For once, my mind doesn't race with what I should say next. It's content yet buzzing with excitement at his presence.

"I hoped I'd get another chance to talk to you," he says. "There's something else I meant to tell you the night of the picnic."

My cheeks pink as I recall the way he touched my jaw and the something else I couldn't name in his eyes. His shoulder brushes mine. Is that intentional? Is he going to—*yes, please*!

He continues, "I think something was going on where I pulled up with Jim the day it flooded. It was very well kept with trees cleared. It's the only way I got the boat on land when the water level was so high. And I could swear there were boxes when I left that weren't there when I got back."

Oh my gosh. I scratch my face as it abruptly cools off. Our conversation isn't going the way I thought—an accidental shoulder bump and I go heart-eyes. I give my head a little shake. *Stop being weird, Bea Pearl.*

"Most of the land around the river is farmland, so it's probably already cleared for fields. Did you pull up on the same side of the river as the boat ramp or on the side where his shirt was found and where you pulled Jim out of the water?"

"Boat ramp side."

I perk up. "Only the Lake George side of the river was searched extensively because of the way the currents flow. Can you take me there?"

Colin looks over the river and skips a rock. It bounces three times before sinking. "That's the problem. I can't find the road. Everything looks different now that it's not flooded, but the road I could've sworn I was on is paved and curves west. I can't find it. I've looked for it every chance I get. Do you think we should get the police involved?"

I consider it. That makes the most sense. Sheriff Oakwood will be able to muster a bigger search party and cover a lot more area than just Colin and me. Only *if* the sheriff believes me. If they blow me off, will the vicious cycle of distrust and doubt start all over again? I shake my head. He knows about Colin saving Jim, but still won't believe me. I'm sure he figured it out same as we did. He's not stupid, so there must be a reason that side of the river wasn't searched as well as our side. "It's me against the Flat Earth folks."

"Don't forget me. I still want to help, that hasn't changed."

I shiver, either from the breeze on my damp skin or from the anticipation of what he's saying.

He takes off his shirt and slips it over my head. I open my mouth to protest but his shirt is warm and smells so good, I decide against it. And I *finally* get to see those chest and arm muscles! They're better than I imagined.

"I hear an engine."

I freeze when I hear the low rumble of a truck engine and the muted *boom-boom* of a stereo. "They wouldn't leave without me!" I yelp, taking off running. All the pokey, prickly leaf matter ignored in the face of being left. Colin is right behind me. The clearing where we parked is ahead of us through the trees.

"They're gone," he says.

I burst through the tree line, twisting my ankle as the ground abruptly changes from hard, compacted leaves to soft sand. Off guard, I fall so fast that Colin trips over my foot, sprawling on top of me. "Ooof!" The air squeezes out of me—he's heavy.

"Sorry! You okay?" He gets to his knees.

I'm incredibly glad I have his shirt on because the tumble shifted my swimsuit top. I twist away from him and put everything back where it belongs. When I peek at him, he's looking everywhere but at me. My embarrassment fades at his chivalrousness.

The sand squeaks as he moves. "Wanna make some sand angels?" He grins and offers me a hand as we both stand. "How's the ankle?"

"What? Holy crap, my ankle! Ow!" I shift to take the weight off it. Then I hear the sound of a boat motor. "Sara and Beth."

"Want me to flag them down?"

"Too late." The engine rumble is already receding. "The way this river bends, they won't see you. And knowing Beth, she'd probably let me ride until she spots a gator then throw me in front of it with a bucket of chum as my parting gift."

"She must be the wasp."

"One and the same." I try to put weight on my foot again.

He grins and drapes my arm over his shoulder and scoops up my legs. I need to focus on something besides these very delicious muscles. "Totally can't believe Honey rode off and left me. Did she forget I was here? Was she that caught up in her new boyfriend? I don't believe it."

"Maybe the wasp told her you'd already left?" Colin heads away from the river and toward the woods.

"That makes sense." I say, a sliver of my brain wondering if I'm truly safe with the last person who saw my legally declared dead brother alive. Most of me is trying really, really, really hard not to notice how close his mouth is to my face. "You feel real for a water spirit." I tentatively graze my index finger on his bare, sun-warmed shoulder. I examine the shadows between his neck and chin, imagining how the soft, scratchy skin would feel against my lips. Not a very helpful way of calming myself down but I've pretty much forgotten about the pain in my ankle, or even that I have ankles.

He laughs softly. "How many water spirits have you felt?"

"True," I sigh. "Why don't you change into a horse? That would be easier than carrying me like this."

"A horse? What?"

"Oh, I guess you aren't a pooka-type water being. That's good news actually. I wouldn't want you to drown me."

A chuckle rumbles in his chest. "You are something else, Bea Pearl."

"Something else?" I repeat, confused.

"I meant it as an expression. But yeah, if I'm a water sprite, what does that make you?"

For some reason that simple question scares me. Bad. "I exist." Fear pinches my voice, making my words come out small and disfigured.

He must sense my panic because he quickly says, "Of course, okay, the existence of Bea Pearl is not to be discussed. To Bea, or not to Bea, is not the question. Weather, politics and religion only." As he talks, his jawline scratches against my temple, snagging on the curls escaping my braid.

I smile at his *Hamlet* reference and let out a steadying breath. "It's like two miles back to the house. Are you going to carry me all that way?"

"Nah, we'll just take my four-wheeler."

"What? You have a four-wheeler?"

He carries me down the deer path, approaching a thicket of pines, where lo and behold, a blue four-wheeler waits. "How do you think I got down here?"

"Became one with the river? Wait, so you are stalking me."

"I was down here already. Y'all drove right past me."

"Really?"

"Yup, you were crouched low in the truck bed." He helps me get comfortable on the back, climbs on himself, and we take off toward Lake George. There's no talking over the motor, just the wind and bugs rushing past.

I don't know what to hold onto. Obviously, the best place would be around his waist. I chicken out and prop myself on the metal bars behind me, daydreaming about what it would feel like to be gutsy enough to wrap my arms around him. Warmth collects between us. The inside of my knees rubs against his legs. I want us to ride forever and ever but the closer to home we get, the more I can imagine Momma's reaction. I don't want Colin to see that. To see my broken family, and subsequently, to see too much of my broken self. He makes me wish for the Old Bea to return.

I tap him on the shoulder. We're close enough to Lake George that reality might slap me in the face. We slow down and he turns his head. "Hey, do you mind dropping me off here?"

He shifts in his seat so he can see me better. "What? Your ankle may be broken."

I bite my lip. "It's barely throbbing, so it'll feel better when it quits hurting."

He gives me the same look I give my dad when he tells me that. "Okay. If you're sure?"

I'm not sure about anything but he helps me off the four-wheeler anyway. "Thank you."

He looks at me, touches my shoulder. "I'm glad I was in the right spot to help you home today."

"Me too." I pull off his shirt and hand it to him, then turn as if I'm heading home. I wait until he drives off to start hobbling. I don't want him to see how bad it hurts to walk.

With the help of a bamboo pole, I'm able to make it to the house without crying. Momma, Daddy, Honey, and Lucas are on the front porch, and they all come toward me as soon as Toby barks. Momma looks as if she was crying which makes me feel worse than my ankle does. Jim's disappearance has already given her so much pain, and I don't want to be the one that gives her more. I prefer the refusal to acknowledge our gaping hole to this fresh anguish.

"Oh, Bea!" Honey cries, hugging me tightly "We are so, so sorry!"

I lose my balance and almost fall down.

"She's hurt, Honey!" Lucas says, as he grabs an arm with Daddy.

"What's wrong?" Daddy looks me over. My swimsuit is dry from the ride. Arms, legs, and feet sting with cuts from sticker bushes, and I can only imagine what my hair looks like, blown dry by the breeze, the braids surrendering to a losing battle.

"My ankle. Can I sit down?"

They lead me to a wicker chair on the front porch. Honey is now full-fledged crying and Momma's face is white with dark, worried circles under her eyes.

Since Honey can't talk coherently, Lucas fills me in. "When we got out of the water, Beth was the only one there with our stuff. She told us that you were ranting about how she wasn't right for Junior. Y'all had words and you told her you were going home. Your stuff was gone, so we left too. We tried to catch you on the trail before you got too far ahead, but we didn't see you on the path and didn't see you once we got back here. All of us were really worried."

I shake my head. "We did have words." I'm not about to re-peat what she said about Jim in front of my parents. "So, I went for a swim. I left my bag and flip flops on my towel."

"They weren't there," Honey sobs. "I should have never left you with her! I knew she was poison. And now you had to walk miles and miles with a broken leg!"

I squeeze Honey's hand. "I'm pretty sure it's just sprained. And it's not your fault."

"We're taking you to get checked out," Momma says quiet-ly. "And you're not to go to the river again."

"What!? That's not fair."

"Life's not fair," Momma goes inside the house to get her keys and purse.

"Is this because of Jim?" I yell through the open front door. "Are you punishing me for him being gone?" I really need to learn to keep my mouth shut, glutton that I am for punishment.

But not right now. I'm desperate for answers. "What aren't you telling me? Why do you want him dead?"

Momma strides out the door. Her footsteps are gun reports on the hollow wooden porch. She flattens her hand and slaps me.

My head jerks back in shocked surprise. The anger is fading from her eyes and I can see she regrets it, but I'm too outraged to care. My cheek burns and my eyes water.

"What you did at the restaurant was uncalled for. Don't you *ever* touch his stuff again." My mom's face collapses in on itself, hurricane-swept and shuttered.

Daddy takes the keys from Momma's other hand and tosses them to Lucas. "Take Bea Pearl to the ER." Then he ushers my pale, stiff mother inside, her eyes glittering harshly.

Honey and Lucas help me up into the truck. I need all the help I can get because my bottom jaw seems to have permanently come unhinged. Does she mean the beer?

"Sorry y'all had to see that," I whisper once I can speak, my voice heavy with misery.

Honey squeezes my fingers. "None of this would've happened if we had just ignored Beth." Her voice wavers.

If Lucas wasn't there, I would probably let myself break down into a teary pool of anger and wretchedness but instead I focus on relieving Honey's guilt. "How would you have known until y'all got back home? And where is everyone else?"

"Tim borrowed my truck to take the girls home," Lucas tells me.

Honey hands me a wrinkled sundress she pulls out of her beach bag. I slip it over my head.

The angry pink on my cheek fades by the time we reach the county hospital, though my ankle has darkened like a summer thunderstorm. It's badly sprained, not broken. I will have to wear a clunky brace but at least I won't be starting my sophomore year in a cast. I'm secretly relieved there's an easy excuse to use if anyone asks why I'm not cheering this year. No one wants to know the real reason is because I lost myself.

Losing who I used to be is why I reacted in fear when Colin said, 'You're something else, Bea Pearl', because I really am something else.

I'm someone else.

Losing Jim made me lose myself. Around Honey and Colin, my old self peeks through sometimes. My abnormally normal self. Which is weird because Colin didn't know me before.

To the Flat Earth people, I am too quiet, miserable, and delusional. I don't want that to be my entire future existence. In addition to finding Jim, my lost self needs to be recovered as well. I bet they're together somewhere.

Or maybe I'm just approaching the state line of Crazy.

"We can bedazzle the brace," Honey says skeptically once we're back in the truck, heading out of town.

"Bea, you want me to take you home or do you want to come to our house?" Lucas asks.

I hesitate. I don't want to face Momma's anger again, but I should be home. "I don't know."

Honey holds my hand. "Your mom was really scared for you. And also, what they found in the restaurant."

"Found? Is that what she meant about not touching someone's stuff? What happened? I didn't see anything when I filled the cooler this morning."

Honey and Lucas exchange a look. She grips my hand tighter. "Mama wants you to come over to our house. Is that okay with you?" she asks.

I swallow hard. This scares me. Her mom, Mrs. Grace, works for the Department of Human Resources. Why does she want to talk to me?

"Your dad thinks it's best."

I nod and bite my lip to keep it from trembling.

13

The Eye & The Voice

Mrs. Grace makes sure I am comfortable on their screened-in back porch, getting me a padded ottoman for my ankle, turning the fan to the highest setting, and bringing us sweet teas. Honey can't sit still and I'm sure I look nervous right along with her.

"Relax, Girls," Mrs. Grace turns on the bug zapper. "Bea Pearl's safe."

"Thanks for the tea," I say. She beams at us then sits across from me.

Honey takes a deep breath, fidgeting with a throw pillow.

"Jeez, I feel like you're about to break up with me," I joke feebly.

Mrs. Grace tucks her bare feet underneath her. She's wearing teal leggings with a floral tunic and looks so at ease with the world. I ache with the wish that she was my mother. At least for now. Instantly, my thoughts shift and I feel intense guilt toward my own broken mother who—when she's not working—can barely be bothered to comb her hair. "I'm not here in any official capacity. I'm listening as a friend to your mother, who's having an awfully hard time lately. As are you."

I nod and focus on the lattice pattern on a pillow, tracing it with my eyes until I feel the tears recede. My own private flood is contained.

"Tell me what you intended with the restaurant."

"Um, the beer? I only had one." I glance at my best friend, wide-eyed. "Honey didn't drink any." Honestly, I can't remember if she did or not. It feels like forever ago instead of just this morning.

"Beer?" Mrs. Grace looks from me to Honey who shrugs. "No, the photos of Jim in the restaurant."

"What? What photos? I didn't see anything this morning. I woke up minutes before we left for the Sandbar." I look to Honey. "You didn't see anything either, right?"

Honey shook her head. "I didn't go inside though."

"The restaurant was already unlocked, and I went straight to the kitchen." My heart thumps as if it wants to crawl out of my chest, it hurts so much. I rub my bee necklace in agitation. "What's going on?"

Mrs. Grace picks her phone up from a side table. "Your dad sent me these. He was preparing for a police report, but your mom was adamant that you did this." She hands me her lit up phone.

It's picture after picture of Jim, blown up on canvas and propped up against the walls. Grainy close ups of him eating, laughing, shooting hoops, and stretching before a swim. I start shaking my head and don't stop.

"Your mom heard the front door at three last night." Mrs. Grace's voice is gentle, as even as a breeze through a willow tree. "She said when she got up at five there were muddy footprints tracking from the front door to Jim's room, back to yours."

Now the shaking has moved from my head to my hands. My grip on her phone tightens so I won't drop it. I can't stop staring at each picture. My feet were muddy still when I woke up. Did I go to Jim's room before I came to bed? Probably. It's gotten so second nature, that I do it now without thinking. Every night before bed, I check for open windows and disarray, try to keep it nice for him when he gets back.

"Bea?" Honey's voice squeaks the tiniest bit. I hand the phone to her and slide my trembling hands up and down my ribs, hugging myself.

"Did you go outside early this morning?" Miss Grace asks.

I nod.

"Did you hang these pictures up to get your parents' attention? Honey told me that you aren't happy that they had him declared dead."

Oh my God, if she says something about closure, I'm going to rip the feathers out of one of her throw pillows. "Would that make anybody happy?" I take a deep breath through my nose and let it hiss out my teeth. I see why my parents asked Mrs. Grace to talk to me. If this conversation was with them, we would have already passed the snarls and gotten to the shut-down, shut-out silence. If I was speaking to the sheriff right now, he would already have me arrested. He doesn't believe in innocent before proven guilty when it comes to me.

Mrs. Grace nods. "Poor word choice on my part. I apologize. Won't you tell me what happened?"

I rub my fingers on the nubby trim of the nearest pillow. "I had a bad dream and took a walk to clear my head. I walked through the irises."

Honey's mom's eyebrows crease for the slightest moment. "Irises... ah, near the well box? That seems an odd place to go for a walk."

"They're… pretty." I shrug, not wanting to say I was look-ing for clues. It seems so farfetched in the light of day when it was so possible in the dark.

"Did you see anything from the restaurant while you were out there?"

I shake my head. "Well, wait. I heard a crash. But I figured it was a raccoon or a cat in the garbage bins."

"No lights?"

"No, ma'am."

"And you didn't see anything later this morning when you went in the restaurant's kitchen?"

"No, but I didn't turn on any lights. I went straight to the back."

Mrs. Grace gnaws a little on her lip, a daintier version of Honey. "But there's so much natural light in there from all the windows."

"Mama," Honey says with an edge to her voice. "She says she didn't see anything."

I give her a tight-lipped smile in thanks. Though why *didn't* I see any of this? From what's on Mrs. Grace's phone, the dis-play was covering an entire wall. And if I didn't do it, who did? And why? The motive Mrs. Grace has pinned on me does make sense, although I hate to admit it. But there's no way I took those pictures. It's not my style. But who else would have those? "Can I see the pictures again?"

Honey hands me the phone.

I scroll through quickly, my suspicions confirmed after the first three. My voice is shaking now, but this time with excite-ment. "I know where these pictures are from," I announce.

"Where?" Honey and her mom both say, echoing each other as they straighten, interested.

"Yearbook."

The next day, school is everything I imagined. Whispering takes place behind my back. Clusters of students watch me while pretending to focus elsewhere. Even the teachers look at me weird. Do they think I'm going to have a conversation with an invisible Jim? Re-enact being swept down a flooded river as I hold my arms above my head and spin in circles, bumping into folks in the hallways like they're trees in a flooded forest, screaming as I go? I snort.

A giant yawn crawls out my mouth, so huge my jaws audibly crack. After Honey brought me home after eating dinner with her family last night, I fell asleep thinking about who stole pictures from the yearbook and why. I also wanted to know what exactly happened between Colin and Jim in the flood. If that wasn't enough, my dreams jumbled everything together to form sand dollars with icy-blue eyes and giant chickens pecking at clam shells with wooly eyebrows.

Rubbing my eyes, I stop walking, letting students stream around me. The display case across from the office is bare where Jim's jersey hung. I'm not going to return it. It belongs to me more than the school. Anyways, if I tell the principal a water spirit gave it to me, at the hands of mean girls, I'll just be adding to the rumors. And getting myself in trouble.

In first period, I overhear Ashleigh Wilson telling Ashlee Fredricks that I stole it because I was going to use voodoo to bring Jim back from the dead. Good grief. No wonder everyone's looking at me funny.

Honey and Beth are the only ones who talk to me all day except when the teachers take roll. Lenise smiles and waves but gets disapproving glares from others for her effort.

I could do without Beth talking to me. Even more, I wish I could make an effigy of her. I'd start by duct taping her mouth shut and fixing her eyebrows. While waiting on Geometry, not my best subject to begin with, she saunters down the aisle. I can't help but smile when she drops her pen near Junior's desk then makes a huge production of bending over to pick it up in a short skirt. The funniest part is Junior doesn't notice a thing, too deep in conversation with the guy on his other side about fishing.

Beth glares at him, knitting her drawn-on eyebrows, and then she sees me smile.

Crap.

I duck my head and pretend to read about the area of a circle, but she walks over to my desk anyways.

"Wow, nice accessorizing, Beatrice. Trying to go for sympathy votes? Aww, won't work. Did that happen on your hike yesterday?" She points to my boot. "I heard you had a long walk since Honey abandoned you." She looks around. "It sounds like even your *best friend* doesn't want to be around you." She tsks.

The buzz of conversations dies down. Do I cower or find myself? Remember the old Bea Pearl who had a brother who believed in her?

"Funny story," I say calmly, making my choice. "A hot guy on a four-wheeler drove me home. And not cool stealing my flops. You know they won't fit you."

Her nostrils flare and I'm happy to hear a few snickers from other classmates.

"At least I didn't kill my brother," she spits, and glares at Junior before she stalks to her desk like a cat with tinfoil on its tail.

I stare at her back. Then sounds come roaring back to me and I run out of the classroom, anxious to make it to the bathroom before puking. I can't look at anyone.

I hide in the library for the rest of the day, avoiding librarians who would send me back to class and searching for any information on Jim's "death." Two freshmen girls, who obviously lost the memo that you're supposed to whisper in a library, inadvertently fill me in on more of today's Gossip of Bea Pearl. One, I talk to water fountains. *Only if they contain water spirits*, I correct to myself. And two, Principal Higgins was going to punish the person who stole Jim's memorial jersey until she found out it was me. She didn't want to cause any more problems for my parents. For that, I am grateful and partly relieved she doesn't buy into the voodoo rumor.

"I'm proud of you, Bea Pearl," Honey says as she hunkers down next to me in my library burrow. I have no idea how she found me, but she forces me to explain why I'm here. Reluctantly, I tell her my conversation with Beth. "I 'abandoned' you. Really. I'd like to abandon my shoe up Beth's double-wide rumpus."

"What does she know that no one's telling me?" I ask, my voice way steadier than expected. "Do you think she knows why Jim went down to the river?"

"How would she know?"

I shrug.

Honey pats my hand. "I know what will cheer you up."

I raise my eyebrows and look at her suspiciously. "If it has anything to do with Junior, I'm so not interested in hearing it."

"Nope! Mrs. Ell has a sub today. Guess who conveniently left the lock jammed to the yearbook room when the sub went on a wild goose chase for Principal Higgins?" She beams at me as she zips up my book bag, then nudges it closer to me with her foot.

I grin as I slide the strap over my shoulder and wobbly stand with her. "Won't you get in trouble when the sub talks to Higgins?"

Honey walks with me toward the door, a bounce in my step for the first time since Colin dropped me off in the bamboo woods. "I had a freshman deliver the message, telling them it was from Beth, who is an office aide, after all," she explains.

"Which I'm sure is how she got the key to Jim's jersey," I grumble, choosing to ignore the pointed looks from other students in the hallway instead of feeling persecuted like I was earlier. I wonder if distracting me while the jersey was stolen was the real reason Sara encouraged me to dance with Junior. Ironically or maybe karmically, Beth's feelings got in the way. "And probably the pictures of Jim she plastered all over the restaurant."

Honey links her arm in mine to draw me closer. "I thought that at first, but Beth isn't in yearbook, and she's never bragged about getting into the yearbook room. I don't think she has a key to it." By this time, we've reached Mrs. Elliott's—Mrs. Ell's—door. I'm looking around all fugitive-like until Honey steps on my good foot. "Stop it. Jeez. The truth belongs to us—to you—so act like it."

She's right, it does belong to me. I throw my shoulders back and step inside the empty classroom. Just past the computers, Mrs. Elliott has a room attached to hers that contains the school's archived yearbooks. More importantly, there are boxes upon boxes of pictures, all the ones that didn't make it in the yearbook itself. Also, a random, massive container of powdered lemonade that has crystalized into some semblance of lemonheads. We both take a scoopful before going inside. It's tradition for everyone who works on the yearbook staff. The sourness on our tongue melds into the vanilla of old paper and the faint cigarette smell from the seniors sneaking in to smoke.

Last year, I spent every spare minute in here because I was obsessed with photography. Most of the yearbook staff contains juniors and seniors with two students each from the freshman and sophomore class: one to be the eye of the underclassmen and take pictures (me, freshman year) and the other to represent the voice. Honey is the voice again this year, but I can't pick up a camera yet. My life won't go back to normal with a Jim-sized chunk missing from it.

"Who's your photographer this year?" I ask, walking to the far wall and pulling down a box labelled with Jim's senior year.

"Lenise. She doesn't do the artsy-fartsy shots like you, but she showed me some candids she took at the Back to School dance, and they're good. Everybody looks happy which is perfect for a positive school image, whereas you always captured the truthfulness." Honey grins and slides a box out from the shelf perpendicular from me.

My head twitches a little. That description is so familiar. "Oh."

"Did you find something already?"

"Think back to the pics your mom showed us on your back porch. Isn't that how Jim looked?"

Honey purses her lips. "Yeah, but Jim always looked like that. And we're talking about Lenise. One, she wasn't on year-book staff last year, and two, she wouldn't do this to you."

I nod, a deflated wave flushing through me, like every morning since this spring. I miss Jim at the breakfast table splashing milk everywhere while eating his cereal like it was a race to the bottom. Especially, I missed him the night I won first place in 4-H for my black and white photograph of the limestone banks of the Chatothatchee. Momma and Daddy left me at the Farm Center suddenly. All the while, I wore a goofy, I-thought-it-was-okay-to-be-proud grin because I didn't know the awful news yet. My parents rushed to the police station and learned that Jim's shirt had been found. Without Jim inside it.

"Hey, you okay? We need to stop?" Honey crouches on the floor next to me where I'm sitting cross-legged, hugging the box to my chest like a life raft. Why didn't Colin save me when he saved Jim? I could be with my brother now. I could've helped somehow.

I sniff and nod, clearing the what-if cobwebs out of my brain. "You find something?"

She hands me a picture. "Found this in the box from Jim and Lucas's junior year."

Jim and that ball cap guy from my daydream pose in front of lockers. What's it called if you aren't asleep and daydream at night? Or was I asleep and dreamed the dream in a dream and that's why I didn't see any lights coming from the restaurant? I shake my head to clear it.

"I've seen this guy before." Was this the picture I needed to find that night of the back-to-school dance? So much happened that night with the jersey and the fight with my parents that I forgot that weird feeling when Momma took my picture with Honey. Had I seen this last year and not give it much thought because I didn't understand its significance?

"At Lake George? Looks like he's a friend of your brother, so probably so."

"Maybe he can tell me why Jim was down by the river that day." I study the guy with the baseball cap. Maybe that's why he was in my waking-dream. "Can you find their junior yearbook so we can see who he is?

Honey darts to the floor to ceiling bookshelves and runs her finger along the gold-embossed spines as I look into the box of pictures that didn't make it into the yearbook in case she missed a clue.

Expectation and the chemicals from all the ink are making my head spin.

"Found it." She plops next to me. She flips to Jim and Lucas's class, but the mystery guy isn't in there.

I sigh in frustration. "Start at the beginning with the freshmen. He's probably just in a different grade."

She scans through the freshmen. Then the sophomores. Thank goodness Georgefield isn't a big city and we can go through it quickly. The anticipation is killing me.

Honey skips over the junior class but stops.

"He's got to be in the senior class, Honey. I just know it."

"I sure hope so." She turns the page.

Everyone in the lower grades has a black-and-white head-shot for the budget, but the senior class is in full color. As she turns to the next page, we both gasp.

"It's him."

I trace the row over to read his name. "Daniel *Paner*? What? Beth has a brother?"

"I don't think so. There's a resemblance, but unless they have different parents and are half siblings..." Honey taps her forehead. "Wait. I think I recall Lucas saying something about a cousin causing drama for Jim when they first moved here."

"Why haven't you mentioned that before? Don't you think that's important?"

"Well, no. It wasn't a big deal—just a flexing of muscles type thing. It was like a year before the flood."

My eyes widen. "Maybe *he's* how Beth seems to know something I don't. How do we find him?"

14

Honey Beas & Bloody Shirts

We cross the Chatothatchee. The *dum-da-dum* as we drive over the bridge echoes in my chest cavity at narrowly getting out of trouble. I'm not usually a fan of pity pardons, but I was glad for one from Principal Higgins today. Amidst the sleuthing epiphany, we didn't hear the sub come in. Frustration oozed from her like sweat on a dog day by the wild goose chase. When she saw the pictures surrounding us, she accused us of making effigies. Apparently, *she* listens to freshmen gossip. Though it didn't help that I had knocked over a container of straight pins we use on our project boards when she busted open the door.

"How are we going to prove Beth's family did something to Jim?" I ask. I've been dribbling the idea around like one of my brother's basketballs ever since learning the identity of the guy in the picture and my memory-dream.

Honey pulls into a parking lot for a silk flower shop. Carefully, she examines her chipping nail polish as I stare at the funeral wreaths in the shop window. "You didn't kill Jim," she says.

I blink and fiddle with the air vents. "Beth seems to think so. She knows something. But, Honey… what if I did?"

She swallows like the time at Sara's ninth birthday sleepover when she stuffed eleven jumbo marshmallows in her mouth at once.

"What if I couldn't save him?" An ant carries a potato chip across her dashboard. "What if I distracted him and made him fall?

"That's a huge difference."

"Is it? Dead is dead as my parents were sure to let everyone know."

"Of course, it is." Her fingers knot themselves on the wheel. "You are my friend no matter what happened. At the same time," she hesitates, and something gnaws at my insides. "I think I agree with your parents. I think not accepting he's dead is messing you up and…" She pauses again and looks at me, tears in the corners of her eyes like dew on wisteria before the sun bakes it off. "And I don't want anything to happen to you. You know?"

She smiles and that gnawing thing completes its metamorphosis and emerges with wings wet.

"We can't be HoneyBea without Bea. We can't go off to college and share a trailer in Auburn if you're not there. Otherwise, who knows how many boys I'll make out with behind azalea bushes covered in poison ivy. I *know* the saying is 'leaves of three, let them be,' but I just can't tell without you."

I sob but it turns into a laugh when it hits the air. She leans across the console to hug me and I hug her back.

"But I do want to help you find out what happened to him," she says into my hair.

I nod. That's all I can ask for. We let go and sit back in our seats. "There's a random picture of Jim with Beth's cousin. Someone plastered posters of Jim made from yearbook pictures in the restaurant, someone took his jersey out of its case, and someone broke into his room to search for something. Is that really all I know?"

"And nothing really points to Beth." Honey's pointer finger ticks back and forth like a metronome.

"Except her horribleness."

"Her waspishness." She cackles as she cranks up her car.

We turn on our road, and the car is quiet as I mull things over. "Crap, she hid my favorite flip flops. I can't go down to the river in this stupid brace."

"Text my mom and let her know where I am."

I unlock her phone and send the text, wondering if I'll see Colin down there. "What about Momma's decree of 'the river is forbidden'?"

"Oh, right." She presses her lips together in thought as she passes her driveway and continues down to Lake George. "We aren't going *in* the river. You can stay in the truck and I'll look around for your stuff."

Daddy is with some fishermen on the dock when we get home. "Your mom said no river," he reminds us.

"I can't go down the sandy slope in this brace," I point out. "So, I figured I'd look in the edge of the woods and Honey could search closer to the water. We'll be careful."

"And those were expensive shoes. I'd hate for Bea to spend her hard-earned money to buy a new pair," Honey adds.

I beam at her. She knows that's the best way to get through to Daddy.

"All right then. You working tonight?"

"Just hostessing, so I don't have to be on my feet a whole lot. I'll be back by five thirty at the latest."

He nods his assent, and we trade out Honey's car for Jim's truck. She drives us down the path.

I squint as we head southwest into a setting sun. "Should've brought my sunglasses," I say as I pull down the visor. My finger brushes against something sharp. "Ouch." Blood wells on my index finger. "Apparently Jim kept his fish hooks up there."

"Look in the glove box for napkins." Honey reaches over and pulls out a wad of fast food napkins. She hands them to me as I cup my finger, trying to keep the blood from dripping on Jim's upholstery. I don't want him mad at me for staining his truck when he gets home.

"What's this?" I ask, detaching a sheet of loose-leaf after I smear blood on it.

She tries to glance my way but as we're in the narrow, woodsy leg of our journey, she has to keep her eyes on the dirt road.

"It has one of his turtle-doodles on it. You know, the ones with the shell of a basketball?"

"Open it! What if it's a clue as to what the heck y'all were doing down at the river!" She parks at the sand atop the river bluff.

I unfold the sheet of paper. It has one column of random letters and two columns of numbers that go halfway down the page. The final two numbers sit without accompanying letters at the bottom. That's it. No explanation.

"Basketball stats?" Honey asks, leaning over.

"Not a clue, maybe we can ask Lucas?"

Honey opens the truck door and hops out. "Oh, what if it's a secret illegal gambling ring that Jim was trying to uncover? You stay there."

I roll down my window. "A gambling ring for high school basketball that has clandestine meetings in swamps? Hmmm, just a little farfetched. Even for us."

"Oh! Maybe instead of an illegal cockfight, they're fighting swamp monkeys?!"

I laugh. "That sounds like a great school mascot: the Fighting Swamp Monkeys."

"Love it! I'm gonna see if we can officially change our mascot from the Georgefield Panthers to the Georgefield Fighting Swamp Monkeys. Genius!"

We both laugh. I smooth out the piece of paper, trying to memorize Jim's handwriting. "I can't believe I haven't found this 'til now." I searched his truck for clues months ago but overlooked the stack of extra napkins.

"Especially with that hook just waiting for its next victim. How did we never search through McDonald's napkins to find it?" Honey walks toward the river.

Indeed, why would anyone search there? If it's actually important, maybe this is what the person who trashed Jim's room was looking for.

Honey's soon out of sight. A breeze shifts through the Spanish moss clad oaks and the sweetgum trees flutter their broad leaves. Something stirs the palmettos nearest the truck and for half a second, I'm hoping that it's Colin. Instead, a squirrel emerges, scrawny tail flicking, turning over an acorn in its tiny paws.

I run my tongue along my molars and sigh. Colin doesn't live here, and he's not really a water spirit. For the longest time, he was the only one to believe me about Jim being alive. I wish he was here to talk things over with him and his odd logic.

A fat bumblebee buzzes in one open window and out the other. Then Honey comes up from the sand bank holding my towel in a bundle. She walks past the cab and dumps something in the bed.

"Beer cans," she says by way of explanation when she climbs in, handing me my towel and flops. "What a wasp."

Momma brings me a stool to perch on at the restaurant's hostess station which looks like a peace offering. I smile my thanks before she walks back to the tables. I'm relieved and let down at the same time. Relieved because I don't know what to say to her and let down because she didn't ask about my first day back at school or how my ankle feels even though she's my mom. If she thinks me capable of murdering my own brother, trashing his room, and then setting up a photo gallery, I guess I understand. I glance around the dining room. Where did they put the canvases? My hope that Lucas knows what Jim's numbers mean is dim.

From five thirty to six thirty it's pretty slow with mainly early bird diners. If I'm hobbling to their tables, there are no worries. I'm glad I'm a hostess tonight, because they can put down some fried catfish, keeping the servers constantly on their feet. Both servers are wearing a pathway back and forth from the kitchen to the tables.

It's after seven when Beth's mom and dad walk in. My shoulders relax when I don't see Beth behind them. Mrs. Paner also has drawn-on eyebrows, using them dramatically as she glares at me. As I seat them, she demands to see the owner.

Really? There hasn't been a chance for anything to go wrong yet. I hobble to the kitchen but look back at them before rounding the corner. Mr. Paner is on his phone, hunched over the table, his free hand clenching as if he's trying to keep his temper. Mrs. Paner is holding up the silverware like she's looking for water spots, but when she glances at her husband, worry settles on those Cruella deVil eyebrows.

"Need something, Bea Pearl?" Daddy asks. "You're supposed to be taking it easy."

"Paners want you."

"'Kay. Need to talk to him about kudzu control anyhow. Did you know he's found a market for that as potpourri? Crazy what folks will buy. That man finds opportunity anywhere." He tosses a dish towel onto his shoulder and strides toward them.

Almost sounds like Daddy admires him. As I head back to my stool, I figure someone who can turn an invasive plant that can grow a foot a day and swallow cars and houses whole into money deserves admiration. Though I wonder if Mr. Paner's determination is what's hurting his family with the way his wife and his daughter use their meanness as armor.

I'm wiping menus when Daddy comes up from their table. "Apparently you maliciously embarrassed their daughter in front of an entire class today at school?"

"Does 'she started it' sound too petulant?"

Daddy crosses his arms. "Do I even want to know?"

"I said her feet were big *after* she made fun of my sprained ankle. Not a huge deal." Oh, she also called me crazy, made fun of the fact that I have a missing brother, and she thinks I'm the killer, but I'll keep that part to myself.

"Girls and their feet. Is she the one who hid those expensive shoes of yours?"

"Yes sir." Of course he makes that connection. "Honey found them, by the way. I can put that money I was going to spend to replace them in my college fund now." I may have slathered that on a little too thick. Inwardly, I cringe until Daddy winks.

"That's my girl. Just lay low and I'll tell them you got your pay docked or something."

"Can you ask Mr. Catfish to spit in their food for me?"

"Not funny," he says, walking back towards the diners.

I'd laugh if Mr. Catfish did.

Momma has me refilling saltshakers when Emma Kate and her mama approach the hostess desk. After our last conversation, I'm sure I'm the last person she wants to see, so I stay put, taking my time. When my name floats over the restaurant clatter, it startles me enough that salt spills everywhere. "Crap." Do I throw it over my left shoulder with my right hand or vice versa? What could Emma Kate's mama be telling mine? If she tells Momma that I asked after Jim, Momma is liable to freak out, go tight-lipped and scary-glitter eyes. I freeze, listening past the normal clinking of silverware and conversation, wondering if Daddy needs to be here for damage control.

"Bea Pearl!" Emma Kate calls out, then waves when I look in their direction.

My smile catches on my lips.

Momma motions me over. I glance at her face, framed in wisps of brown hair newly threaded in silver, escaping from her ponytail. She gives me a tired smile, but still, a smile. I toss the salt over my right side. How can I warn Emma Kate's mama not to say anything about Jim in front of Momma? I take a deep breath, hoping she knows how dysfunctional we are at the moment. I cross my fingers that she will stay out of it and won't mention anything. But then what could she want with me?

It seems to take forever for me to limp around the three tables between me and the hostess desk where they wait. Momma's expression grows impatient. Especially when Mrs. Paner calls for her from their table.

"Bea Pearl, you remember Emma Kate, don't you? She won the hot dog eating contest at the picnic."

"Yes ma'am. Hi, Emma Kate." I nod hello at her mom.

"She wanted to ask you something about cheerleading. Lemme go see what Liz Paner needs." A shadow of a frown crosses her face. "And then I'll fetch your to-go order," she says to Emma Kate's mother with a smile.

Momma hides her grief-stemmed crazy nicely in public.

I let out the breath I've been holding. No one mentioned Jim, and it's just something ordinary like cheerleading.

Emma Kate's mom purses her lips together. Emma Kate tugs her hand. "My daughter can be very persuasive," she begins.

My eyes widen. This isn't about cheering.

"And it's been on my mind since we spoke at the picnic. To appease her," she looks at Emma Kate and smiles, though she lowers her voice, "I tested the blood on Jim's shirt."

Hands shaking, I carefully set the salt on the hostess desk, so it doesn't spill again. No need to stack bad luck against myself.

"It wasn't identified earlier because he was declared a victim of the flood since you... Well..." She avoids my eyes. "But Emma Kate says you're positive he's alive, so I ran some tests against the hair she brought me. And the other blood's not a match for yours."

"That's why I pulled your hair as we left! So she could test the blood DNA against your hair DNA! Wasn't that super clever of me? Mama says I watch too many detective TV shows. If I don't grow up to be a gymnast, I might be a detective. I'm a super smart thinker. Whoa. If I'm a gymnast-detective, does that make me a ninja?"

Shell-shocked, I'm surprised that Emma Kate thinks so highly of me. And that the blood was never properly identified. Isn't that the first thing that happens in a CSI episode? Did someone tell her not to check it? Who? "Do you know whose it is?"

She shakes her head, glancing around. Background conversation has me leaning in to better hear her. "All the tests revealed was that it's male, no relation. But listen, I don't want folks to give Emma Kate or me a hard time, so don't tell anyone what I did for you. I promised my daughter I'd look into it, but not at our expense. He's laid to rest and needs to stay in peace."

I nod. Sadly, it's understandable. Not many want to be branded as different. "Thank you." But I don't agree with the peace part.

Momma walks up holding a to-go bag and I plaster a smile on my face. "Keep practicing those cheers, Emma Kate!" I go for enthusiasm, but my voice sounds high-pitched even to me. Emma Kate surprises me with a hug and then she leaves with her mama.

Momma gives me an odd look but doesn't say anything. I lurch in the direction of the bathrooms before she can change her mind and ask questions, my brain whirling like a pinwheel on a Peanut Festival carnival ride at all the possibilities. Did Colin get hurt when he pulled Jim in the boat? He didn't mention it, and wouldn't it need to be a rather large amount to stain a river-soaked shirt?

Maybe the bigger question is if it wasn't Colin's, who else could it be? Does this go back to when Mrs. Lou Ann told me at the police department that I was hurting myself by looking for Jim?

15

Steam & Clouds

As soon as I get into Honey's car the next morning for school, the first thing out of my mouth is to ask what Lucas knew about the mysterious numbers.

"Top o' the morning to you, too," she returns crabbily, using the rearview mirror to put on her mascara.

I make the hurry up motion with my hand.

"He didn't have a clue. Not basketball—or any sports—stats."

I sigh. "Not helpful."

Honey finishes her makeup and hands the paper back to me. "Don't get discouraged."

"You think we'll find Jim alive?" I look at her in surprise.

"No, I'm pretty sure we'll find out who's messing with you," she says over her shoulder as she backs out of the parking lot.

Let down, I know I can't hold it against her. She believes the earth is flat and will keep believing that until I prove her, and everyone else, wrong.

The rest of the school day isn't much better, but I didn't think it would be. If I keep my expectations low, I can't be disappointed, right?

Beth gives me an excellent Disney villain sneer in Geometry but drops it when Mrs. Adkins approaches her desk. I'm doodling ninja monkeys in my notebook instead of working on our assignment, and ignoring Junior who watches with weird open-mouthed, fishy looks as if he wants to say something. Since I have no interest in speaking to him, I don't give him the opening he's obviously looking for. Assuming from the way Beth glared at him yesterday, she thinks he was the guy who rescued me on the four-wheeler.

Bits of the conversation between Beth and Mrs. Adkins float my way, and I can't help but overhear how upset Beth sounds in response to whatever our teacher just said.

"Please don't call my parents," she whispers, looking scared and earnest, an odd contrast to her usual distain. "I promise I'll get my grades up. Daddy's been really stressed with work and won't like it if he's called in."

Momma and Daddy told me about the Paner's when they first moved here. Beth's dad was a farmer somewhere in Louisiana but moved here after something happened. I can't remember exactly what Daddy said, but I think it was something along the lines of farm insurance fraud. It makes sense to me. Folks who act as high-n-mighty as that family usually have something to hide.

Without her sneer, Beth looks almost... human. And I can understand all too well how stress can disrupt a family. Easily, I put myself in her too-big shoes, thinking of how strained my mess ups make my parents. If I'm not careful, I might just find myself feeling bad for her. Mrs. Adkins returns to her desk at the back of the room and Beth catches me looking at her. I give her a sympathetic half smile.

Hmm, never noticed before how she and her mom have that same horrible skin-a-cat-alive grin.

Between classes, I hurry along as fast as my brace will allow, desperate to sit in the somewhat safety of my desk and use a textbook to shield myself from all the curious looks.

As I pass by the gym doors, my steps slow. I feel drawn there, recalling what Lucas said that day at the Sandbar about Jim losing his scholarship. I should check with his basketball coach to see if he knows something. I would love to add another missing piece to the puzzle of Jim Before He Disappeared. Eagerness for any sort of clue makes my hand shake as I grip the strap of my book bag.

I shoulder-open the heavy gym door. Girls walk out of the changing room in packs, whispering together when they catch sight of me. The hollow, rubbery *thunk* of basketballs echoes in the cavernous room. Glancing around, I retreat back to the door when there's no sight of Coach Thompson.

Someone calls my name, startling me. My P.E. teacher and former cheerleader sponsor, Coach Green, jogs toward me. Yesterday, I gave her my pass to be sidelined in class because of my ankle, so I'm not sure what she wants.

"Bea Pearl! If you can walk that fast in a brace, I expect you back on my squad by next week."

I stop, smiling apologetically.

She smacks her ever-present gum. "Whatcha running from?"

Surprised, I stare at her for half a second. "Ma'am? Nothing...," and then I think about it and the words just shoot out like steam from a tea kettle. "I guess from being branded as crazy, or…. No, I'm running from disappearing. I want to be important enough to someone so that if I disappear, they'll look for me until they find me, and they'll never just call me dead and be done with it."

As soon as the words come out, I wish I can reel them back. Especially after I glance at Coach Green's face. She stops chewing her gum.

She *never* stops chewing her gum.

She blinks owlishly then chews faster than a gum commercial on fast forward to make up for those lost seconds. Just looking at her makes my jaw ache.

"Whoa. Most kids say boyfriend or bad grades. But yeah, I can see that. Okay, all right. Umm, you wanna go see the counselor?"

Beyond mortified, I shake my head, wishing for a random patch of quicksand. "I meant Geometry…grrr." I weakly shake my fist in the air. "May I go hide now, I mean, class? Go to class?"

She pats me on the shoulder and I skip-hop away.

The house is empty. I wave bye to Honey after she drops me off from school. Sitting on the front porch with Toby, I enjoy his simple doggy presence before heading across the parking lot to begin my shift. I wish I could say that everyone avoiding me at school feels like all the seclusion I need. Instead, I am exhausted since I spend all day wound up and more tense than if everyone yelled at me at once.

Friday is a good night for tips, and I'm looking forward to the weekend so I can dedicate more time to uncovering the events around Jim's disappearance. Maybe, I'll even prove I'm not crazy nor a murderess.

And maybe, just maybe, I'll find the puddle Colin's been hiding in all week. It's confusing how fast I got comfortable with him popping up out of nowhere.

Toby's chewing on something so I pull it out of his mouth to throw for him. He shimmies his rear end in anticipation. Looking at the object covered in dog slobber, I see that it's not a toy, but rather a wallet. "Oooh, where did you get this from, you bad boy?" I open it up to check for a driver's license and suck in air. Jim's face looks back at me. "Where did you get this, boy?"

Toby whines and tries to take it from me, but I hold it out of his reach. I scramble to a standing position and hobble to Jim's closed bedroom door. It's always closed. I know the only time Toby goes in the house is with me. Where did he find this? I clean off as much slobber as I can, but it's soaked into the leather. This was my last birthday present to my brother. I open it back up to look at his face. Everything inside is brittle and blurry like it was once wet. I scan the dates on the receipts tucked inside. Searching for anything that will tell me he's still alive.

Nothing.

I put it on my nightstand then leave the house, crossing the parking lot and restaurant gangway. Did Toby find it washed up from the river in the woods? Had Jim left it at the house? Is this Jim's way of reassuring me he's still alive? I feel like he's so close, but I can't see him. Only his pieces remain, the shadows he casts, like a sun too bright I can't look directly at it.

Momma's at the hostess desk. We don't make small talk as I check the schedule to see which tables are mine for the evening. I want to ask about the wallet, but I'm afraid she'll either flip out on me again or she'll take it away. While we haven't technically apologized to each other, we both know that won't ever happen, we just brush the whole incident under the rug. The exact thing we did with Jim's disappearance, too, now that I think about it.

Nodding to Mr. Catfish and the two servers in the kitchen, I fill water and sweet tea pitchers. Mr. Catfish is the only staff who knows about the Jim gallery, thank goodness. He was actually the one that discovered it, and he and my dad cleaned it up before the servers arrived. I guess Momma was too busy accusing me to help.

Daddy pops his head in, "Bea Pearl, your mom just seated a party at table three. They're from the government."

"Oh, how mysterious." Despite my sarcastic response, I'm curious. Is the FBI in town to infiltrate an illegal Swamp Monkey fighting ring? I grin. Honey would love that. Or, hope beyond hope, has the sheriff found new evidence that Jim is still alive and brought in help? Was the wallet Jim's way of letting me know? Should I retrieve it and hand it off as evidence?

My hand holding the water pitcher trembles. I round the corner. As soon as the table's in my sight, I stop dead in my tracks.

"Hey, watch it!" The other server narrowly misses dumping coleslaw down my back.

"Sorry," I mumble, not willing to take my eyes off the table. Five people are seated in apparent deep discussion. Two men have their backs to me, two men face me, but it's the one on the end, in profile, that makes me freeze like a bug-eyed deer in headlights.

It's Colin.

My mouth goes dry. I've spoken to him many times but now that others are around, the ability to talk escapes me. I wipe my palms on my apron. Truth be told, I wasn't entirely convinced he was real; just a coping mechanism of my broken brain.

It takes fifteen steps to reach their table. "Hi, welcome to…" No one turns my way, so I try again a little louder. "Welcome to Lake George Restaurant. My name is Bea Pearl and I'll be …"

"Oh! You're the girl Colin's been hiding from us!" One of the men on my right responds, a good-natured grin appearing through his beard. They're all wearing polos with Fish and Wildlife embroidered on them. That must be what Daddy meant by government.

"We thought you weren't real," another says, giving Colin a mock stern look.

Colin's been talking about me? I blush. Colin grins at me and suddenly, all that anxiety slides away and it's just like we're on a riverbank again, sans dangerous limestone and Bea-eating alligators.

The man on Colin's right claps him on the shoulder. "Colin's been a huge help this summer tagging all the sturgeon coming through the Chatothatchee."

I take their drink orders and scurry back toward the kitchen so I can catch my breath. I feel a hand on my elbow and spin around, thinking Colin came after me.

Instead, Junior hovers close to me. Why am I always getting these two mixed up? Because I let my hopes get too high, that's why.

"I tried to talk to you at school today," he begins.

A polite smile sits awkwardly on my face, "Oh, I'm not too good at math, haven't even cracked the books yet to start homework."

"Not that, though I can tutor you if you need help."

"Ah, thanks. You needed to talk to me?"

"Yeah." Then he just stands there. It takes an inordinate amount of willpower to keep my toe from tapping.

"Um, I'm at work so I need to…work. I'll see you on Monday? One of the other girls has your table, right?"

"Yeah—"

I dash off as fast as I can in the brace.

My tables keep me busy so the only time I speak directly to Colin is when I take his order. His table is a lively one. They take turns telling stories when I check on them. The man on Colin's right is his uncle, and Colin tells me about his school program that earns him credit while he's out in the field. Jealous. That explains why he isn't enrolled at Georgefield High.

Around nine, many of the families head home for the night and Lucas sets up his guitar in a corner. A different crowd starts pouring in. Couples dance, the lights dim and there's less for me to do since I can't serve alcohol.

I lean against the wall corner, trying to take some of the weight off my ankle as I wait for an order of fried pickles to be ready. From this vantage point, I can see Lucas, most of my tables, and still hear Mr. Catfish bellowing when orders are up. I'm very aware when Colin catches my eye, excuses himself from the table and walks my way. I can't help my smile but don't know where to look. My heart pounds.

"Hi," he says, putting his hands in his khaki pants' pockets.

"So, you're real."

"I do exist."

Wow, that smile can really melt my bones. Turn them straight into Bea stock. *Get a grip, Bea!*

"How's your ankle? Noticed you're still favoring it."

My jeans are flared enough to hide the brace. "It's starting to ache," I admit. "But it's a lot better. Thanks again for rescuing me."

"Anytime. I discovered where the sheriff found Jim's shirt. Want me to take you there tomorrow?"

"Are you serious?" I want to hug him, twirl around, jump into the air. Wave my pom-poms. Wait, that's not me anymore. Maybe tomorrow would be a good time to ask if he got hurt pulling Jim in. I don't want to spoil tonight.

"You want to dance, don't you?"

"Get out of my head!"

"Well, come on. I like this song."

The hand he holds out is very tempting. Anticipation for tomorrow buzzes in my head, a fat and happy bumblebee tipsy on honeysuckle. Not only do I get to hunt down more clues for Jim's disappearance, I also get to spend the day with Colin! Can it get much better? The music is already seeping into my skin. I'm reaching for his hand when Mr. Catfish calls out:

"Order Up, Beep!"

"Let me take these fried pickles out first," I tell Colin.

We've been physically close before like when he pulled me to safely from the Shelf, when he gave me his shirt when I was shivering in the riverbank, when I fell and sprained my ankle, and when we rode in on the four-wheeler. But none of those times are like this. I don't feel my feet move. Each of our steps, each twist, each bend, is totally in sync with each other. Twirling until I assume we gravitate above the floor. It's as if we're dancing in a giant bubble with iridescence around us and the outside world is just a muffled, glittery dream.

Until another server's voice hisses jarringly in my ear. "I'm not doing your work even if you are the boss's daughter." Pretty sure she had a crush on Jim and blames me for his disappearance.

It takes me a second to emerge from my cloud of bliss. I'm chilled once Colin heads back to his table, peeved at that other server when none of my tables need anything. Well, they only need to give me a hard time about dancing with a boy in front of everyone. I grin, because that's something the old Bea Pearl would have done. Not this brotherless, shadow-quiet girl I am now.

Back in reality, my ankle throbs. After checking in with my tables, I head to the bathroom. In an anteroom with a couch before the actual bathrooms, I spot the perfect place for a little quiet time to sort things out. I fidget until I find a position that doesn't ache so badly.

The door swings open, making the noise from the restaurant sound like breaking the surface of water. It sounds almost raucous compared to how muffled it was just a second ago.

"Who is he?" Junior demands.

Really? Always stealing my quiet time. "Can I get you something?" But I don't move to get off the couch. I'm not assigned to his table, so I'll save anything he needs for the rude girl.

"That guy you were dancing with. He's the one with the four-wheeler you were bragging about to Beth?"

This guy sets my teeth on edge. "Don't think 'bragging' is the word I'd use…"

"I don't like him."

"That's unfortunate, but none of your concern."

Junior takes a step closer. I fight the urge to shrink away. I've never noticed before how much space he takes up. "You need to be careful around him. I don't trust him."

"Junior, you don't even know him!"

"I know he was around when Jim died. Disappeared. Whatever."

Whatever? If I was one of those feral cats that lives in the restaurant garbage bins, my ears would be so flat back to my head a flea couldn't get past me.

"You don't believe me. But the second I saw him here, I knew he looked familiar. I just couldn't place him 'til y'all were dancing. So, please. Be careful, okay?"

"Not that it's any of your business, but he's actually gotten me out of some situations lately." I gulp air at the thunderous expression on his face, the anger creasing his eyebrows like a vicious storm front. "He's helping me find my brother. Not that anyone around here is willing to do the same," I spit out in fury, then regret it. I don't want that getting back to anyone who'll try to stop me.

"Do you know why he's helping you?" All of a sudden, he straightens, his calm demeanor smoothing away the intensity in his forehead. "I'm just saying I don't want to find scraps of your bloody clothes when I'm fishing in the river like I found Jim's." He leaves, the door swings wildly as if it wants to sweep away all the unpleasantness Junior just dumped in here.

I didn't know he was the one who found Jim's clothes. I mull over what he says about seeing Colin this past spring. Not that Junior's doomsday rant is anything but jealousy.

Junior pokes his head back through the door, startling me so I let out an annoying little squeak. "I was trying to tell you I got you a little something. A present that I left on your porch. But you got me riled up."

His head disappears, leaving me with my eyebrows cocked and mouth sideways in surprise and skepticism.

I rub my temples, then experimentally wiggle my ankle. Leaving me a gift proves all this is coming from jealousy. When pain doesn't shoot up my leg, it's time to get back to work. The Fish and Wildlife table is empty, but they left me an awesome tip and Colin scribbled his good-bye and where to meet tomorrow on a napkin. Smiling, I tuck it in my back pocket and think about it for the rest of my shift and until I fall asleep that night.

16

Rabbits, Yellow Jackets, & Turtles, Oh My!

Momma's ridiculous decree banning me from the river isn't forgotten, I'm just going to ignore it. Honey's babysitting the Lopez twins again, so I mention it to Momma at breakfast. I let her assume I am going to meet her there. I know it's a lie by omission, but I'm not going to let her anger keep me from uncovering clues about Jim's disappearance. I lost my nomination for Daughter of the Year a long time ago. Pretty much around the time she thought me capable of killing my own brother.

Colin mentioned that we need to take a boat downriver since the spot is hard to get to by truck or four-wheeler. I dress in my usual T-shirt and shorts over a swimsuit with my hair in a braid, and then I drive Jim's truck down to the boat ramp on the other side of the Chatothatchee.

It's a pretty, late September Saturday, so the ramp is packed with trucks pulling boats on trailers, eagerly waiting their turn to unload. A few of Daddy's friends watch me from a truck as I drive past and my scrambled eggs lurch in my stomach. It's not like I'm going to ask them to not mention to Daddy that I'm here. *That's* not suspicious. Regardless, I am on a mission and I'm going to stick to it and just take my punishment when it comes. Who knows, they may get really drunk and forget they even saw me. Driving from one end of the lot to the other, I park close to where boats slide off their metal braces then I roll down my window to wait.

A tapping on the passenger window startles me. Colin stands there in a US Fish and Wildlife T-shirt and swim shorts with a lazy smile and his hair a morning mess. *How on earth could this boy be real?* I hop out of the cab.

"Good morning," he says, walking around to my side.

"Hi." My hands flutter so I stick them in my shorts' pockets.

"Boat's already in the water. It's too nice a morning to sit around the house, so I got here early."

"I'm pretty excited, too." Argh. That's not what he said, but seeing his face makes me think that's what he meant. And, really, who doesn't love boat rides?

He holds out his hand and I hesitantly place mine inside. I hesitate because of my recent faux pas. What if he just wants me to hand him something? I'm not holding anything except Jim's truck keys since my beach towel and driver's license are still in the truck. I let out a sigh of relief when he squeezes my hand gently and unselfconsciously. He holds it all the way down the embankment to the river and until I board the boat. Once I'm seated, he fiddles with the engine, gets it going and we putt-putt out of the no-wake zone.

The boat rises on plane, skimming lightly over the river. There isn't much use trying to talk over the engine and the wind. I'm content to admire the limestone cliffs covered in ferns, the Spanish moss hanging from cypress branches just touching the water, mullet jumping, and damselflies spreading bits of rainbow-colored light everywhere. Even though I've lived here my entire life, I still can't get over the beauty of the river. We come to a shallow area near the river junction where the Talakhatchee joins the Chatothatchee. Colin slows to avoid cedar stumps sticking out of the water.

"Did you know adult Gulf sturgeon eat next to nothing when they're here? They only eat when they return to the Chatothatchee Bay near the Destin area and that part of Florida. They're migrating back downstream now," he says.

"Is that what you were doing here this past spring? Monitoring their upriver migration?"

He nods.

"It's too bad they're threatened. They're amazing and prehistoric-looking."

"Yup. I'm sure since you pretty much live on the river, you've seen them jump?"

"Yeah, that's the only time I've actually seen them except in old black-n-white pictures."

"We believe they jump to communicate."

"That's neat. Jim used to tell me it's because jumping's fun." My smile is wistful. No one lets me just talk about Jim. Before I can send out invites for my own pity party, I sternly tell myself to enjoy the moment. I start by asking every sturgeon and river related question I can think of and he points out areas they've set up monitors and sensors as we pass them. The surprise and enthusiasm on his face makes me feel selfish since I have been too overwhelmed by own problems to listen to what interests him.

I never thought he'd stick around long, because, well, he's beautiful and I'm a broken, frizzy-haired shadow-girl searching for the dead. Should he be mistrusted like Junior thinks? Who would the old Bea Pearl listen to? Not having my friends to trust means the only thing I can hold onto is the now, and the now is sunshine and a river breeze and Colin.

"His clothes were found a lot farther downstream than I expected," I observe as we pass the Sandbar.

He steers the boat closer to the bank. The riverbank is mainly debris stuck in tree roots and cypress knees, so I'm a little worried about how I'll navigate without wrenching my ankle again.

He's studying the river's edge, too. "Let's go down a little farther to see if there's a better place to pull up. No slipping, okay?"

I should've worn water shoes rather than flip flops, but it's too late now. He ties the boat to a cypress knee and helps me out. "Is this it?" I ask. "How do you know? It looks just like any other part of the river."

"You see that boulder on the opposite bank? That's what I was told to look for."

I look around, a little disappointed at how normal everything seems. What do I expect? A big X marks the spot would be nice or a note carved in a tree from Jim that says, 'For your next clue on this morbid scavenger hunt, walk five steps backward, quack like a duck and follow the white rabbit'? *Riiight. Quack, quack.*

"Oh, look at the rabbit."

Whaat? I skid around so fast I slide on river birch leaves, grabbing his arm for balance.

"Are you scared of rabbits?" he asks incredulously.

"Haha, no. I'm just afraid of my inner monologue."

"You thought I was an imaginary something-or-other, yet you still feel that some things are too weird to say out loud?"

That can easily be taken the wrong way but when he moves my hand from his arm to hold in his, I assume he's teasing me. "Water spirit," I mutter, distracted by his warm palm snug to mine. I've gotten so use to people shying away from me that his casual touches almost undo me.

He tugs me closer to his side. "Do you prefer me as an imaginary water spirit or as a real person?"

"It's nice to know I'm not the hallucinating-crazy type." I wonder if he's heard the rumors that everyone thinks I'm the reason Jim supposedly died.

"You're not crazy because you have faith in your brother when no one else does. If I was missing, I'd want someone to look for me."

"Me too," I say in a tiny voice, a little shaken at how close Colin is to my biggest fear. I tense, thinking he might pull me in close. A comforting hug or even an oh-my-goodness kiss. Can I handle that? Goodness, yes.

But he just pulls me closer to the trees.

"The guys at the hardware store said the fishermen who found the shirt scraps told them it was high in the branches about head height. They only noticed it in the first place because it was a Lake George T-shirt. When they pulled it down, they spotted the blood stains on it. They brought it to your dad, who verified it was Jim's."

"With someone else's blood besides Jim's. And not mine either like everyone assumes. It's male, no relation."

"How do you know?" Colin looks surprised.

"You're not the only one looking for clues." I take a deep breath. "Could it be yours?"

Colin jerks. "What do you mean?"

I rub the back of my neck. "When you pulled him out of the river?"

Colin kicks at a fallen, rotting log. "You think I hurt him? I told you he was already hurt when I pulled him in."

"No! I'm asking if you were bleeding already? Maybe a branch got you? I don't know."

His eyes are wide as he shrugs, but he's not looking at me. The hurt there makes my heart lurch. I'm sorry I asked.

"I...I don't know. Things were happening really fast, Bea. I mean, I got scraped up, yeah, but nothing serious enough to get stitches."

Before I can respond, a low buzzing tickles my ears. An angry thundercloud of yellow jackets fills the air. "Oh, crap!" I grab his hand, yanking him towards the river. We dive in with the mad buzzing at our heels.

The coffee-colored water is murky but not enough to lose sight of Colin. He really could be a water spirit now, suspended in the river with his hair fanning out and shirt floating up to reveal tantalizing glimpses of tanned stomach. I sigh as well as I can underwater.

He points to the surface and I shake my head. I can't hear the yellow jackets anymore but that doesn't mean anything. If we could stay here like this, I'd rather not ever surface. The burn in my lungs tells me otherwise. With a couple smooth kicks, he propels up and breaks the surface.

When he doesn't duck back down, I join him. "I'm sorry. I'm just trying to figure things out." His facial expression has me feeling lower than four flat tires.

He nods, then thankfully grins. "I can't believe you threw me in the river," he says, splashing water in my face.

"Whatever. I saved your life."

We smile at each other, treading water when his expression changes abruptly.

"What is it?"

"Something just hit my leg."

"A fish? Or something bigger, like a turtle?"

He barely stays long enough to hear me, free-styling with one arm as he drags me with him toward the boat.

I can't help but laugh, even as I get a little water in my mouth. I spit it out. "You pretty much work for Fish and Wildlife, and you're freaked out by something touching you?"

He tugs me closer. "Maybe it's because I know everything that's in these waters."

Somehow, he pushes me into the boat. If he really was a water sprite, he would know everything in these waters. Then he could tell everyone for sure that Jim isn't still in the river. When I don't get out of the way as he pulls himself into the boat, he falls on top of me.

I detangle myself and sit on the boat seat, primly facing him. His face changes from concern to self-aware so fast, I bust out laughing.

He laughs too. "Do you always go swimming with all your clothes on?"

"Seems like it. All the cool—no, excuse me, crazy— kids are doing it."

He leans forward. "Bea, I don't think you're crazy."

"Do you think he's still alive?" I blurt out before I can stop myself. It's another one of those questions that shouldn't be asked because I don't want to hear the answer.

"I... Honestly, I don't understand why everyone's so quick to assume he's dead."

"Right!?"

"On the other hand, where is he if he's alive? Where did he go when he left this boat?"

I nod, tucking my hands under my legs as I look around the johnboat with renewed interest. The last place I saw my brother alive was in this boat.

"Which creek were y'all going to, do you remember?"

"Yes, it's the same one that flows to the Shelf. That limestone ledge where we first met."

Colin starts as if he's going to say something but then changes his mind. "Something was—or maybe is—down there that was so important to Jim that he risked rising flood waters to get it."

"We should see if that something is still there." That part of the woods fills me with a dark sort of fluttering in my belly and throat. I'm nervous that the natural beauty could turn wicked and dangerous as quick as a flood surge that rips away brothers and slams you into tree trunks. Last time I went down, the fear distracted me from the search. Perhaps I can do it as long as I have someone with me.

"Don't get too excited. Any clues have more than likely washed away in the floodwaters. We have no idea what it might be."

I nod impatiently. "Sure, okay. Can we go?" A sobering thought strikes as I recall how uncomfortable he looked earlier. "That is, if you want. If you have time." He might be ready for better company than yours-truly.

He looks at me in surprise. "Sure. Uncle Rob lent me the boat for the whole day once I told him I wanted to take you around. You made a good impression on him last night."

I pick at the invisible algae on my arm, trying to hide my pleased grin. "Oh, well, okay. Bet it was the fried pickles. Everyone likes those."

17

Wild Scenarios & Pointy Beaver Sticks

We speed back upriver, past the Sandbar, the boat ramp, and all the boats out enjoying this beautiful weather.

"Your boyfriend is giving me a go-to-hell look," Colin yells over the motor.

"Not my boyfriend," I correct, looking around. Yup, there's Junior, trawling along the far bank with a couple of buddies in an aluminum johnboat. If stares were drill bits, our boat would sink, full of holes.

"I don't know if he agrees with that." Colin cheerfully waves at them.

"He warned me away from you."

"Really?" Colin flares his nostrils and bares his teeth in a menacing look.

I laugh.

"Yet here you are."

My head bobs. I swallow hard.

"If only he had offered to help you find your brother, he could be here with you and I'd be the one staring enviously as the two of you race off in search of clues."

Envious? I can't tell if he's kidding or serious. Is that why he offered to help me find Jim—he wants an excuse to hang out with me? Maybe he feels guilty that he didn't finish saving him before. Also, is he implying that I'm only hanging out with him because he's helping me? Surely, he knows I like him. Yes, I'm admitting it. *Bea Pearl, you like this boy a lot.*

I don't know how to respond. Staring at the bow as it cuts through the water, I pretend I don't hear him over the Evinrude. I'm a coward. A twitchy, awkward coward.

We pass brick trestles that tower through the brush on each bank. They once supported the bridge for the railroad tracks back in Georgefield's glory days. Though the glory days seem to be returning. Daddy was telling Momma about another restaurant opening up on the other side of town. Different food than ours so no competition, but apparently Georgefield is the safest place around. Folks and businesses are moving here, wanting to be a part of that sort of community. I hug my knees to my chest. Well, safe if you don't count my missing brother. Come to think on it, having a mysteriously disappeared teen might be bad for a wholesome, progressive image.

Passing the next bend, spring water tumbles—miniature waterfalls—off the jutting limestone shelf. Colin throttles down once we approach the limestone and the bank turns sandy from the creek.

Last time I was here was the first time we met. The time those mysterious eyes watched me from the bush. "There may be swamp monkeys around here," I say as he helps me out of the boat.

He laughs.

"That's what I thought too, until I saw the skull."

"Hmmm, I'll have to ask Uncle Rob about that."

Again, I can't tell if he's serious or not, but really, who can blame him for being skeptical? Then as a thought hits me, I grab his arm. Already, I'm more comfortable around him. I like it. Wonder if he does too.

"Do you remember something else?"

"If there was a new species, would that be worth something?"

"Well, yeah, it could. Like to conservationists and scientists who wanted to study the new species."

"Okay, here's a wild scenario and don't you dare laugh. What if Jim discovered a group of swamp monkeys and found out they could make him rich. He needed money for school, so he came back to save them when it flooded. Instead, he was kidnapped by the people who wanted to skip Jim as the middleman and capture the monkeys themselves?"

To his credit, he doesn't laugh though he does look dubious as one eyebrow disappears into his dark brown hair. "First off, it would be a *troop, barrel,* or *circus* of monkeys, depending on the species, and I don't know if anyone would be kidnapped over monkeys…"

I look at him as if he's teasing me. "Seriously? A barrel of monkeys is a scientific thing?" I consider what he said. "What if it was a weird hybridization—a missing link— of monkeys? This river is known for its biodiversity."

Colin winks. "Maybe if they were genetically modified Flying Monkeys."

I stick out my tongue, and he tugs my braid. One thing is for certain. If monkeys can survive out in the wilderness along the rivers, unseen for over half a century, then it's totally plausible for my brother to exist out here, too. "Jim and I were upstream," I say, changing the mood.

"Lead the way."

The creek has a firm, sandy bottom, making it easier to navigate by walking in the creek itself than along its banks.

Splashing in the knee-deep water feels safer for some reason. Flip flops in hand, I keep my eyes peeled for anything out of the ordinary as we walk under a fallen tree, shrouded in scuppernong vines. "You must have equipment around here since you were in this area the day I was down."

He nods. "Good thing too, since you would have been gator-bait without me. Why were you down here?"

"If the swamp monkey idea amuses you, you'll really love this next bit. I dreamed a water sprite gave me a fossilized sand dollar, telling me to come down here so I could find my brother. Now, I bet you really think I'm crazy, huh?" I don't want to turn around to see his expression.

"That explains why you said I wasn't real."

"And look, I'm back here again, trying to find my brother. So, I've included you in my madness."

"I like your madness."

I turn around to cheese at him when something sharp punctures the bottom of my foot. I cry out in pain as I trip over a submerged tree branch.

Poetry in motion.

"Bea, are you okay?"

"Stupid beavers, leaving their crap everywhere," I mutter, dripping wet for the second time that day.

He laughs gently. "You're been falling for me ever since we met."

Truer words never spoken. The tips of my ears heat up.

"How's your ankle?" He extends his hand. I take it but don't pull myself up yet. Something's not right.

"Ankle: sprained. Pride: I think it's broken. But there's something in my foot." My voice wobbles. Whatever is sharp didn't dislodge when I fell. I can still feel the pressure so it must be in pretty deep.

He kneels in front of me in the creek and I study his hair. What if I was brave enough to reach up and run my fingers through his windblown hair? It would be beyond embarrassing if he kindly but firmly stops me. It would be unnerving if he doesn't. Because then, what else? I can't handle either the rejection or the encouragement, so my lungs forget to breathe.

When he gently picks up my foot, a foot long stick, bark stripped, protrudes from my sole. Gravity pulls at it now that it's out of the water and my pulse reroutes itself from my heart to my foot. Blood gushes. I whimper.

He looks me in the eye. "We need to get you out of this water."

Maybe I'm in shock because I ask, "Sharks?"

He tries so hard not to smile that his mouth goes upside down for a second. "Not so likely in ten inches of freshwater. I'm more concerned about marine bacterial infections."

Oh God, I'd rather punch a shark in the nose than deal with flesh-eating bacteria. My okay sounds like a mouse squeak halfway down a rattler's throat. I brush wet sand and clam shell bits off my palms and knees.

He sets me on a nearby log. My fingernails dig into the wormy, soft grooved bark. He holds my foot down.

"Shouldn't you elevate it? Stop the bleeding? I'm feeling woozy."

"Right now, your blood is cleaning out the wound."

I may have exaggerated the gushing and wooziness because after a few minutes, the pain doesn't get any worse. When he does let me elevate it, the bleeding stops though my heartbeat is still in my foot. Our backs are now on the soft leaf litter, our legs over the log. Sunlight filters through the maples and birches, the birds' chirping makes for nice background music, and the occasional dragonfly catches light like rubies, sapphires, and emeralds.

He rubs his knuckles against mine. "How do you feel now?"

"More peaceful than I deserve."

"Yeah, I know exactly what you mean."

He doesn't say anything more, but I wonder why he thinks he doesn't deserve peace.

"Should I take you back home?"

I sit up and shake my head. "This is as good as place as any to look around for clues."

Colin tears off the sleeves to his shirt. I open my mouth to protest, but biceps. He wraps the material around my foot before sliding my flip flop back on. I feel like Cinderella on Survivor.

"Lead the way," he says.

This section of the woods looks ordinary. It's a little flatter than near the river with more pawpaw trees, maples, and hollies and less cypress and river birch. There isn't even that much undergrowth to hinder our view. The canopy blocks most of the sunlight from reaching the ground. I point towards the southeast. "This way is our cut through from the field behind the house to the river."

"Anything upstream?"

I shake my head. "This creek flows from a swamp, which is runoff from Lake George and underground springs. It would've been impossible to get through it during a flood, so we would have gone through the higher field."

"If Jim was down here because he had hidden something, he might have buried it. But there's no way of knowing where it would be because the floodwaters and six months' worth of rain would have obliterated any signs of fresh-dug dirt," Colin says. "Or he could have been meeting someone."

I blow my escaping hair out of my eyes in frustration. Every time I have a glimmer of hope, reality keeps snatching it back.

"Now if we had a treasure map..."

"Ha. And a parrot. Hey, I almost have a peg-leg." Something tugs at a loose flap of my grey stuff. "Wait. Can you read coordinates?"

"Like GPS?"

I nod like a bobble-head on an unpaved road.

"The depth-finder on the FWS boat would work. Why?"

"I found some numbers in Jim's truck. We thought they might be some kind of sports stats, but Honey's brother said no. What if—Wild Scenario Number Two for the day—they're latitude and longitude coordinates for Jim's...whatever it is?"

Colin nods. "That makes more sense than Wild Scenario Number One. Do you have the numbers?"

I mentally retrace my steps. Honey handed it to me before school. I was disappointed Lucas wasn't helpful. What did I do with it? "It's either in my schoolbag or the jeans I wore yesterday."

"Do you want to look around here any longer or head back?"

I scan the woods and creek once more. "You're right. It's pretty doubtful we'd find any clues after so much time has passed. I'm not magically remembering anything else like I hoped I would, so let's go fetch that treasure map."

We head back down the creek to the river and the boat. My eyes are glued to the ground for more beaver booby traps as I hobble along.

"It's past lunch. Maybe I can get together something for us to eat while you get the numbers, and we can meet back up at the boat ramp?" Colin helps me climb in. "I still have the boat for the day so we may as well make the most of it."

"I'd like that. As long as I'm not keeping you from anything important."

"If something more important comes up, I'll turn into fog and creep away. Sound good?"

"Guess so, as long as you don't expect me to eat raw minnows and algae salads."

"What?"

I shrug with exaggerated nonchalance. "Or whatever it is that water spirits eat."

"Oh, I figured water spirits would eat sunshine and drink tears from weeping maidens."

I laugh as we circle back towards the boat ramp. The glare on Junior's face as we pass his fishing spot again sobers me. My laugh cuts off and hides in the back of my throat.

As Colin walks me to Jim's truck, I struggle to find that tiny bit of light-heartedness we had before. I think we both deserve it. Colin's reaction to my question about the bloody shirt shows me how much guilt he's holding inside when he didn't do anything wrong. I bump my elbow into his arm, and he bumps back. I grin as he opens the driver's side door and my mouth wobbles as the grin dissolves.

"What's wrong?" Colin asks, seeing my face. He steps in front of me. "Whoa. The truck wasn't like this when you left, was it?"

I shake my head and duck under his arm that's still holding the door open. Jim's truck is chaotic. The glove compartment and console are emptied, everything strewn about the cab. "Jim's room got trashed after I found the receipts. His truck gets trashed after I find the not-basketball-stats."

"Those GPS numbers you were just telling me about?"

I nod.

Colin pulls out his phone.

"Who are you calling?"

"The police."

"Calling them won't help." I tug his arm down. "The sheriff and my mom will say I did this. They always do." I scan the parking lot and boat ramp. It's busier now than it was earlier. One pickup truck in particular catches my eye. It looks like the one I ran into that August morning I tried to keep the phone from ringing. In hindsight, it's a strange thing to realize it was a call from Colin that I was running to.

"Who knew you found the receipts and the numbers?"

"Honey and Lucas, but I trust them with my life. I trust them with Jim's life."

"Bea Pearl, are you in danger? Can I take you back home?"

"No. The only way to get out of this mess is to find Jim. And I'm supposed to be with Honey so I can't very well show up with you. I'm going home and getting those numbers. And then, we will find Jim."

Colin touches my jaw and nods. "I'll be here when you get back."

18

Dreamlike Memories or Memory-like Dreams

I'm driving past the field between our property and the William's when Honey's car approaches from the direction of my house.

Oh crap on crap on whole wheat bread. We roll down our windows as my truck and her car pull beside each other.

She raises her eyebrows and bares her teeth in chagrin. "So, umm, next time you're 'babysitting' with me, please let me know. I just got you in major trouble."

I wrinkle my nose. "I meant to…"

She lays her arm across the open car window, propping up her chin. "Where were you since you obviously weren't with me? Your hair looks like you've been swimming. Did you go hang out around Beth's pool with the rest of the cool kids?" She fails to maintain a straight face.

I snort at the absurdity and squirm, wanting so badly tell her about Colin.

"You were with a boy! Not Junior, though? There's a boy you like, and I don't know about it? Bestie Beatrice Pearl! You can't keep things like this from me!"

I stretch my face but it's no use, I'm cheesin' big time. And really, I'm sure Junior or anyone that saw us dancing at the restaurant will mention him to her. "His name is Colin and he's here with the US Fish and Wildlife." Wow, it feels good to finally tell her.

"Slap me with a swamp monkey. How old is he? He doesn't go to our school, does he? I'd notice a new guy."

"He's still in high school. It's a co-op or something."

"How'd you meet him?"

"He saved my life."

Honey pretends to swoon, the back of her hand flicking to her forehead. "How romantic! When do I get to meet him?"

"He's waiting for me now. I'm running home to get—oh! Those last numbers in Jim's truck may be map coordinates."

"Wow! Seems like I've missed a lot this morning. Though I hate to tell you, don't expect to be able to leave your house. Ever." She pauses, glances at the road before looking up at me again. "Does he know about Jim?"

"Yeah, he was actually here this past spring when it flooded."

Honey raises her eyebrows and looks past the truck. "There's a car coming behind you. And your parents might be rounding up a search party. But!" She holds up a finger and raises one eyebrow. "I want a full report on this Colin fellow."

"Yes, ma'am. That's if I'm still allowed to use a phone."

"I'll keep my eyes peeled for smoke signals." She grimaces as we roll up our windows.

My stomach churns the closer I get to Lake George. The possibility of reversing and high-tailing it on out of here is tempting. Colin and I could run away in his uncle's boat, head on down to Panama City where we'd live happily ever after chasing dinosaur fish. I tap the steering wheel. No, it's time to put on my big girl panties. I'll take my punishment now, so it won't hang over my head for the rest of my life. And the car behind me makes it difficult to turn around on the narrow road.

As soon as I pull up to the house, Momma and Daddy stare me down from the front porch. Toby has his paw over his snout as if he feels bad for me. The way they're always mad at me makes me wonder if Jim was their favorite or if things have changed since his disappearance. Have they ever liked me, really?

I brace myself and limp toward the house. Mama birds feign broken wings to lure predators away from their babies, and it feels like I'm doing the same. Without the pretending. The baby I'm protecting is a fragile little egg of truth that Jim is still alive.

Momma looks at me, white faced. Same old mixture of sorrow and disappointment. I wonder if she wishes it was me that disappeared rather than Jim. Is she disappointed because I'm the one that made it back? The one that still exists? Is it more of my delusions that we were ever a happy family?

Daddy finally speaks after I climb the couple of steps and face them. "You didn't answer your cell phone."

"It was dead. On the charger in my bedroom." Conveniently, so I wouldn't feel guilty about avoiding their calls.

They both stare at me.

"I'm sorry but…"

"Honey just left."

Nodding, I swallow, eyes on the ground. The silence hangs between us as they wait for my excuse. I don't offer one. Daddy's sigh is so heavy my shoulders slump with it.

How am I going to let Colin know I can't make it back? I never thought to get his number. Will he be worried something happened to me? Or, horror-of-horrors, think I didn't want to hang out with him. If the situation were reversed, I would be devastated.

"You need to shower before your shift starts," Mama says finally, calmer this time than when I returned from the Sandbar. "I can smell the river on you."

I frown. "My shift doesn't start 'til five-thirty."

"The schedule changed. You're working concessions this afternoon, too."

I cross my arms, glaring at the ground. She changed the schedule last minute. On the other hand, if working an extra afternoon shift is my only punishment for disobeying her, I'll take it.

Though not being able to continue my search for clues in Jim's disappearance is all the punishment I really need.

There's no word from Colin. Not a call, or a rain drop for the rest of the weekend. Each night I sit on the dock or on the bank of Lake George, braving mosquitoes and risking Momma's wrath, waiting for him to magically appear out of the dark.

But he never does.

I'm going to explode from all the guilt, anger, fear and frustration. So much so that I need to keep my arms wrapped tightly around myself, so I won't burst into a million fiery little embers.

During break at school—the only other place Momma allows me to go besides work—Honey touches my elbow. The unexpected touch makes me jump. I'm too focused on holding myself together. So tired, my grip is slipping. I hold myself tighter.

"Bea Pearl, what's wrong?"

I shake my head and bite my lip.

Honey puts her wrist to my forehead. "You're burning up!"

I shake my head again, wincing at the pain and stiffness throughout my body. My foot is on fire. Then I can't stop my whole body from shaking.

I am broken. Everything around me is fractured.

"Okay, I'm taking you to the nurse." She puts her arm around me. I'm grateful for her help in holding myself together. It hurts to walk.

I'm underwater. All the sound and light around me are muted as if I'm holding my breath in a brown-green world. A cool hand replaces Honey's now hot one and I smell the faint antiseptic of the nurse's office. Too tired to listen, to exist here, so instead I let myself drift off in the cool, comforting currents.

Jim and Toby crouch down beside me in the front yard, my hair in pigtails, a hand-me-down Mickey Mouse shirt to my knees. Jim poked a piece of pine straw down a hole, fiddling for chicken chokers. When the straw started vibrating, Jim snatched it up and I reached out to catch the ugly little grub. Toby smacked me in the leg with his thick, ropey tail.

Frost on the windows. I held my breath to keep from fogging it up. I had to see what Jim was up to, stealing out of the house at night. A tiny flame, then the cherry glow of a cigarette. Jim was sneaking out to smoke? He was always against smoking, saying it would slow him down on the basketball court. Then I heard a rougher voice. Deeper, more mature than his. I pressed my ear to the chilly glass but couldn't make out the words. Then someone turned on the hallway light and I was backlit. I ducked down.

Honey and I caught each other flitching corn off the stalks in the farm between our houses. Partners in crime, we vowed to be best friends forever. That taste of sweet, milky corn on the cob. The excitement of having a best friend to share everything.

We hid behind some pine trees, painting each other's arms and faces with pokeberry juice as Honey and I spied on Jim and Lucas as they fished off the bank of Lake George. But when the talk turned to gross stuff about older girls we ran off, vowing to each other that we'd never let boys talk about us that way.

But then, years later at school, making a shield with our locker doors in the sixth-grade hall, some girls were talking about Honey that way. I didn't say anything. I didn't say a word. Worse, I giggled, too.

Jim's last win at the End-of-Summer Picnic swim race. I went looking for him to tell him congrats and finally found him as he disappeared behind the well box. Someone was already there, waiting. Back to me, a ball cap pulled low. The sun was too bright for me to see. I blinked but the chlorine in my eyes made rainbows. Fire ants attacked my feet and when I stood back up, the guy in a ball cap handed him an envelope. Jim pulled out money. Lots of money. Too much.

Hot summer days spent exploring the Chatothatchee in canoes, our end-spot always the Sandbar and swinging off the oak. Those magical seconds that exist after letting go of the rope right before breaking through the water's surface.

Then the recycled, sanitized air of a hospital room. The hum of machines, the murmur of TVs and nurses. I don't want to open my eyes. I'm happy here, existing in the memories in my head. But was this the hospital visit in spring or am I back here again in autumn? Picturing one last wildly free swing, I then resolutely make up my mind. I choose awake. Otherwise, who will save Jim?

My eyes open.

Deadly Mud & Awkward Questions

Curled in a ball, Honey sleeps in one of the wood and pleather chairs. It looks like the same chair she sat in when I came in for my ankle. Has that just happened, or will it happen in the future? The freshly remembered betrayal in my memory-dream twists my gut. Bile rises, guilt-thick.

The guy in the baseball cap is Daniel, Beth's cousin. I wonder what connection he has to Jim. I don't remember them ever hanging out as buddies. What was going on between the two of them? I wonder if that was his cigarette glowing through the cold window. Or if it was his blue pickup.

The blinds are closed. There's no calendar hanging from the painted cinderblock walls. The white board is so scribbled with new and old notations that nothing's legible. Remembering my head injury last March, I lift my IV taped arm to touch the right side of my head. No bandage. This must be September. My foot is completely wrapped and aches like a mother. All this because of the giant beaver splinter?

The bedside table holds a flower arrangement, but I immediately zero in on a fossilized sand dollar next to it. Colin. Does that mean he came to see me? The heart rate monitor beeps faster.

"Oh, Bea, you're awake!" Honey untangles herself, stretching her arms into the air. "Uh, my legs are asleep. How do you feel?"

The queasy ball of shame in my throat has me clearing my throat so words can come out proper. "Like we really should get frequent visitor cards."

"Ha! Right?"

"What's wrong with me?" I lift my arm with the tubing.

"You got a marine bacterial infection."

"Seriously? Oh god, is it eating my flesh?"

She makes a blech face and quickly shakes her head. "You're on four different antibiotics so the doctors say you should be fine. How did you even put your shoes on before you went to school? It was so swollen they had to cut it off."

My bottom jaw trembles. "My foot? They cut off my foot? I'm having phantom pains. Oh jeez. It hurts."

Honey laughs. "Sorry, I'm not laughing at you...Never mind, I am. They cut off your *shoe,* silly."

I let out a huge, steadying sigh. "I washed it out with hydrogen peroxide when I got home. I thought I got all the splinters out."

"Apparently it shoved just enough mud up into your foot to make you really sick. After you passed out, they put you under and did exploratory surgery. Dr. Arnie told me and your parents that he's confidant it's all out."

All this talk is making my foot ache. "Were you here when Colin came?" I gesture towards the sand dollar.

Honey smooths the slept-on side of her head. "Yes and let me tell you how much it freaked me out when that hotness came in here with a river sand dollar. If he's in your dreams, I'm sleeping over at your house."

I grin. "Yeah, I didn't think he was real either when I first met him."

She hesitates like she's thinking of how to word something unpleasant.

"What? Just tell me. Not like I can get out of this bed and stomp away from you."

Honey smiles but it doesn't reach her eyes. "It's just, I don't know. Something about him is…"

"Have you been talking to Junior?"

She nods.

I roll my eyes. "He's jealous, that's all it is." And weird. I never did find any sort of present on our porch.

"Maybe. But we've known Junior our whole lives." She frowns. "Well, I did just learn the other day that Sheriff Oakwood is his mama's brother, but that's beside the point. This Colin guy, while he is the hottest thing I've seen in real life—or in my dreams, is a stranger. Junior said he remembers Colin acting sketchy at the boat ramp the day you and Jim got swept down the river. Also, I don't think it's right or fair to you that he's encouraging you on this hunt for Jim. Yeah, he told me what y'all did the other weekend. And maybe I'm guilty of encouraging you, too. I just want you to find out why Jim went out there for closure. Get on with your life, be the Bea you were before Jim disappeared. I mean, what's his angle?"

"I think it's because he likes me," I admit softly, surprised at the vulnerability in my voice. It doesn't seem a good enough reason when I say it out loud, as if I'm not worthy. If I tell her he was the one who rescued Jim, she'll just turn it around against him. I sink back into the pillow, blowing the hair out of my eyes. Honey is abandoning me. Giving up on me like everybody else.

Honey sighs heavily. "Oh Bea, I hope he does." She holds my hand for a second before moving toward her purse. "But... Junior gave me something today to give to you."

I huff in annoyance as Honey reaches into her purse but then yelp when she opens her hand. Resting on her palm is a lumpy freshwater pearl. *My* pearl.

"Junior said he found it in Colin's truck."

I take it from her hand, rolling it between my fingers. Rememorizing its surface. "Yeah, right. What was Junior doing in Colin's truck?" Colin would've told me he had this when he confessed, right? Maybe he didn't understand how important it is to me.

"Junior said he saw it in the truck's console at the boat ramp, so he rescued it for you when no one was around."

"So, everyone's just making themselves at home in everybody's trucks, huh?" Bitterness twines through my words like thorny sticker vines. "Junior has been getting around a lot lately. Could he be the one that broke into Jim's room *and* truck? Don't you think he could be lying? Maybe he's had my pearl this whole time."

"Bea, you're being ridic—"

"I'm tired," I say. The remnants of guilt sharpen my words.

"Sure, of course. I'll just sit here."

"No, its fine. You can go."

Honey looks startled. "Honest, I don't mind. I've got some homework to do."

"You should go home." I roll over on my side, facing away from her. Every movement sends pain flaring up my leg, the IV tape pulls at my skin.

"I'll be back after school tomorrow to bring you the assignments you're missing. Love you, Bestie Bea. Glad you're going to be okay."

I mumble a response but don't relax until the door shuts. When Momma and Daddy visit, I feign sleep. They don't stay long. When the nurse announces an end to visiting hours, I let out an involuntary whimper.

Colin never came. Pearl in one hand and clutching the sand dollar as tight as I dare without crushing it in the other, I drift off to a restless sleep.

I wake up the next morning when the nurse checks my IV bag, amazed that I've slept through almost an entire night in a hospital.

"Rise and shine, Sugar Pie. Let's get you freshened up. You have a visitor waiting to see you." The nurse helps me brush my teeth and wash my face but when it comes to brushing my hair, I can see her getting frustrated.

"Who is it?" I take the brush from her and pull my hair up into a messy bun.

Her eyes twinkle. "Oh, just some boy."

I glance at the clock. School has already begun so I hope it's Colin and not Junior.

"There you are, pretty as the month of May. I'll send him in."

My heart skips up into my throat when Colin walks in the hospital room. Oddly enough, I've only been inside with him that one time in the restaurant, and the walls seem to close in on us in an intimate way.

"I didn't know which flavor algae you liked best, so I picked a flower instead." He hands me a white marsh mallow blossom with a dark pink center.

"Blue-green's my fave."

"And I took you for a filamentous girl." He studies me until my cheeks warm up.

"Thanks for the sand dollar."

"Your friend acted like she saw a ghost when I brought it in. Hope it didn't freak you out, too."

"Not at all. I was glad to see you had been here." My cheeks are probably glowing now. I'm having a hard time resisting the urge to scratch.

"I've rescued you from gators and Grendels, but not mudkins."

Laughing, I stretch my arms, too giddy to stay hooked up to this bed. "Yeah, who knew? Squishy between the toes: yes. Potentially life altering and deadly: no idea. I'm glad you aren't mad that I never showed up last Saturday. I got grounded for sneaking off to the river."

He crosses his arms. I wish he would come closer. "Yeah, Honey filled me in. Sucks to hear you got in trouble."

"Did y'all have a good talk?" I hold my breath.

"She doesn't trust me because she's very protective of you. She's a good friend."

"Hmmmph." I roll the pearl in between my fingers, then hold my palm out to him. I don't want to see the hurt in his eyes again, but I have to know. "Have you seen this before?"

He sits on the side of my bed and plucks it out of my hand. I don't scoot over, enjoying the way our legs press together. "Freshwater." His eyes dart to my necklace and he smiles. "The pearl to your bee?"

I grin. "How'd you guess?"

"You fiddle with it when you're anxious or talking about your brother."

"Very observant."

He nods, pleased. "Why'd you ask if I'd seen it before?"

I bite my top lip. "Junior told Honey he found it in your truck."

His face stiffens and he looks intently into my eyes. "What do you think?"

My heart thumps, thinks it over, thumps again. Then races. "That he's jealous. Because he can see how much I like you."

Colin stops breathing. "Is that so?"

I nod.

Then he kisses me with such intensity I honestly melt into Bea stock. His lips are soft and just the tiniest bit salty. He tastes of boat rides on breezy days. The hint of stubble scratches my skin in the best way possible. I thought dancing with him was magical, but it doesn't begin to compare to this kiss.

He backs away enough to murmur against my cheek, "Thank you."

I shiver though my lips burn as if I just ate spicy crawfish. "I don't care a gnat's toenail what Junior thinks."

He laughs into my hair, giving me a fierce hug.

"But the idea of him rummaging through your truck makes me wonder if he's the one who trashed Jim's truck and bedroom."

"How do we find ou—"

An ill-timed knock on the door interrupts him. Colin quickly stands as Momma and Daddy walk in with a take-out container from the restaurant.

"Morning, Beep!" Daddy says. "Thought you might like something better than hospital jello for breakfast. Oh, you already have a visitor…"

With my cheeks glowing like flares, I introduce Momma and Daddy to Colin, which is really, really weird.

"Okay, yeah. I remember the FWS eating at the restaurant the other night. Nice to meet you." Daddy shakes his hand.

Momma crosses her arms. "Are you why my daughter defied me and went out on the river when I expressly told her not to?"

"Momma! Really."

"Are you responsible for her foot being impaled? For her getting infected so bad?"

Daddy squeezes her arm, and she presses her lips together.

"I'm really sorry that happened, and glad she's on the mend." Colin smiles at me, then clears his throat. "I need to meet up with Uncle Rob soon. But I'll be seeing you again, Bea Pearl. It was um… nice meeting you, Mr. and Mrs. Montgomery."

He leaves and I expect to immediately get bombarded with horribly awkward questions.

"Seems like a nice kid," Daddy says. "But what about that Junior boy? Now he can fish."

Ah, now it begins. "Not going there."

When the small room falls silent, no one knows where to look. Daddy's arms are crossed over his chest. Momma's are clasped before her, thumbs twirling. This standoffishness isn't us. Isn't our family. I can't remember the last time Momma smiled at me. A real smile, not one with blame and grief hiding in the corners of her lips. Months?

Then it hits me that I've done this to us. My quest to find Jim and my refusal to accept that they want him dead has put this huge wedge between us and it's wearing us down. If I don't change something, it will destroy what's left of this family. So, I have a choice, lose the family I have left, or lose the hope that my brother is still alive.

Momma breaks the overbearing quiet when she clears her throat. "The nurse said she'll come by in a little bit and take out your IV. You'll be on pill-form antibiotics for the next ten days, and they want you back in for a checkup in a week."

"And seriously, no river this time," Daddy cautions.

I wipe my tears off with the corner of the hospital bed sheet and nod. How can I choose which family members are the most important? It would be so much easier if I give in and let Jim go. I wouldn't be branded as crazy forever. My parents and I could have a better relationship. But I'll know. I'll know I killed my brother by giving up on him. And then the rumors about me will be true.

I can't let that happen.

Once they unhook me from the IV bag, I dress in regular clothes and gather my things, slipping the sand dollar in my shorts' pocket. They leave me alone as I wait for my parents to come get me and fill out discharge papers. Time weighs heavy. I can't get comfortable in the sticky pleather chair. My mind wanders until I recall Emma Kate's mom telling me about the blood on Jim's shirt that didn't match my blood type. I wonder if there's anything else she didn't tell me.

I open the room door and look down the hallway. It's empty except for a nurse entering a patient's room a few doors down. Not knowing the last name of Emma Kate's mom should deter me but I walk down the hallway anyway, scanning doors for helpful signs that say things like "Bloody Shirts Analyzed Here" or "Clues That People Won't Share". I'll settle for one that says "Blood Work" though.

Getting into shenanigans is more fun with Honey. I'm usually the one talking her out of things like sneaking into hospital labs. But desperate times call for desperate measures and I desperately need to find something to prove this Flat Earth world wrong.

There's a plain, boring, old sign for "Lab", and I figure it'll do. Peeking through the frosted glass of the laboratory door, I can't make out much. If I do get caught, I'll blame it on disorientation from the antibiotics or something.

Taking a deep breath, I push the door open. Just that little bit of exertion has me feeling weak in the knees and off balance. A tech looks up from a spinning centrifuge. "I'm a friend of Emma Kate's," I say, hoping he won't think it's odd that I'm obviously older than her. I bet I should have said something like tutor. "Is her mother around?"

He adjusts his glasses and points to the back of the lab, towards a hallway that leads to offices. I thank him even though her name once again stumps me. The last door says records. Hmm, maybe it's better that I don't run into Emma Kate's mama.

The inside of the records room smells like a library, though a heavily disinfected one. I head directly for the "M"s. When I find a file labeled "Alan James Montgomery", I want to dance. Instead I lean against the shelves to take weight off my foot. Thank goodness for small county hospitals that don't rely completely on computers to store information.

When I open it up, there's nothing in it about testing the blood. The last thing is when he broke his arm in the ninth grade. I flip through again, in case it's not in chronological order.

I suck air through gritted teeth. Of course, there's not a file. Emma Kate's mom didn't want anything to do with my delusions.

Sliding it back in the drawer, another file further back catches my eye. I blink. Those mudkins really must have done a number on my brain if I didn't even consider the possibility of my own file.

My hand shakes as I reach for it. Whether from nerves or exertion, I don't know. I locate the page noting my wounds from March. The head wound that needed six stitches, a subcutaneous hematoma on my shoulder. I frown until I realize that must be the fancy medical term for bruise from hitting the tree. And various gashes on my forearms and shins possibly from being dragged down a river. There's also a note that they correlate with defensive wounds.

Scrunching my eyes, I try to get my brain to work. My heart pounds as if it's trying to escape. Or trying to tell me something. Defensive wounds? I swallow. Am I misremembering due to the head wound? Was it possible that I fought someone at some point?

20

Body Language & Fried Moths

The silver lining in contracting a marine bacterial infection is that a whimper gets me out of school. As long as I'm at the house for lunch and dinner, they never know I sneak out the window and meet up with Colin at the river. They think I sleep and do schoolwork all day. I don't have to pretend to be hurting though, because it's true.

Colin and I decide to track down the coordinates to try to figure out why Jim was down at the river in the first place. Then we want to search the other side of the river since that will be more of a needle-in-a-haystack, or literally, one-person-in-a-wide-wide-woods venture.

Two sets of numbers at the end of the columns don't have letters next to them: 310328 and 858639. If we put decimals after the first two numbers, they become coordinates. The first set is north, the second, west. When Colin plugs them in, I'm ecstatic to see it's pinning a spot near where Jim and I were heading the day he disappeared.

We're in the woods above the Shelf again. This time there are fewer passionflowers and more goldenrod and wild clematis, fewer hummingbirds and more monarchs.

Colin's leading the way with the depth-finder and I'm close behind. "Have you ever gone geocaching?" he asks.

"Never heard of it."

"It's something we do back home. Kinda like a scavenger hunt you play with lots of people you never meet. You follow the coordinates and find stuff they leave, but you have to leave something, too. Sometimes you find cash but usually just small stuff."

I frown. I know he's only here while the sturgeon are migrating, but the thought of him going back home doesn't sit well with me. "You think Jim risked a flood to find a geocache?"

He shakes his head. "I'm just saying that's what this feels like."

He turns toward the spot where Jim lost his balance in the sand and went underwater. "All right. This is where the coordinates meet. I'd say start up high, like in a tree, because if it's still here, it has to be where the floodwaters couldn't reach."

We look for hours in every tree in the coordinate radius but as the sun approaches its midday spot, I grow more nervous. My neck aches from looking up. "Maybe this is more like Pokémon Go. It's here, we just can't see it. We need to change our approach or augment our reality." I rub my neck and retie my hair as he grins at me. "Like, maybe it's in something that's been here for a while." I turn in a slow circle, stopping when I see an old fencepost covered in broken strands of barbed wire. The mess is a frenzied jumble of granddaddy longlegs frozen and contained in rust.

"You're lucky you didn't get knocked into that when you were down here with Jim."

Examining the silvery wood, I bite my lip when I glimpse a black, waterproof pouch wedged tight in the cracks. "Found something." Using a stick to knock away spider webs, I gingerly pull it out, careful to avoid the lockjaw barbed wire.

"What's inside?"

I unzip it, tipping it into his cupped hand. A clear plastic baggie falls out.

Colin unrolls it, holding it up so we can see inside. "Don't think this is incense."

"Jim risked a flood for drugs? I... he wasn't on anything...What's going on?" I'm so confused. I know my brother. Don't I? Lucas mentioned a rumor about Jim dealing that day at the Sandbar.

Colin hands me the baggie, then looks at his watch. "It's almost noon. I need to meet up with Uncle Rob."

I don't want to touch it, but I shove it in my back pocket anyways. "And I need to be home before my parents check on me. Do you wanna meet here again tomorrow?"

His arm circles around my waist, pulling me close. "Don't lose faith in your brother. We'll figure this out." His kiss affects me the same way as the first ones so I'm in a happy little daze when we stop for air.

"God, you're beautiful," he says in a low, throaty voice.

As soon as he steps deeper into the woods toward his boat on the river, I head to the house.

Being a daughter of good intentions and good behavior, a prepared lunch waits on my parents when they come in the house. Though I really want to be by myself so I can think about that not-incense now hidden in the very back of my sock drawer. Jim's wallet isn't on my nightstand anymore. Either the wallet fell, or Momma picked it up. She never asked me about it, and I couldn't find it after searching everywhere in my room.

Or worse, I never found it in the first place. If I just imagined it, I obviously don't want to bring it up.

"Thanks for lunch, Beep," Daddy says before biting into his turkey sandwich.

"Should we be thanking that Colin fellow for this change in attitude?"

"Momma. Jeez."

"We don't want you getting too attached to him. Your dad spoke with his uncle the other day. He won't be here much longer. There are a lot of nice boys that live here."

Daddy gestures at me with his sandwich. I stop him before he can say what I know he's going to. "Yes, Daddy, Junior is a good fisherman. But he's not very interesting. Maybe to a bluegill, but not to me."

I searched Jim's bedroom the moment I was back from the hospital but couldn't find anything that tied Junior to being in there.

"You shouldn't be interested in boys anyhow. Schoolwork, that's what's important."

Mentally rolling my eyes, I instead smile at them. "Speaking of which, Honey's going to bring by the work I've missed once she gets out of school. That okay?"

They nod and their concerned smiles make me feel a little guilty. I rub my eyes and excuse myself to go lie down.

Once in my bedroom, I intend on making a mental list of all the possibilities of the contents of the baggie. Surely, I know my brother. And I'm going to search for his wallet again, because I know it was real. Or, I *wish* too much that it was real.

A picture sits on my bookshelf. In it, Jim and I are down at the sandbar, sitting on a tree trunk, our feet in the river. The low water uncovered a fallen tree, remnants from a previous storm, making a fun obstacle to jump off and swim around. Holding the frame to my chest, hot tears run off my cheeks and seep into the pillow.

On that day, Jim broke pieces off the branches and we made boats. Hollowing them out with muscle shells, we used sticks and sassafras leaves for the sails. Then we pushed them out into the current. Mine was ahead. I cheered, jumping up and down on the hard-packed sand until there was a splash next to my boat.

Kerplunk. Then another splash and my boat listed. I looked at Jim and saw his hands were full of cypress balls. I pushed him and he laughed and laughed. The next one he threw sunk my boat. The one after that hit me in the forehead. Furious, I scraped up two handfuls of wet sand and threw one at him and the other at his boat. And when his boat capsized, a giggle bubbled out. After that, we built boats and sank them for the rest of the afternoon.

All of a sudden, the sky clouds over from a summer afternoon showers. The thunder rumbles so long and low it vibrates my toes. I'm by myself, sitting on tree roots with my feet in the water. I'm searching, searching the opposite bank. A deer drinks from the river. She doesn't see me since I'm so quiet. She lifts her head and sniffs the air. I do the same. My heart pounds when I smell sandalwood and mint. Jim's scent.

I breathe deep. I want the smell to linger forever in my nose. The white-tail darts away which fills my heart with sadness. A boat enters my view and two figures paddle downstream. This is the reason why I was waiting. One of the figures wears a baseball cap of unknown color because everything is black and white and gray. A lanky guy sits behind him. Sandalwood and mint fill my nose again, and my heart thumps so strongly, The pulse makes my ribs ache. Clutching my chest with a gasp, I look down to see if a broken rib protrudes from the skin. Nothing.

When I look back up, the river is empty. And still. Somehow even the current has stopped. The pain in my chest is so unbearable I fall into the water. Only my face is wet though my whole body goes under. I cry out and waken to long shadows on the walls and Honey's voice coming from the living room.

I fell asleep on the picture frame and one of the corners pokes into my chest. My pillow is a Rorschach mark of watery mascara from my tears. I wish it had been a memory, but currents don't stop. and I haven't seen Jim since March.

I wipe the rest of the mascara off my face with my T-shirt, yawn as I tie my tangled curls into a ponytail on top of my head and then open my bedroom door to greet Honey.

"Hello, Sleeping Beauty! How do you feel?"

I sit back down as she dumps books on my bed. "Achy. Nothing compared to the mortal anguish now that you brought all this."

Honey waves her hand dismissively. "You missed some kinda drama today. Beth said something rude about you being sick and Junior just walked over, calm as could be, and knocked the books out of her hand."

"Did he get in trouble?"

"Of course! But Mrs. Adkins heard what she said and gave Beth detention too! Isn't that great?"

"Junior shouldn't feel the need to defend me."

Honey frowns. "But it's romantic. He got in trouble for you."

Why can't she get this? "But I don't like him."

"Because of Colin? Bea, I understand that he's amazingly hot. But he'll be gone soon. Do you even know where he lives when he's not here in Georgefield?"

I grit my teeth. Everyone's constant reminder makes it very hard to forget. "No, I haven't asked him."

Honey leans forward, scrutinizing my face. She squishes my cheeks together. "Y'all kissed!"

I blush and bat her hand away.

"Well, tell! I want details!"

"It was amazing and that's all I'm going to say. We were at the hospital so I'm glad no one saw us."

"Oh, people did." Honey laughs. "You thought I could tell just by looking at your face? That's awesome. I could be a body language expert, and no one could lie to me."

Unfortunately, I'll need to test that out. I'll be forced to keep things from her as my search for Jim continues. What kind of person does that make me? A girl who lies to her family and best friend for the sake of a missing brother. I don't know if I'm doing the right thing, but the option of forgetting Jim seems even worse. "Who? Please tell me it wasn't High-flying Sara and her evil sidekick, the Wasp."

Honey snorts. "Nope, Lenise's cousin is a candy striper, and she was coming to check on you since the heart rate monitor was going off!" I cover my face as she collapses from the giggles. She sits up to tug my pillow away. "Ugh, I would have died if I had gotten that kind of information about my bestie from either one of those two. I'm supposed to be the first one to know these things. It's in the Best Friends' Handbook." She gives me a mock-aggravated look. "On that note, Nick and I are official."

"Congrats." I barely stifle my yawn.

"I've worn you out. Get better soon so we can double date!"

I walk Honey to the porch and plop onto the wicker loveseat. It's getting dark earlier with moths already flocking around the porch light. Toby jumps up to sit on my good foot. There's so much I want to discuss with Honey. So many things have happened lately. But I can't and I feel I'm losing my best friend. Is this going to be our extent of our conversations now, the tiresome drama in school and dates with boys? It's cheap and shallow and makes me so surprisingly sad.

"Did you and Honey have a fight?" Daddy asks, walking up from the restaurant.

"No sir, everything's fine. I'm not used to being so sore. First the ankle and now this. It sucks."

He nods and pats my shoulder. "I got your shifts covered for the rest of this week so focus on getting better."

"Thank you."

He sits next to me on the loveseat. I look at him curiously but he's watching the frogs hop on the windowpane.

"Do you remember when we used to sit out here after a storm and count the frogs together?"

I nod, my throat tightening. He's speaking so softly I lean toward him.

He clears his throat like his is bothering him, too. "It's been a long time since we've done something like that."

One side of my mouth pulls into a smile. "Yeah, I use a calculator for all my math problems now."

He turns to face me. When did he get old? The hair around his face is more salt than pepper. Worry lines tunnel deep into his skin. Jim has his nose and eyebrows, the latter do the same quick bounce when he acknowledges you. I have my dad's eyes.

He squeezes my knee. "Beep. I've wanted to ask you, but your mother—"

He sighs, looks again at the frogs. "Have you remembered anything about the day Jim…disappeared?"

His eyebrows do that jumping thing as he faces me, waiting for my answer. I'm confused as to why he chose to say disappear instead of died. My vision blurs so I look down at my twisting fingers. Splay them on my legs so they'll stop shaking. "Why did you and Momma have him declared dead?" I can barely squeeze the words out, my throat is so tight.

I don't want him mad at me. Especially if small quiet moments like this are still possible. Just Daddy and me sitting on the front porch, listening to the bug zapper and soaking up each other's presence. But I feel like they owe me this. *Bea Pearl, it's you against the Flat Earthers.*

"You know your mom and I will love you no matter what."

My heart hiccups because I don't believe that's true.

Everyone wears grief differently. Daddy wears his like waders—he's covered in it, but loosely. He can slip it off easy enough. Momma wears grief like a wetsuit. It hugs every part of her, and no one can reach that back zipper.

If there's some truth to the idea that I accidentally caused Jim's death, Daddy may forgive me, but Momma won't. She already looks at me as if Jim's ghost hovers near. He haunts her through me. That's why I have to find him and protect that mad, fragile bud of hope from all the Flat Earthers.

Then Momma will love me again without having all that blame in her eyes, obstructing her vision.

Daddy lays a hand on top of mine. "It was for the best. The only way we could move on."

If my throat grows any tighter, I won't be able to breath and tears will spill. "You mean the only way *y'all* could move on. Don't include me."

When his mouth tightens, I wonder if it was more for Momma's sake than both of theirs. But if I don't try my hardest to find out what happened to Jim, I won't be able to live with myself. I pull my hand from under Daddy's and fold it primly in my lap.

He clears his throat, and his voice becomes crisp. "I know it's none of my business, but Junior's at the restaurant asking if he could come over. Something about whatever y'all went over in Geometry today?"

I huff, causing the hair around my face to fluff out. That boy doesn't give up. On the other hand, maybe he'll confess how he's connected to Jim's disappearance. "All right, but tell him I'm still achy so he can't stay long."

Daddy kisses the top of my head. "Lemme get the ledger from your mom and then I'll head back over and let him know. And the request still stands, if you remember anything, I'm here for you."

I nod. "I haven't seen Chief Hoyle fishing in a bit," I say, taking advantage of Daddy in a sharing mood. "Did he get a new hobby? Take up golf or something?"

Daddy gives a low chuckle. "Cow pasture pool is what he calls it. Not likely. No, a buddy was telling me Oakwood's been sending him around the county, busy with a new task force." His eyes leave the frogs to harden on mine. "Why?"

"Just curious." I shrug. "He used to pay me a nickel a cricket for bait when I was little—thought about that when we were reminiscing," I lie, feigning fascination at the moths twirling around the light until Daddy goes inside. After he walks back toward the restaurant, I remember something from freshman English, when we read Don Marquis's *lesson of the moth*. In the poem, a moth tells "archy" the cockroach the reason moths are attracted to light.

> it is better to be a part of beauty
> for one instant and then cease to
> exist than to exist forever
> and never be a part of beauty

Then the moth fries himself on a cigar lighter. Is it better to have moments like this with my dad that soon cease to exist, than to live the rest of the years we have together without them?

It's like Honey's Last Popcorn of the Summer milestone. It's the moments—the instants—that count, right?

Junior walks towards me through the dusk. His stride is so different from Colin's with his head looking down to the ground and his scuffed-up work boots shuffling on the concrete walkway.

"Hey. Did Honey give you your pearl back?"

I'm sure this isn't what Mrs. Adkins went over in Geometry today, but it's a great opener. "You didn't find it in Colin's truck, and you know it."

"How can you believe him over me? *He* did this to you." Junior gestures to my stitched-up foot.

His intensity causes goose bumps on my arms. I rub them to warm my skin. "No. That's not true either. What were you looking for in Jim's room?"

His eyes widen. "What're you talking about?"

"You couldn't find it, so you trashed Jim's truck next."

His jaw drops and he sits on the love seat, turning toward me. "No, I didn't trash anything. Are you okay?"

I search his face. He knows something but his alarm does seem to be genuine. And Honey's kinda right. I have known him all my life, so I change tactics. "Tell me about that day the floodwaters surged."

He leans forward and rests his elbows on his knees. Toby lays his chin on my knee. "A bunch of us went down to the ramp to see how high the river had gotten. We saw a guy putting a boat in despite the current almost snatching the boat off the trailer before he could get it loose. The water was too rough to be out on the river, and he was acting all shifty. I didn't really think too much about it until after your parents realized you and Jim were missing. Then, you were found with a concussion and later, I found Jim's shirt covered in blood. That's when I figured the guy with the boat might have had something to do with everything that happened. Because," he takes a deep breath, rubbing his palms on his blue jeans. "I don't think you killed your brother. That's why I left you that present."

I pull a loose thread from the hem of my shirt. This doesn't make any sense. "If you thought there was foul play then why did Sheriff Oakwood pronounce Jim a flood victim?" I don't understand why the sheriff was so adamant that Jim drowned rather than look into the idea that someone picked him up. "You told him, right? Why didn't he believe you either?" What Honey mentioned earlier popped back in my head. "He's your uncle. Why wouldn't he listen to his own nephew?"

An odd look passes over Junior's face. "'Cause right after the river crested, Colin went back to Mobile, I heard. Uncle

Chuck said he questioned the guy with the boat. I thought it was weird, but I didn't have concrete proof," Junior shrugs.

But Colin told me no one got back in touch with him. Something's not adding up here, but I can fill in the blanks after hearing what Junior has to say. The events surrounding Jim's disappearance were nearly forgotten until Colin came back. As soon as Junior saw I had feelings for Colin, Junior began to make a tale to try to scare me away from the new boy. How juvenile! Once again, my opinion of Junior plummets.

Though now I know where Colin calls home. Mobile is only three hours away which is close enough for a long-distance relationship to work. Speaking of a lack of proof: "Why do so many people think I hurt Jim?" I don't really think he'd know; I'm more or less just musing out loud.

He scratches his neck. "Ain't that what you told..." He shakes his head as if puzzled. "Guess not, now that I think about it."

What is he not telling me? I touch his leg even though it feels wrong. Resting my hand on his jeans, I ply him for more information. "Told who?"

He looks at me in surprise, his brown cow eyes jumping around my face. "Beth."

Sitting back, confusion causes my head to whirl like the junction's carousel, though I'm not surprised she's the one spinning it. Surely Beth wasn't the thing Jim told me to run from. It only makes sense that it was the flood surge. "Beth wasn't there."

Junior watches my hands until I scoot them under my legs. "She said you confessed to her that you pushed him. Her daddy told Uncle Chuck she wasn't to be involved, and the sheriff listened since the two of them play poker once a week."

My nostrils flare. "Why on earth would I have told her, of all people, something like that?" I itch my nose, then rub Toby to mask my agitation.

"She said you felt bad about knocking her in Jim's grave?" He brushes my thumb with his.

I jerk my hand back. Part of me knows I should feel terrible for knocking her into an open grave, but that regret disappears once I hear that she planted rumors of my fake confession. "What do you mean they go way back?"

Junior's leg jiggles. "Oakwood brought the Paners here, you know. They were buddies at LSU."

I shake my head. "No, I didn't know that." Unsure of what that could mean, I go back to what he said earlier. "What present are you talking about?" I don't actually want anything from him, but it's a little weird that I didn't see one.

"Jim's wallet, of course."

I sit up straight. It's real? My lips tremble and tears fill my eyes. "Toby had it. Where'd you get it from?" I lean in and grab his plaid shirt. "What do you know about Jim? Is he still alive?"

When he shakes his head, his cow eyes look mournful, his jaw clenched. I let go of the fabric and shrink back.

"If I tell you all I can, will you get me that list of numbers belonging to Jim?"

"So that's what you were searching for when you broke in?"

His fists clench. "I ain't the one! But give me that list and they'll leave you alone."

"Who's they?"

"Bea Pearl. Please."

I stand and lean into his face, my pointy finger inches from his nose. "I'm going to find proof. So much proof it slaps you and that good-for-nothing sheriff upside the head. So much proof it suffocates this entire town that refuses to believe in me, and Jim. But I'll get you that list." Momma washed my jean shorts with the paper inside a pocket, so the list is now hard-to-decipher, fluffy bits. I don't see the harm in giving the list of numbers to him since Colin and I already removed the baggie. I just don't know how to connect the two events yet.

I enter the house to retrieve it. I hold my hand out when I return to the porch. "Tell me."

Junior's eyes bug out when he sees the condition of the paper. "What did you do?"

"It got washed. So what?"

"Damn, girl."

"What was it?"

Junior's leg jiggles even faster. "Jim stole something he shouldn't have. That's all I'm gonna say. Did you ah…read it?"

"Just a bunch of random numbers. Figured it was a math assignment," I lie. "What did Jim steal? Did the note you had me give him have anything to do with this? Tell me what's going on, Junior."

The screen door shrieks as Momma opens it, causing me to jump. "Junior, it's getting late," she says.

He stands. "Yes, ma'am. My mama just texted me to come home. Bye, Bea Pearl. Hope you heal soon and be careful around that new kid."

"Shut it." Momma doesn't need to hear his ridiculousness.

He shrugs and walks toward the parking lot.

"We didn't raise you to be rude to folks on our own front porch. You apologize to him tomorrow. He's been a big help around here."

I do my best not to roll my eyes as I stand and hobble around her to go inside. When I tell her to be careful of him, she looks at me like I'm irrational. I'm so tired of folks looking at me like that.

Backwoods T-ball & Murderous Hogs

The next morning, I sneak out my bedroom window to meet up with Colin. I need something real right now. Yesterday's dream of the nonmoving river and—oddly enough—the wounded look on Junior's face haunted me all night.

My heart goes into overdrive when I see Colin; it's amazing I haven't had a heart attack yet. His head is down, looking at something at the river's edge when I walk up from the creek. His brown hair frames the intent look on his face which makes my insides tingle. "What do you see?"

He looks up at me. His mouth, that delicious mouth, splits into a smile. "Watching a little school of gambusia."

"Mosquitofish?"

He nods, pulling me to him to kiss me. When we stop for air he says, "I found something for you." Something hard presses into my hand, and I'm surprised when it jabs me.

"Wow! A shark's tooth. Thank you."

"Fossilized. I found it on the river yesterday. Amazing that it's still so sharp, huh?"

The flat sides are as smooth as a worry stone while the edges are serrated like a steak knife. He wrapped wire around the top of the tooth so I can string it on my necklace. He fastens the clasp for me. His fingers brush against my neck, teasing the tiny curls. I'm going to lose my mind and I'm fine with that.

"I have another surprise for you." He bounces on the balls of his feet as I turn to face him.

I laugh. He's as excited to give me something as I am to see what it is. I close my eyes and cup my hand. He squeezes it instead. My eyes fly open.

"I found the road."

My mouth trembles as I suck in in surprise. "To Jim?"

He nods. "They built a chicken house in front of it, so I kept driving passed where I thought it would be. Yesterday afternoon, someone was coming out of the road and I knew it was the same spot. Want to go for a ride?"

"More than anything." I blink back sudden, hopeful tears. I'm touched by the fact that Colin hasn't stopped trying to find the way to the last spot he saw Jim.

"Figure we'll take the boat to the ramp and load up in my truck since your parents can't see you leave." His forehead knots as he brushes a thumb on my cheek. "There might not be anything there, Bea Pearl."

"But there might *be*," I whisper back, before turning toward his boat.

As we ride to the ramp, I lean over the side and let my fingers trail in the cool water. Once we pull up, we trailer the boat and take off in the truck.

"These woods are posted private property," I say nervously as we turn at a sharp angle after the chicken house, leaving paved roads and bouncing along red clay ruts.

"It looked deserted back in the spring, though. Maybe it's just some old family homestead and everyone alive lives elsewhere."

"Or someone's going to appear with a shotgun and hunting dogs." The trees are so thick there's nothing to see except the winding road before us and a swirling red cloud behind us. Through the windshield, vultures circle in the sky.

"There's an abandoned house up ahead," Colin says.

"How do you know it's abandoned?"

"No roof, just the brick base and hearth. There aren't any electricity lines out here and the water is from those old-fashioned pumps. I don't think anyone would live out here."

We make a turn and the trees thin out. In a clearing, there's the house as Colin described. It doesn't look habitable, but I don't think it smart of us to assume it isn't. He stops the truck and turns off the ignition. The vultures are now circling right above us.

"Something's dead." I point upwards.

He shrugs. "Could be anything. I pulled the boat up over this way." He walks away from the house toward the thicker trees.

I pick up my pace to stay close to him. "Oh, there's that water pump you were talking about!" I walk over to check it out. I love old things so can't resist pumping the handle to see if it works. It does. The handle moves easily as if it gets regular use and the water flows out cleanly.

"Colin, someone's been using this recently…" And then I freeze. My backbone feels as icy as the water rushing into my hands when I hear the *shick-shick* of a wooden pump gliding along a shotgun barrel.

A man in profile stands at the tree line, pointing his ugly gun at Colin. I crouch behind the water pump. The man doesn't act like he saw or heard me. He spits out something nasty and approaches Colin, who raises his arms. Colin doesn't look scared at all. On the other hand, I am terrified.

"I'm not here to cause any trouble," Colin tells him in his horse whisperer voice.

I can't make out what the man says but when his arms tighten around his gun, anger makes my ears ring. I'm not going to let some backwoods inbred shoot Colin, who's here because of me. I find a metal pole lying in the grass and pick it up. Circling around, I do my best to stay out of the man's line of sight.

"You fool kid, this is private property. Coming to steal my stuff. I'm gonna feed you to my hogs. They gunna love you..."

Creeping closer, I make out more of his greasy, stained hat and blue jeans. I'm close enough to see the sweat rings on his shirt and smell the unwashed stench emanating off him. And then his feet grab my attention. I expect bare feet or old boots the color of mud. Instead, he's wearing nice sneakers. I stand behind him and swing the pole like I'm a t-baller at bat. His head makes a *thunk* sound and he goes down like a smelly heap of cow turds.

Colin stares at me. "Wow."

I drop the vibrating pole and point at the man's feet. "Those are Jim's shoes." Crouching over him, I pull my T-shirt up to cover my mouth and nose. "Do you think I killed him?"

Colin touches the man's wrist. "No, he's just stunned. You saved my life."

"Well, you've been saving mine, so I figured I owed you. Now we're two for two."

"Remind me never to get on your bad side. That was pretty awesome, Bea." Colin picks up the shotgun, then holds out a hand to me.

I let him help me up but when he doesn't release my hand, the tips of my ears tingle.

"We should probably get help."

"I don't think so. Maybe if I could ever get ahold of Chief Hoyle. No offense to your suggestion, but the sheriff will just pat me on the head and send me home. And that's if he's feeling generous. He thinks I'm delusional and Jim is dead. This rotten-mouth vagrant will tell him I attacked him over sneakers." I pause as it sinks in. "And everyone will believe him over me." Depressing.

"What do you want to do with him?"

The fact that Colin is not treating me with kid-gloves strengthens me. "Tie him up. We can question him about why he's wearing my brother's shoes when he comes to."

Colin stands watch as I run back to his truck, finding nylon twine in the toolbox. He trusses him up and I wait impatiently for the pile of poo to wake.

Searching what's left of the old homestead, I catch glimpses of dusty, spider-filled moonshine jugs and broken beer bottles. Nothing points to a hiding place that's Jim sized. All the while I wonder how I'm going to get that horrible person to tell me what I need to know.

A jagged sliver of mirror reflects sunlight. I pick it up. My hands are shaking as if I'm still holding that metal to the man's head. I stare at my reflection and notice my eyes are too big and bright while my face is drained of color but my cheeks are splashed a deep pink. How would I feel if I had killed that man with one sloppy pole strike? How could I live with myself? Although he threatened to feed Colin to his pigs, I still didn't have the right to take a life. It would make me the same type of person as that horrible man.

"Bea, he's moving."

On guard, I kick his feet as he stirs to get his attention. "Listen up. You're wearing my brother's shoes. He's been missing since March and I have to find him. Please tell me if you know anything about him."

He leers, showing off his rotten stumps of teeth. I gag. "Not talkin' to no coo-coo in the head bit of a girl. Especially one who knocked me in the head. Gonna get th' law on y'all."

"You know who I am?" It's sad that my reputation has reached even this deep in the woods.

"M'cuzin tole me."

"Who's your cousin?" Colin asks.

The creep's grin broadens so I decide to let Colin beat the crap out of him.

"We are trespassing, Bea. And we assaulted him."

"Because he held a gun to your face!" I glare at Colin then I try not to breathe in through my nose as I lean in toward the man who we propped against a tree trunk with his hands tied behind his back. "Listen, I am about to go crazy on you if you don't tell me where my brother is." I stop for effect, making sure I have his full attention. "I will kill every one of your precious pigs. And feed them to my dog."

His bloodshot eyes widen then narrow. "You leave my girls outta this. Fine. I found him in my woods. M'cuzin came after the flood to check on me and recognized him. Said he was the one who knew the rivers."

"Wait, what?"

He glares. "We're puttin' that SOB to work."

So, fast it's a whirl, he shoots out a leg alligator-tail-style and knocks both of us to the dirt. We scramble after him, but he seems to have disappeared into the woods.

"That took an unexpected turn," Colin says as we circle back around.

I'm still in shock and frustrated that he escaped us. And it feels like I busted a stitch in my foot.

"We need to find out who the cousin is."

"I bet I can go to the courthouse and see whose name is on this property. I'll say it's a school project or something.". I pause, replaying what Rotten-mouth said. "He said 'puttin' that SOB to work'."

"What?"

"Colin! He said 'putting' not 'put'. Jim is still alive! I knew it!"

"I wouldn't pin all your hopes on that guy's verb tense," Colin says cautiously, but I'm not listening. I refuse to give up on my optimism.

Gleefully, I jump onto Colin and kiss him with all the joy and happiness I can muster. This is the first kiss I've initiated so a surge of doubt goes through me as Colin takes a step back in surprise. He quickly rights himself and kisses me back with equal intensity. Soon we're breathing heavily.

"Um, I know I started it, but this place is a little creepy."

He gives a shaky laugh and loosens his arms. I slide down until my flops reach the ground. I shiver deliciously.

Then bite my lip, hugging my arms around my middle. "Do you think I made the right decision to not get help? Because now he's gone."

Colin rubs my arms, warming me. "We need more proof that someone actually has Jim. He could claim he found the shoes in the woods after the flood just like your *ex*-boyfriend found Jim's shirt."

I smile at his emphasis on ex. "Never my boyfriend, but at least now you're on the right track."

"I figured you had some other guy on your mind now."

This guy gives me more shivers than a snow cone in January. I nod, trying to think of something flirty to say, but nothing awesome comes to mind. He reaches for my hand and rubs my thumb as we stand in the clearing surrounded by wildflowers and ferns nestled in the shadowy places. This is possibly the most romantic moment in my entire existence. A cool breeze ruffles our hair. Colin reaches with his free hand to touch my cheek and move a stray curl from my face.

This minute is lovely as long as we can conveniently forget the fact that there's a snaggle-toothed, probable kidnapper loose in the woods that might be holding my brother captive with his human-eating, murderous hogs. These two things alone dispel much of the romance of this secluded little meadow. Adding to the evaporating romance is the fact that Colin might be leaving soon. If I think about it too much, I become as shaky as a cotton ball at a boll weevil convention.

"Why?" I ask.

Colin seems to understand what I'm asking. "Why? Because damn, Bea Pearl, you're the kind of girl who exists somewhere between birthday candles and Christmas lights. You're the brightness that lights up the darkness of everyone's disbelief."

Ah. My bones melt straight to Bea stock. I lean in for a tight embrace. "What should we do with the gun?"

"We definitely can't take it with us. We'd get in serious trouble if we were found with it." Colin lets go of me and picks it off the ground. He presses a button in front of the trigger and a shell falls out. "Let's just take it up the road and hide it some-where." Colin puts it in the cab of his truck.

I nod wearily. "Tomorrow I'll go to the courthouse and find out who owns this land."

A little way up the rutted road, Colin hides the shotgun in some wild azalea bushes. After that, we return to the boat ramp and across the river to the Shelf. We share a pinkie toe tingling kiss that could have knocked my socks off if I'd been wearing any. And then, I drag myself back up the field to the house.

Daddy has his back to me, replacing flowers I must have acci-dentally stepped on when I climbed out my bedroom window. Thinking fast, I change paths and dart in the back door.

And jump in surprise as I startle Momma in the kitchen.

"Oh! Bea Pearl! I thought you were still in your room."

Crap. "Huh, must have shut the door behind me. No ma'am, I just fed Toby."

"You have grass seed all over you."

"I was throwing sticks for him."

"Good, he needs the exercise. Just don't overexert yourself it. Do you want to eat dinner here or at the restaurant?"

"I think I'll just eat here, if that's okay. But y'all don't have to keep me company. I'll eat with Toby." This way I can feed him for real, so Momma doesn't think it suspicious when he acts hungry. Wait, he always acts hungry, he's a dog. *Don't over think this, Bea Pearl.* "Is it all right if I go into town tomorrow? I need to do some research for a class project."

"We have your checkup tomorrow, so you can do your homework afterwards. As long as you go to school that morning. Though I'm sure you'll be fine if you feel well enough to play with Toby."

I don't know what to say without making her suspicious, so I yawn and massage my shoulder. "Okay. I think I'll lie down before dinner; I might have overdone it with him."

"Call the restaurant if you need us or want me to bring back something for you to eat." She walks out the door calling for Daddy.

With the house all to myself, I slump against the fridge and let out a huge sigh. The lies come too easily lately. I don't like it, but what else can I do? Walking down the hallway, I stop in front of my door but don't turn the knob. There's an almost physical ache when I think about how much I miss Jim. I got so close to finding him today. I've followed the trail to his wallet and then his shoes. Now I just need to find *him*. Instead of going into my room, I continue going down the hall until I am outside his door.

Opening the door, I step inside. After the break-in, I put everything back like he left it. Even a glass still sits on his nightstand, the water long since evaporated. When I'm in here, I completely forget he's gone and get so confused when I walk out into the world and can't find him. Sitting on his bed, I hug a pillow, my eyes filling with tears as my nose fills with the dust that covers everything.

Jim is being held prisoner by that nasty man's family, and I'm helpless to do anything except sit on his comfy bed, crying and sneezing. My nose starts running so I open up his nightstand drawer to look for tissues. Instead I find his wallet.

Momma must have found it on my nightstand and put it here. Even though that means she was snooping in my room and probably thinks the worse of me for having it, I'm glad the wallet is back where it belongs. Glad it's not just a figment of my hurting imagination. Maybe if I get all the pieces of Jim back together again, he can return to us whole. I close the drawer as Honey calls.

She fills me in on the day's news that I don't give two craps about, especially when I find the giant canvases of Jim in his closet as I'm hanging up his confiscated basketball jersey—returning another piece of him . I must have been quiet too long because there's a pause in Honey's dialogue. "'Kay, I'll let you get some rest. Want me to pick you up for school tomorrow?"

I sit back on his bed after I drag out a picture. "Umm... I've got a checkup at the doctors, then I gotta go look at some records at the courthouse for Daddy, so I'll just take Jim's truck."

"I don't mind taking you to the doctors. What kind of records?"

"Deeds."

"You don't have to go to the courthouse. All those records should be online."

As soon as we end the call, I slide the pictures back in his closet then go back to my room. Whoever made those portraits was spiteful but seeing Jim larger than life gives me hope.

I pull out my laptop and type in the coordinates Colin gave me earlier for the property. There's no stopping the smug smile on my face when I see the land was recently purchased by a shell corporation that is only two clicks away from Paner Farms. I have a connection between Jim and Beth now, but I can't figure out the rest. Like why would Colin randomly bring him to the

property during the flood. Does anything connect Jim to the Paners that would take him down to the river in the first place?

Beth's been working too hard at casting shade on me, and
that seems like something more than retaliation for knocking her
into an empty grave. I mean, it's not like it was an exhumed
grave or anything crypt-keeper-creepy like that.

Curious, I search for Daniel Paner on social media but can't
find anything. Beth and I are obviously not online friends so I
can't browse through her pictures either. Nothing pops up when I
search my brother's name. He never messed around with social
media, but I could keep track of him and belatedly know the location of field parties by the pictures he was tagged in. I chew on
my lip. It's another way he's stopped existing. All at once, I realize I don't know Colin's last name when I try to look for him
online. "Colin Water Sprite" pulls up a lot of cosplay pages.

I sigh.

A ding from the laptop catches my attention. I scowl to see
it's a message from Junior, but I click on it anyway. Maybe he's
decided to answer my questions from last night.

STOP LOOKING FOR JIM. DO YOU KNOW WHAT
YOU JUST DID TODAY?! DON'T LEAVE YOUR
HOUSE WITHOUT HONEY OR YOUR PARENTS.

My heart races. How does *he* know what I did today? He
must've seen me in Colin's truck. That's the only time I left the
house. Taking a deep breath, I log out of everything without responding, then close my laptop. I'm not going to let his jealousy
or his threats keep me from searching for Jim.

Little Bo Beep Finds Her Sheep

In a dream-version of the concession stand, I'm holding an empty waffle-cone in one hand and an ice cream scoop in the other, waiting for the pale-as-moonlight girl with flashy bluegill-scale eyes to tell me her flavor. Instead, she gestures for me to come closer. I lean in, watching her mouth to see if her teeth are small and pointed like a gar's. Her lips move and her sharp little teeth flash, but I can't make out what she's saying. It's as if she's trying to talk underwater.

Oh, *get up*. She's telling me to get up, but my bed is way too comfy. I'm usually a light sleeper, but the physical and emotional exertions of the day along with still recovering from the beaver pike has me out completely.

The sliver of moon is the last bite of a vanilla wafer, so the only light is from the streetlamp in front of the restaurant. A shadowy figure leans over me. The black against gray coloring looks just like my dream-memories. When my lips press painfully into my teeth, I wonder if this isn't a dream anymore.

"Don't say a word or your brother dies." The whispered demand sends daggers of fear down my body. I try to nod but only pull my hair painfully. I hear the sound of duct tape and then feel adhesive over my mouth. He— it's a he, I'm sure— stands, pulling me along, my feet tangle in the sheets. He wears a mask and ties my hands, pushing me out my bedroom window. I fall heavily on the flowers Daddy just planted.

Are Momma and Daddy okay? Where's Toby? I scoot back, trying to hide in the boxwoods. He snatches my feet until my ankles throb. Pulling me over his shoulder like a trussed pig, I half expect an apple to appear in my mouth. Do folks really do that at pig roasts? I wonder why. If I lick myself would I taste like bacon?

Staying in the shadows, he tosses me into a covered truck bed hidden near the restaurant. I panic but stop struggling when I realize it's the same truck—just with a truck cap on it now—as the one I saw the day of the break in of Jim's room. He might be taking me to Jim.

The thought calms me, and I realize that I've truly arrived at my destination: Crazy. My passport is stamped. There is no return ticket. What kind of person calms down when they dream about being dragged out of their bed in the middle of the night with threats of people killing their brother?

If they're threatening to kill Jim, then that means he's alive *now* and I still have a chance to save him. And myself. As fear creeps like roaches up my spine, I focus on Jim until they go away.

I try to look out the windows, but they've been spray painted black. Everything is so dark, almost as if I can't open my eyes wide enough. I scratch at the paint, but by the time I make a big enough hole and maneuver my face to look out, I can tell by the vehicle's shocks—or rather, lack of—we've left paved roads. There are only the dark shadows of trees.

Colin's cuff is still around my wrist. The jostling makes untying difficult, but the knot comes undone by the time we brake to a stop. The mystery man opens the tailgate, then pulls me out by my bare feet. I drop the bracelet in the grass, hoping he doesn't see the movement. I'm marched downhill until the hard-packed grass turns into softer leaves and then through painful rocks. The earthiness of mud is thick in the air. It feels like we're close to a river. When I hear the sound of falling water, I know I have to be dreaming since there are no waterfalls nearby to make such a thunderous sound.

The ground grows slick. My elbow is wrenched a few times when I lose my balance. As a cold mist hits my face and soaks my night clothes, I gasp, suddenly fully awake. We must be behind a waterfall. But where? It has to be somewhere along the Chatothatchee or Talakhatchee but I have never been to this spot before. It's pitch black so visibility is nil, and the roar of water makes it difficult to hear. It still feels like a nightmare.

I twist away from the shadow guy and loosen the tape covering my mouth. "Where's my brother?" My voice echoes back to me, so we must be in a cave. There's a tug at my wrists as the creeper shadow guy ties me to something I can't make out. "I found the guy who took Jim's shoes and I beat him over the head with a pipe," I say, hoping to goad him into saying anything that might be helpful. "Daniel." Maybe guessing his name will unnerve him.

"That's why you're here, you snotty bitch," Shadow Guy snarls.

"Where's my brother?"

He snickers. "You killed him, remember?"

"I didn't mean to distract him. He was walking straight into a section that drops off. He shouldn't have been there in the first place."

"He was there because of you."

"No, I followed him down."

His laugh chills me more than the wet air of the cave. "Are you sure?"

"Yes." No.

He slaps me on the cheek in a condescending way that stings more because I don't know whether to believe him or myself. He stuffs something damp and moldy smelling in my mouth. Bile rises.

"Don't you go anywhere," he taunts. "Gonna let the boss know you're here. And then you'll give him the *real* location of the flash drive you stole from your brother. Before someone else has to get hurt." He runs a dirty, scabby finger down my jawline before I lurch away, my heart pounding. "Like Honey."

I shake my head and grunt. What flash drive is he talking about?

Please don't let them hurt Honey. I've been drifting away from her lately but none of that matters. I would die if she was hurt because of me.

Chuckling, he slaps my cheek again before walking back toward the mouth of the cave, his footsteps grow fainter as the sound of water swallows them. When he crosses in front of the waterfall, his profile is in relief from the feeble light making its way in. It must be close to dawn. No one will know I'm missing until Honey comes to pick me up for school. Only if she is still in one piece.

I feel around, trying to figure out what I'm tied to. Metal. Wood (splinter, oww). Rock. I'm guessing it's a wooden support beam, holding back the earth. I try to push the nasty cloth out of my mouth, but I gag myself, so I leave it, worried that I may choke. What a mess. My wet hair and clothes cling tightly to me, the discomfort dissipating the insubstantial wisps of confidence I have left.

I grunt again, wondering if Jim is hidden nearby. Surely, he would have made his presence known if he was gag free. Tears blur when I realize he must not be here. I feel like I've failed Jim all over again. I tear my family apart in ways the creepy man and his boss never could. They won.

It's.

My.

Fault.

Rocking forward, I press my head against the wooden beam. A thick metal ring restrains my hands in an upright position. Mentally, I go over every item on my body.

My necklace.

With the pearl, the bee.

And more importantly, a shark's tooth. Hopefully sharp enough to cut through rope and despair. I know Jim wouldn't give up on me, so I refuse to be a victim of my own mind. Jim needs me. There's still a chance to save him. And rescue my whole family in the process.

I pull my hands down as low as possible and grab my necklace with the base of my palms. The tooth cuts into my thumb but I continue maneuvering it into a position that will cut through the ropes. Pulling downward makes the rope taut, tight to the point that blood flow is restricted, and my hands grow sluggish. The position also helps cut the rope faster, and I only jab myself a couple more times before the rope slacks and then breaks. Blood rushes back to my hands, prickling my skin and oozing out of my new cuts.

I realize I can see the blood from the excess light pouring in the cave. Day must finally be here. Pulling the gag out of my mouth, I cough, spitting out cotton fibers and other bits I don't want to think about.

Sacks covered with the PF logo surround me. The logo matches the ball cap in my memory and in the picture. Paner Farms grows corn for cattle feed and fuel, but a damp cave is no place to store sacks. They will mildew in no time.

The clues are starting to come together. I remember the packet of not-incense I found at the coordinate site and Kiki telling us at the Sandbar that it's been easier to get stuff. Using the tooth again, I gnaw at the burlap, finally slicing it open. Dried corn spills out. Maybe I assumed wrong. A packet falls out. Then lots more spill all over the floor. Picking one up, I can tell the packaging has the same moss green logo as the scrap I found with Jim's doodled turtle in Lake George's supply room. How did it get there and why is Jim involved? The whole logo reads Magic Swamp Weed Potpourri. Daddy mentioned Mr. Paner was selling potpourri made from kudzu, but why hide it in sacks of feed corn? The package is about the size of a deck of cards, too small a portion for most potpourri dishes. Who even uses potpourri these days? I tear one open and it looks the same as the non-incense we found hidden in the fencepost. I sniff it and gag.

Something rumbles faintly over the sound of the falling water. It sounds like an engine from a boat motor or a truck. I need to out of here when Daniel returns. Looking around, I hide behind a pallet of sacks.

A wind wafts through the cave smelling of mint and sandalwood ruffles my hair. "Jim!"

Heading to the rear of the cave, I realize the darker space is actually a tunnel. Part of me wants to stay in the light near the water. I don't know where I'm heading, but at least I know it's toward my brother.

The dark tunnel is long and cold. It reminds me of every lonely nightmare I've had since the spring. Then the scent of mint curls around me and I know I am so, so close.

So close to a wall.

I smack into something hard. But it's metal, not rock. Feeling around, I find a handle, and twist as I push.

The weak morning light blinds me. I blink as I check out my surroundings. I'm in a dugout hole with steps built into one side and a lift like a simple elevator on the other. The door behind me shuts with a loud clang. I wince.

"Who's there?"

That voice—I almost faint with relief. I fly up the rocky steps. "Jim! Oh Jim! It's me! It's Bea Pearl!"

"Beep?"

The hesitant hope and joy make me come undone. I search for him in the thick woods around the exit. My brother is tied to the steps of a rusted trailer like a dog.

Rushing to him, I hold on to him like my life depends on it.

"What! They got you? They said they'd leave you alone."

He almost pushes me away, but I hold tight. "What're you talking about? I found you! You're alive!" He's felt like a dream-memory for so long that he doesn't seem real.

"They said the town held my funeral. That everyone thought I was dead."

"I believed!" I sob. "I knew you were still alive! It just took me too long to figure everything out. I'm so sorry." It feels so good to just be near him again. When I reach out my hand no longer sinks into nothingness.

"But Beep, little Bo Beep, I didn't want you mixed up in this. I hoped you stay safe at home."

He's real, he's alive. "It's no home without you there, Jim. I can't hold our family together by myself. I can't." He's still crouched down. I'm trying to pull him up but he's not budging. And he's fussing at me. "Are you okay?"

His hands are on my face, in my hair. "My leg's broken. I set it with a splint, but it healed wrong."

His pants are grimy and torn. No telling what kind of infection he has from sitting in a filthy-looking trailer for months. He's lucky to be alive. "I'm so sorry."

"Don't worry, they gave me antibiotics," Jim says, seemingly reading my mind. "They need me alive because I know these rivers too well. They were running aground with all the underwater debris and the shallows. Destroying boats and getting too much attention."

Ronnie Haster's hunch-punch money from the abandoned boats. That wasn't such a silly memory after all. I squeeze his hand. "Why do they need you to navigate the rivers?"

Jim drops his head in his hands. "I started running errands for them along with the eco-tours at first. They gave me bigger jobs as time went on. Boxes of potpourri to bags of feed grain. Part-time on the weekends to the dead of night. Making some extra money since I was going to have to pay for all of college. I lost my scholarship."

I nod.

"Small things started adding up. When I realized I was making too much money for transporting bags of corn, I found trouble. To me, it was weird that all the transporting was done on the river. Originally, I thought they were just trying to get back to their roots like when they lived in the bayous. But it's spice, drugs." He shook his head. "Once I knew, I tried to get out."

So that foul-smelling stuff was spice.

He continues. "I knew too much by then. They wouldn't let me out. So, I tried blackmail, recording Paner and Oakwood talking and—"

"No wonder the sheriff was pushing Momma and Daddy and the entire freaking town so hard to get you dead and me branded as unstable. Where's this recording?"

"That's what I was trying to get the day it flooded. I didn't make it, so my evidence is gone. Nothing could've withstood those floodwaters."

"We sure didn't. But…I did find a packet of spice in an old fencepost."

Jim stares at me, eyes wide in his dirty face. "You did? Had it gotten wet? There's a flash drive hidden inside the kudzu. Bo Beep, this is it!"

I smile at the sound of my childhood nickname. One long ago Halloween, I dressed up as Little Bo Peep and fell so madly in love with my costume that I wore it constantly. At least until I hit a growth spurt and tearfully had to pass it on. "I opened the baggie, but it smells like roach spray. I didn't dig around in it. That means the flash drive is hidden in my sock drawer."

"How's Mom and Dad and everybody?"

"Miserable. Lucas stayed here, didn't go off to school. Everybody at the restaurant is fine. Georgefield is actually thriving, which is weird when our family is—no, was—rotting away."

He nods. "That's because Paner isn't selling the spice around here. They're sending me way upriver or way downriver to distribute."

"Why?"

"Because Oakwood wants to build up Georgefield. He has some pretty high aspirations other than his sheriff duties."

Pieces of the puzzle are coming together. "Then I wouldn't be surprised if he's the one, not Momma and Daddy, who put the whole town on gag order when it came to talking about you. Folks think I'm crazy so I'm either avoided or talked about."

"You seem okay considering the circumstances."

"Everyone thinks I'm in denial or grief stricken. And I'm having a hard time knowing what's real or not."

"Man, sorry."

"Like I might have seen you in a boat this past June."

"You might have. Occasionally we'd go out in the day if there was a rush on it."

So, it was a memory. My brain just didn't know how to process it. "And an entire wall in the restaurant was covered in blown-up pictures of you."

"I would've liked to have seen that." He tries to laugh but it comes out as dry and crackly as dead leaves.

"And I think swamp monkeys are watching me."

"Uh, I can't help you with that one."

I grin. "It's all right. Honey doesn't believe me, but she hasn't given up on me yet. And there's this guy…" I feel my cheeks redden. "This guy…who inadvertently, is the one who delivered you to the rotten-mouthed guy I brained yesterday…"

"You brained? Wait, you're dating a guy who helped kidnap me?"

"No, well, I don't think we're dating. We spend a lot of time together, but we mainly search for you and…other stuff…" My ears are on fire.

Jim raises an eyebrow.

I take a deep breath. "The floodwater surge that separated us in the woods that day swept you out, but Colin happened to be there and pulled you in his boat. He saved you from drowning but then brought you to the property owned by the Paners. On accident."

Jim's eyes widen in shock.

I snap my fingers. "I bet that's why he was able to land the boat without crashing into trees. The river's edge was already cleared out to make it easier to transport the stuff—the spice."

"Makes sense."

I shake my head anxiously, trying to reason everything out. "Do you remember the note I gave you from Junior? What was it about?"

Jim sighs heavily. "The note was a warning. Junior got me the job and started to worry when things weren't adding up. He overheard his uncle on the phone the night before he sent the note but didn't want to text me in case Oakwood had tapped his phone."

"But he had your wallet. And gave it to me as a "present". He also knew about your paper with the numbers on it."

"I told Junior I was building a case, so I started writing down all the drop locations. Quickly, I realized they would simply change them when I quit. I knew I needed to find more concrete evidence, so soon after that, I got the recording on the flash drive."

"And they thought the flash drive got lost in the flood until I found the paper and tried to figure it out. I guess they brought me here as leverage to either find the 'real paper' or tell them where to find the flash drive?" I use air quotes since Daniel thought I had lied to Junior.

Jim shrugs. His face looks older, bearded. He's thin and pale, but alive. My brother is real, and he exists. I hug him again. "I'm so glad I found you and you're in one piece." I unclasp my necklace and use the shark's tooth to cut through his rope. I'll need to remember to thank Colin for his present next time I see him.

"Wow, does that feel good." He massages his wrists. Deep gouges and calluses circle around his hands like grotesque bracelets.

"Do they usually leave you alone like this?" The trailer doesn't have a skirt on, so I've been keeping an eye out for feet or wheels. "Surely you could've found something to cut through this rope."

"The guy you call Rotten-mouth usually has his hogs out here."

"A pig! I threatened to feed them to Toby."

Jim laughed. "I've seen what these hogs can do to a gator. There's no way I could've outrun them with this gimp leg."

"Let's go home."

"That would be great, but I don't think it'll be that easy."

Of course, escaping with Jim's malformed leg is a whole set of problems that I didn't foresee. We don't have time to sit around and cry about it. "I hear an engine. You think it's boat or four-wheeler?"

Jim cocks his head to the side. "Sounds like a four-wheeler. To the cave?"

"To the cave."

The dark isn't so bad with Jim leaning on my shoulder and daylight pouring. Once we go through the waterfall, I hear the engine much more clearly. As if it's right on top of us.

"Can you run?" I ask Jim.

"No, but you go ahead. I don't want you caught again because of me."

"Yeah, right. I'm not leaving you again." I give him a shove right over the ledge.

Bad Guys & Government Property

Over the limestone ledge and into the river he falls with a look of shock, and I jump in after him. I hope he can swim even if he can't walk or run as well as he used to.

We surface. He sputters. "What the hell? A warning would've been nice."

"A warning would've elicited more of your woe-is-me-save-yourself crap. You're done sacrificing yourself for me. Now, let's make like a mullet and swim before they know to look for us." Once again, I'm in the river swimming in my clothes. Swimsuits have not been a sound investment this year. Thank goodness I wore a sensible T-shirt and shorts to bed rather than a flimsy nightgown.

We swim with the current to the other side of the river. I figure that's the best course of action since we have no idea how far the Paner's property stretches. I assume since all the places Colin could have landed during the flood were their property, they

must own a huge area of rural riverfront. It's probably very secluded with no close neighbors if they're running drugs.

Jim struggles to keep up. These past six months of captivity
have changed my strong lifeguard of a brother and my heart goes
out to him. My anger at what has happened to us gives me
strength. I know that if anyone gets in our way, whether it's a
snaggle-tooth, creeper, alligator, or water moccasin, I won't stop
until Jim is safe.

We're so close to the opposite bank when engine vibrations
pulse through the brown water. "We might need to hold our
breaths for a bit," I warn Jim who's wheezing like a punctured
pool raft. We swim deeper but it's much slower going, and I have
a hard time keeping track of him in the muddy water. I stop
swimming and flail a leg behind me.

Nothing connects.

Panicking, I fight against the urge to surface and instead spin
around underwater, blindly reaching out. I haven't gone through
all this just to lose him now. I want to yell out his name, but I
need to conserve what little air I have left.

My left hand brushes against something so I reach out again,
hoping it's not the rough surface of a gator or the bumpy bark of
a submerged log. I suck in a little river water when something
grabs tight to my wrist. Feeling fingers rather than teeth, I pull,
relieved when Jim's shadowy figure comes into view. My eyes
sting from the mud, my throat and nose burn, but I kick as hard
as I can, dragging Jim behind me.

Fortunately, the boat passes by. When I haul Jim to the surface for air, I'm thankful the current has pushed us closer to the
bank. A few stokes later, we can touch the gooey, muddy bottom
with our feet. Dr. Arnie is not going to be happy with all this
mud I'm packing around whatever stitches I still have left.

"Where are we?" I ask Jim, helping him up the sandy bank
where he collapses. Gasps wrack his entire body. I plop down
next to him and inspect my foot.

He nods, barely, blinking to adjust his eyes. "That creek up-river. From where we. Uh… jumped in. Cow Bridge Creek. Now that we're on. Our side of the river. It shouldn't be too hard. To find something familiar. Though we're so far downriver. I don't know how the walking will be."

I don't like the idea of walking miles through woods barefoot. Swimming upriver is out of the question. "What if we look for one of Paner Farms' grounded boats? We can fix it up and get home that way."

"Maybe. Any left after the flood will be even worse for wear than usual."

I help him up after he catches his breath. "Well. Lucky for you I have a lot of experience coming up with Wild Scenarios, so I'll think of something to get us out of here. Let's keep moving."

Jim nods and I help support his weight so he can walk with his injured leg. It is reassuring to be this close to him, and feels like a dream come true.

"Momma and Daddy are going to be beside themselves when I walk up with you. Hopefully they'll forgive all my lying and sneaking around these past weeks. Momma forbade me from going to the river, can you believe it? Completely your fault."

"Bea, you were kidnapped from your bed. I think that excuses everything."

"I'm so happy we can be together as a family again. I really missed you."

"Okay, enough of that little sister mush, let's get on home. I've been living off canned sardines and dreaming about Mr. Catfish's fried pickles for months." He proceeds to list everything off the menu with such relish, my mouth is watering too.

Then Wild Scenario Number Two for the day hits me like twig across the face. "Ouch." I bat the underbrush away and rub my cheek. "Speaking of fish, what about sturgeon?"

"Beep. They're threatened. And Mr. Catfish would never put roe on his menu."

"Not to eat. Gross. The Fish and Wildlife Services have placed monitors all up and down this river. What if we find one and disable it? That might send a signal, so they'd come fix it. Then, hello! Boat ride home!"

"Sounds good to me. Destroying government property for a good cause."

Sticking out my tongue, I ignore how pale his face is. "Not destroy."

We're sun burnt, horsefly-bit, and starving when I finally spot a small buoy with FWS stenciled on it and a silvery thread peeking out of the water. Yanking on it, I finally pull hard enough that something comes loose, and I fall back on my butt. Hopefully that'll do the trick.

"Now we wait?"

"And cross our fingers that Colin or his uncle are paying attention."

We find a shady spot underneath a grove of river birches where we're hidden from sight but can still see a boat approach. Catching up on six months of fear and loneliness helps my worries slide off my back like a snake shedding old skin. Lots of pent up anger leaves my body as well. Thinking of what we both went through—and the pain my parents hold tight to themselves—when all Jim had to do was refuse to help them. Why didn't he just knock Daniel upside the head with an oar on one of their deliveries and be done with it? Why didn't he come back home?

My nostrils flair and I bite my lip hard enough to break skin. "Why did you stay away?" I'm trying to push the anger down. The words come out raw.

He looks startled. "They threatened you. As long as I did what they wanted, you were safe."

Tears well and I blink to get them to go away. "Together, we could have figured it out. I'd rather you had been home."

Jim's Adam's apple bobs. "Daniel told me Beth caught you breaking into the school's office to change my grades to help with my scholarship eligibility. She told me she wouldn't press charges against you as long as I stayed dead."

"I didn't even know you lost your scholarship 'til recently. Beth is working with Daniel, I guess." I snort. "She told the sheriff I drowned you. Though we now know the families are working together. As long as you stay dead, I stay delusional and untrustworthy so I can't argue against them and you continue working for them to protect me. What a neat package of madness." Then I shush him to keep him from responding. "I hear a boat again."

He cocks his head to the side.

As soon as it comes into our line of sight, we both huddle behind a cluster of saw palmettos. "It's Honey! I see Honey." I stand, about to wave my arms when Jim yanks me back.

"Look who's steering the boat," he hisses.

My heart falls out my toes and sinks into the mud. "Junior. She doesn't know he's one of the bad guys. Wait. Is he if he tried to warn you?"

"I don't know. But he's helping Oakwood if he tried to get those numbers from you."

As they pass us, I let out the breath I'm holding. "Do you think Honey's in danger?"

"Who was the other guy on the boat?"

"Her new boyfriend, Nick."

"Ledger? Football?"

I nod, slightly amused at how guys sort themselves by sports.

"Then hopefully she's okay," Jim says.

What is Junior capable of to protect his uncle? There are so many bad things that could happen on the river that could be made to look like an accident.

The sun moves. Bugs whine and bite until I coat our skin in a thin layer of mud. A stick snapping behind us makes me jump.

"See, Uncle Rob thought it was a raccoon, but I figured it's a Bea Pearl tampering with our sensors."

I whirl around at the sound of Colin's voice materializing behind us. I run to him and leap into his arms.

A throat clears behind me. Giggling, I make introductions, thrilled that I can introduce my brother to Colin.

"Sorry for only half rescuing you this past spring," Colin says as he and Jim shake hands. "I could've saved you and Bea Pearl a lot of worry."

"They were already after me. The flood just made it easier for them."

"Jim can't walk well. He's leg was broken and healed wrong," I point out to Colin.

"I have the four-wheeler up this deer path. We're a few miles southeast of Lake George."

"Why'd you come by land and not by river?"

"Something's going on at the boat ramp. My uncle tried to launch the boat once he noticed the sensor was disabled but some folks are blocking the ramp, saying their truck broke down."

"Relatives, I'm sure, of Rotten-mouth or Creeper," I say.

Jim mumbles something about getting a head start up the path since he's slow. As soon as he disappears around the trees, Colin scoops me off the ground and holds me close.

"You went swimming in your clothes again?"

I laugh, tucking my face under his chin before he sets me back on my feet. "You're rescuing me yet again. So aggravating." I follow Jim up the barely discernable path, not wanting him out of my sight ever again, with Colin close behind.

"You rescued yourself by signaling me and drawing me right to your location. And—wow—you found your brother. What happened? Honey told me she went to your house this morning and there were signs of a struggle outside your window." He holds out his leather bracelet. "I think you dropped this."

He ties it to my wrist as we walk, causing shivers to run up my arm as he traces the faint rope marks still indenting my skin. "I can't believe you found it! Where was it? It was so dark when they snatched me, and I had no idea where I was. I used the shark's tooth you gave me to cut through the ropes. Thank you again for the very practical gift."

"Hell, Bea Pearl." Colin squeezes my hand. "It was near the road we took to the homestead. There was a deer path we overlooked the other day. I went down it a ways but couldn't see anything."

"Jim was near a cave, hidden by a waterfall. I never would have found it either if I wasn't taken to it."

"We split up to cover more ground. When I got the call from my uncle about the sensor, I had a feeling it was you."

"'We'? You and my parents?"

"No, me and your ex-boyfriend. The one thing we have in common is you."

My skin chills even though I'm still close to him. "Junior's the one who got Jim involved in all this, and he found out Jim had evidence against Paner and Oakwood."

Colin looks shocked. "Evidence against the *sheriff*?

I nod. "We just saw him and Honey in a boat. She may be in trouble."

Colin frowns. "He seemed genuinely worried about you and asked if he could come along to help."

"Yeah, I bet he was worried. Worried y'all might find me. He must be working for the Paner family, too." I sigh and scratch at bug bites on my arm.

Jim stops so suddenly, I plow into him. Colin snatches the back of my shirt to hoist me up as I grab Jim's arm to keep him upright.

"You okay?" I move around to face him, mouth dry when I look again at his malformed leg.

"Someone's here." His eyes dart around. The fear in them makes my stomach drop.

And then I feel the same watchful stare as that time on the limestone shelf when I dreamed of scaly-eyed water sprites and met Colin.

Something crashes overhead. The three of us look up in time to see a brown blur streak through the leafy canopy.

"What was that?" Colin exclaims.

"Has to be a fox squirrel, right?" Jim asks unconvinced. "Though I've never seen 'em that big before."

Laughter bubbles up like methane gas trapped in muddy, leafy river bottoms. I'm laughing so hard, tears run down my cheeks, turning the dried clay back to mud. "That, my lovely, skeptical people, was a swamp monkey."

A Mix of Melancholy & Joy

Lake George reflects the whirl of reds and blues in the fast approaching dusk. Momma and Daddy are on the front porch with Chief Hoyle of all folks when we pull up in the parking lot filled with every police car and townsperson of Georgefield. It feels funny that all this is for me. I've been slipping away all summer, but now that I've actually disappeared, they've taken notice. My existence *does* matter to them.

Momma, Daddy, and Toby run toward us as soon as Colin slows the four-wheeler to a stop. I hop off as Colin helps Jim down.

Momma and Daddy stop in their tracks. Momma lets out a shriek so unbelievably heartbreaking, tears burn my eyes. Everyone acts as if they're seeing a ghost and I guess to all the Flat Earth folks, Jim is one. They buried him yet here he is in the flesh. He looks a little worse for wear, as if he escaped from Hell itself. With Colin and I supporting him on either side, we walk to the house through the frozen statues of people.

I sneak a glance at Jim to see how he's taking all this. He's looking around at everyone, nodding to those he knows personally, confusion on his face when no one acknowledges him. Some folks even look queasy, as if they're about to faint.

"To them, you've risen from the dead, and with that mud you look like you literally just crawled out of the ground," I whisper to him. This isn't the blissful reunion I imagined. Where are the tears of joy? The celebration? The whole thing is off somehow with the amount of quiet and stillness in a gathering this large.

Please don't let this be another dream I wake up from.

Please let this be real.

"Mom? Dad?" Jim says.

Toby breaks the spell when he runs up to Jim. My brother jerkily bends down to scratch his ears. Momma and Daddy rush forward and we hold each other in a tight circle. Love runs through each of us, binding us together again. And here in this exact moment, I realize how right I was to believe in myself. I feel the real Bea Pearl returning, until I'm shiny and new. I knew my old self would reappear with Jim.

Daddy kisses the top of my head. "Thank you," he whispers.

I grin in response, thinking he's referring to bringing Jim back to the family. While my dad has a firm grip on Jim's shoulder, his eyes are only for Momma. He was thanking me for bringing her back, too. I had spent so much time blaming her for not loving me enough, that I missed how bad off she really was. I hug her tighter.

After a while, I wiggle out of the huddle to wave goodbye to Colin climbing on his four-wheeler, broken sensor tucked under his arm. As I start after him, I notice Honey, Nick, and Junior drive up. Junior is going to get an earful. After sending one last glance towards Jim, I march over to them.

Honey runs toward me as soon as she gets out of the truck. "Oh Bea! I'm so glad you're safe! I can't believe Jim's alive! I'm so sorry I doubted you."

"I'm relieved you and Nick are safe as well, since you're with *him*." I glare at Junior, still in the passenger side of Nick's truck.

Honey grabs my arm. "Just because you don't like him doesn't mean you have to be rude. He's been helping us look for you, and he even let us take his boat out."

I twist my arm away. "He's not trying to find me out of the goodness of his heart, Honey. He's the one who got Jim involved with drugs."

"What?"

Junior slumps over to us. "And I'm really sorry."

"Jim has been living in filth and thought dead. Everyone treated me like I was crazy for the past six months and you're *sorry*? *Sorry*!? My family *broke* because of *you*."

"I didn't know he was still alive. I thought if Beth got Jim's evidence against her dad, she and Daniel would leave you alone." He shakes his head and stares at his boots.

I glare at him.

"This just got so out of hand. When I found Jim's wallet in my uncle's office, I gave it to you, thinking maybe it would make you feel better." Junior finally looks at me, eyes wide in confusion. "I've tried to warn you so many times. Didn't you get my message yesterday afternoon? Daniel called Beth while we were in detention and seemed upset at you."

"Oakwood nor Mr. Paner planned my kidnapping? It was Beth?" Pretty sure my jaw hits the gravel.

Junior nods.

The boss Daniel referred to was *Beth*?

Normally, I would be stunned that someone hated me enough to do something so horrifying. Really, I'm just grateful that her actions led me to my brother. "Nick, can you take Junior to Chief Hoyle? Let Hoyle know there's some seriously incriminating evidence in the top drawer in my bedroom."

Nick nods and Junior doesn't fight like I expect him to. Looking resigned, he shuffles away for his punishment. I have no regrets watching him go.

Honey looks over my shoulder. "Bea, I know you're probably beyond exhausted, but you've got a wasp about to land on you."

I spin around, flailing, expecting a sting, but Honey is referring to a waspish person. Beth and Sara march up.

"What are *you* doing here and where's Nick taking Junior?" Beth demands.

I cross my arms. "Junior's turning himself in. And your family should, too."

She laughs but it's as hollow and paper-thin as a hornet's nest. "Whatever. Do you think I'm worried that you got away? Say anything and we'll claim you're just unstable. Wandering around at night in your jammies. Poor, sad, little Beatrice Pearl. It's so easy to make you look pathetic."

Sara claps her hands over her mouth. "O.M.G. Beth. We need to go."

"Uh, no. I'm not going anywhere. We need to tell Hoyle to back off and call Sheriff Oakwood. I'm not going to let this delusional freak mess up everything I've worked so hard for."

"You're working with your cousin, Daniel, aren't you?" I can't look at Beth without seeing Jim's messed-up leg. Tears well but anger dries them before they escape. "Daniel needed Jim to continue transporting your family's drugs, and y'all needed a reason to make him stay once he found out it was spice."

Beth glares at me, hatred pulsing off her, startling me even after all she's done.

I take a step back.

"I don't like you, and your "dead" brother threatened my family. No one threatens my family. Every single thing I did was to prove to Junior how nuts you are so he realizes that he loves me. It's been great watching your fall. Everyone saw that you aren't so perfect."

My jaw drops. "Is that why you spread the rumor about me killing Jim?"

"Hell, she's probably the one who gave you the head injury," Honey says, stepping closer to Beth like she's going to punch her. "Who did you bribe to get into the yearbook room to get all those pictures of Jim?"

Beth narrows her eyes at Honey. "What are you talking about?"

Honey opens her mouth to respond, but I touch her forearm as I think back on how Jim's wallet was put back in his drawer in its usual spot. "Miss Grace told us that the police weren't called when Momma accused me, remember? I don't think many know about it, not even Junior."

Her arms relax a bit, but her fists don't unclench.

"I know who did it, and it's okay." Momma is still cooing over Jim, pushing his hair back, licking her thumb to wipe the mud off his face. Mrs. Ell must have given the pictures from the yearbook to Momma. Maybe that's why I didn't hear anything that night at the restaurant. Momma would have waited until I went to bed. I guess she missed Jim enough to want his presence in his usual spots—the restaurant and his bedroom. An idea that made sense in the middle of the night must have made her ashamed by daylight. There were depths to her depression that I can't even imagine.

"The only ones threatening your family are yourselves," I tell Beth, thinking back to my epiphany at the hospital when I realized I was the wedge fracturing my own family. "I understand why you had to try, but don't you see that seeking to destroy mine won't glue yours back together?"

Beth's eyebrows spasm together, her shoulders tense, but before she can respond or slap either of us, Sara grabs her arm.

"Oh my God, Beth! Shut *up*. Don't say anything else." Sara backs away toward her car, pointing to my family up at the house. "Jim's alive!"

In another situation, I would laugh at how comical Beth looks when her face loses all its color. They take off, losing their heels in their haste to escape.

"They wear the most inappropriate shoes." I shake my head, mystified.

Honey nods in agreement. "Bless their hearts."

We walk over to the restaurant gangway and I fill her in on my day. "Now we'll need to convince Chief Hoyle. I hope once he sees that baggie and the flash drive, he'll realize I'm not crazy."

"Bea Pearl, bringing your brother back from the dead kinda makes you not crazy. Or a murderess."

I smile. At the house, Nick walks off the porch, followed by the officer holding Junior's hands behind his back. Even across the parking lot, I catch Chief Hoyle's eye. He nods while holding up the baggie. And the way he mashes his lips and squints his eyes tells me he's apologizing. For stepping aside for Sheriff Oakwood and not believing me about my brother. My breath comes out in a whoosh. "He'll be able to call for impeaching Oakwood based on what Jim said is in that baggie."

Honey's eyes widen. "If you found your brother, does that mean my best friend is back, too?"

"You think they'll let me cheer this late in the season? I mean, Homecoming is just a couple weeks away."

Honey does a Herkie. "Optimistic Merry Girls…Yes! Especially once we kick Sara off the squad. You can't spell *team* with *kidnapping accomplices*."

We laugh. Daddy calls for me, so we walk arm and arm to the house.

Later than evening, as Mr. Catfish outdoes himself frying up everything on the menu for Jim, I make my way to the pier.

Melancholy and joy, two ends of the emotional spectrum, tumble around my head like sneakers in a dryer, making me twitchy. I can't relax even though my brother is back and safe. For the first time in ages, my family is whole. Momma's finally able to unzip her wetsuit of grief and see the real me again.

The sturgeon are leaving and taking Colin with them. Sitting on the end of the pier, my feet dangle over the edge. I wonder if life is just a constant back and forth of loss and gain. Of finding and losing. What makes my existence on this tiny blue planet worth it?

My family and friends are inside the brightly lit restaurant, but I don't want to join them yet. Needing time to think, I asked Honey not to accompany me outside. Tossing the begonia bloom from the gangway into the water, I try to figure out why I haven't completely let go of the shadow-girl I became while my brother was missing. "Water sprites, please accept my offering. Thank you for bringing my brother back to me. But why does Colin have to leave?"

There's no one outside to witness my silly behavior. No one around to make fun of me.

A throat clears behind me. Spinning around, splinters drag at my shorts. Colin stands before me, looking uncharacteristically grave. "Now that you are real, you can't appear out of thin air and act mysterious anymore." I adore his smile, but there is no trace of one on his beautiful features as he sits down next to me, rolling up his khaki pants cuffs.

"The sturgeon are gone," he says.

"I figured that would happen soon with the weather turning." Already the nights are getting chillier, even though the days are still warm. It's not too cold for shorts but I traded my T-shirt for long sleeves. I desperately want to look at him, but it hurts too much. I've been holding back so many kinds of tears lately.

"Bea, this isn't my home," he begins. I stop him from continuing by covering his hand with mine. He squeezes.

"I know it's time for you to leave. Next rainy season, I'll feel that first rain drop, and know you've returned to me. I'll keep an eye out for rainbows and an ear for the songs of bullfrogs, and then I'll look for you on the riverbank." Looking into his eyes, I realize they aren't the blue of a winter sky, but more like the deep sapphire of warm, salty water.

"I love you," he says.

When we kiss, it's so full of longing and sadness, my heart might shatter. I shut my eyes tight not able to watch him walk away, and he presses something into my hand. He leaves one last kiss on my forehead before I feel the air sigh at his departure. Only when a strong, cold wind blows across Lake George do I open my eyes. but I already know a symmetrically circular beige disc rests in my hand. If its fragile, perfect shape can exist for hundreds of years, then why can't my heart remain intact until next summer?

Finally, I get it. Loss doesn't exist without something important to lose. My melancholy and joy will happen time and time again. Tracing the shape of this fossilized sand dollar, I circle my thoughts through everything that has happened over the last few months. It's up to me to choose whether I exist on top of the circle or bottom, even if the bottom has joy when it swings up again.

This night will not last forever. This night of my lost brother's homecoming. I'll be present and enjoy every moment I can.

Oh, and Colin wrote his phone number on the back of my fossil.

Author's Note

The two rivers in Bea Pearl's world are modeled after real ones that flow down lower Alabama and reach the Gulf of Mexico near the Destin, FL and Fort Walton Beach area—the Choctawhatchee and one of its tributaries—the Pea River. Talakhatchee is the Muscogee name for the Pea River which translates to "pea green stream." (And yes, it has a slight greenish tint!)

The Chatothatchee is modeled after the Choctawhatchee. It's an incredibly biodiverse area (hence Colin's sturgeon storyline), and along with two other neighboring river basins, it makes up the highest level of biodiversity in the United States. The Choctawhatchee is named after the Choctaw Indians. But the Native Americans that lived in this region were the Chatots, though the name was spelled incorrectly on those early British maps. This story is my little way of correcting the clerical mistake and paying homage to the now extinct Chatot tribe.

Acknowledgements

B ack when I was a baby writer, I'd read other books'
acknowledgements and feel a scared kind of awe—*I
don't even know this many writerly people! How can I
ever be an author of a real live book if I don't know enough
people to thank on an acknowledgement page?* (Yes, these are
things I worry over.) From the beginning, I always knew I'd include my parents, Don and Linda, my sister, Megan, and my
best friend, Tabitha. Without the early encouragement, support,
and shenanigans, I mean memories, from family and friends, I
wouldn't have gotten very far.

The more I immersed myself (read: floundered around) in the
writing community, the more I realized what helpful, kind people populated it. A big thank you to the Mobile Writers' Guild
which led me to Carrie Dalby, who was the first author to cri-
tique my manuscript, and Angela Quarles for her query letter
expertise. Much appreciation to the beta readers who helped me
better Bea Pearl revision through revision. This story would still
be full of plot problems without Michelle Hauck's Query Kom-
bat, the subsequent mentorship of M.J. O'Neill, and her
introducing me to Priya Doraswamy of Lotus Lane Literary.

The Existence of Bea Pearl wouldn't exist without the enthusiasm, excitement, and expertise of the amazing Owl Hollow

Press team. Emma, Hannah, and Olivia, you ladies are wonderful to work with and I'm thrilled to put Bea Pearl into y'all's capable wings. I love how the cover brought the story's creepy, swampish beauty to life.

I'm indebted to the past of Lake Geneva and the stories told to me by other generations. To Michael McDowell's Blackwater Saga (and Lake Pinchona) that first showed me how to wrap the familiar into atmospheric stories.

Last, but certainly not least, I'm so very thankful for the love of Josh, Marley, & Gabel. Without whom life would be so much less magical.

Candice Marley Conner

grew up between swamps, a river, and the Gulf Coast, so her stories emerge from gnarled cypress knees, muddy water, and salty air. She is the kidlit haint at a haunted indie bookstore, a Local Liaison for SCBWI, and an officer for her local writer's guild.

Her short stories and poems are in various anthologies and magazines including *Highlights Hello*, *Babybug*, *Chicken Soup For The Soul*, and more. Candice is the author of the picture book *Sassafras and her Teen Tiny Tail*, and she is represented by Katelyn Detweiler of Jill Grinberg Literary Management.

She lives in Alabama with her husband and two children (one of whom is possibly feral).

candicemarleyconner.com

CPSIA information can be obtained
at www.ICGtesting.com
Printed in the USA
LVHW110353220721
693324LV00003B/9